GIVE PLACE TO WRATH

A *ROGER VICEROY* NOVEL

STEVEN C. HARMS

SUSPENSE PUBLISHING

GIVE PLACE TO WRATH
by
Steven C. Harms

PAPERBACK EDITION
* * * * *
PUBLISHED BY:
Suspense Publishing

Steven C. Harms
COPYRIGHT
2021 Steven C. Harms

PUBLISHING HISTORY:
Kcm Publishing, Paperback and Digital Copy, October 2017
Suspense Publishing, Paperback and Digital Copy, June 2021

Cover Design: Shannon Raab
Cover Photographer: shutterstock.com/ EFKS
Cover Photographer: shutterstock.com/ Capture and Compose
Cover Photographer: shutterstock.com/ Malivan_Iuliia

ISBN: 978-0-578-90722-2

ALSO BY STEVEN C. HARMS

Roger Viceroy Series
GIVE PLACE TO WRATH
THE COUNSEL OF THE CUNNING

PRAISE FOR
STEVEN C. HARMS

Killer Nashville Silver Falchion Award Finalist—*Best Mystery*

"A must read crime thriller about revenge and race
relations that is reminiscent of Truman Capote's *In
Cold Blood*… Highly recommended."
—*Bestthrillers.com*

"A rare mystery book that is a true page-turner,
even to the seasoned readers of the genre."
—*Thriller Magazine* (Starred Review)

"*Give Place to Wrath* will leave the reader wanting a
quick release of a second book in the series."
—Sheila Sobel, *Killer Nashville*

"Knit together so well that towards the end of book I was on
the edge of my seat and couldn't turn the pages fast enough."
—*Readers' Favorite*

"Cleverly plotted and anchored by an inventive and ingenious
murder mystery. Shaping up to be an interesting series."
—*Book Review Directory*

"Don't miss this one! It is a well plotted, complex mystery
that mystery thriller fans will love…an absorbing and
very satisfying novel. You won't be disappointed."
—*Mystery Suspense Reviews*

American Book Fest American Fiction Awards Finalist—
Mystery/Suspense: General

Do not avenge yourselves, my friends, but
give place to wrath,
for it is written, "Vengeance is Mine,
I will repay," says the Lord.

Romans 12:19 – Paul's letter to the church at Rome

GIVE PLACE TO WRATH

STEVEN C. HARMS

PROLOGUE

The sixth hole at Pine Creek Country Club is a short but demanding par four dogleg right. Both tee and approach shots require extreme accuracy. It is Pine Creek's signature hole and number-one handicap. The green is a very small, perfect circle that nestles up to the clubhouse, which was built to resemble an English castle set incongruously in the suburbs of Milwaukee. Pine Creek, a narrow and rapid waterway, cuts through the fairway in front of the green. An ancient black walnut tree guards the right side of the hole from its position thirty yards out. Club members have a perfect bird's-eye view of the sixth from the wooden balcony that runs the entire length of the second floor of the clubhouse.

The sixth is also visible from a small grove of oak trees overlooking the course from Talbot Lane a quarter mile away. The watcher made himself as comfortable as possible on one of the larger branches about twelve feet up. Inside his backpack were essential supplies for the task at hand: Pop-Tarts, a thermos of coffee, binoculars, and a remote control device. The sun had risen a few hours prior and the ache in his back was beginning to bore deeper. He let his head rest against the bark of the trunk in a vain attempt at relaxation as he closed his eyes and mentally retraced his morning's activities.

He was an early riser, but the excitement and anticipation of beginning the end game had kept him up late the previous night. So when the alarm blared just after 2:00 a.m. he had startled awake and slammed his hand on the shut off knob, breaking the clock and the skin on his left palm. In just a few minutes he was dressed and left the motel; a backpack slung over his shoulder.

When he neared his destination he turned off the headlights and slowed to a crawl as he maneuvered his vehicle into the grove of trees. Crossing the street, he checked to be sure there were no cars in sight before scaling the ten-foot cyclone fence designed to keep non-members from trespassing on club property. He had selected this particular spot as his breach point because of its remoteness from the other holes and its proximity to the cart path that wove through the course. All he had to do was get over the fence and walk about eight feet to the paved path. From there he could make his way to the sixth hole without leaving footprints in the dew that clung to the fairways between him and his destination. He knew the grounds crew would arrive before dawn and did a quick check of his watch: 3:30 a.m. He had more than enough time.

When he reached the sixth green he opened his backpack and took out a beach towel, a golf hole cutter, a small bundle, and cautiously approached the hole. He spread the towel on the grass and lay the cutter and bundle on top. Very steadily, he lifted the pin from the cup and placed it on the green. Next, he reached into the hole and pulled out the cup, grabbed the hole cutter, and dug out another twelve inches of dirt. Deftly, he unwrapped the small bundle and carefully placed the device in the bottom of the newly deepened hole before replacing the cup and the pin. Satisfied with his handiwork, he took a deep breath before collecting his belongings and retraced his steps to the cart path and back to the point where he had climbed the fence. Along the way he made a brief stop at the bunker guarding the left side of the sixth fairway. The cart path came within throwing distance of the sand trap and an accurate toss was all that was required. He chuckled to himself as the ball landed perfectly in the middle of the sand. He pivoted, saluted the sixth hole, and made his way to the tree on Talbot Lane. A gentle breeze ushered in the late summer morning as he climbed to his position where he now sat straddling a branch, awaiting her appearance. *You have honors, Mrs. Hale. Tee it up.*

Most summer mornings there are at least a few Pine Creek members breakfasting on the clubhouse balcony and today was no exception. Watching their fellow members struggle with the sixth was an enjoyable pastime. Bogies or worse were common and did not elicit any response from the balcony. Pars called for courteous applause. Birdies required a standing ovation, a tradition at Pine Creek since 1946.

It was shortly after 8:00 a.m. on the last day of August, and Mary Hale had just eagled the fifth hole en route to what she hoped would be her best round ever at Pine Creek. The assassin had watched her for a year and knew that she would be by herself, honing her skills. He had been waiting all morning for the action that was about to unfold, and a tingle coursed up and down his arms as he peered through his binoculars and spotted her approaching the sixth tee. From his perch, he had an unobstructed view of both the tee box and the green. Her tee shot landed dead solid in the middle of the fairway, as he knew it would. He watched as she hit her approach shot and admired the high, soft fade as the ball arced over the left greenside bunker, hopped twice on the green, and rolled straight past the pin, settling about eight feet away. He watched her walk up the fairway, back ramrod straight, and acknowledge the balcony with a wave of her hand as she reached the sixth green. She marked her ball and flipped it to her caddie without looking at him. *Only someone of your stature could pull off that little move,* he thought. *If only your ability to pick a husband matched your golf talents.*

Her caddie helped her line up her birdie putt and was standing with the flag in hand about ten feet away. Her backstroke was agonizingly deliberate, and as the putt dropped she pumped her fist—three under through six. The dozen or so members on the
unison to applaud her birdie. The killer softly
the oak tree and then grabbed the switch.
fidence to the cup and bent from the waist,
rieve her ball. That's when the bomb went

climbed down the tree, got into his '75
ay, picking up I-94 West a mile down the

road. "Start counting," he said to no one in particular. The coffee tasted oh so good.

CHAPTER 1

Roger Viceroy jerked violently and let out a guttural moan. The movement and the sound of his own voice yanked him out of the dream. He lay on his back, eyes still closed, and let the image start to dissipate. He knew that it wouldn't fade entirely until he opened his eyes, so keeping them closed was a way to keep her in his arms before she broke loose and jumped off the roof into the abyss. That's where it always ended, and all he could do was lunge and shout her name. *Debbie.* The consuming anguish faithfully followed.

The dawn light seeping around the edges of the curtains inched up the bedroom wall. His brain registered the brightness of an August sun as he untangled himself from the vision in his head, and he wondered again if it would continue to stalk him for the rest of his life.

As he finally allowed his eyes to open, the stab of sun around the curtains' edges made him squint and brought him fully awake. He swung his legs over the side of the bed and sat for a moment. He shut off the alarm, which would not have gone off for another half an hour, and gathered his thoughts. Asleep or awake, her face was never far away even though he hadn't seen or spoken to her for over a year and a half, and still didn't know exactly where she was. As a wave of emotion began its assault, he stood up and attempted to turn his mind to prayer, a daily morning undertaking he had recommitted to at the start of summer. More often than not it had become a two minute exercise of nothingness, but today he was able to muster a few coherent sentences. Lately, these rare moments had turned inward; raw stabs of petitions to God that he was increasingly beginning to question. Answers were needed. Renewal. Reclamation. Conclusion. Something...anything.

He muttered the "Amen," then grabbed the remote and flipped on ESPN to catch the morning edition of *Sports Center*, cranking up the volume so he could hear it as he moved from the bedroom to the bathroom. He stripped off his sleep shorts and turned on the shower to let the water heat up as he gathered his shaving gear. He paused for a look in the mirror. *Not bad for thirty-nine. Could be worse.* His 5'10" frame was beginning to show signs of wear and tear, but he was generally pleased to note that he hadn't yet yielded completely to middle age. There were a few wrinkles around his blue eyes, but thanks to his twice-weekly visits to the gym and the occasional racquetball game, he still had the body of an athlete. A cursory examination of his thick, wavy, brown hair was a weekly ritual as well, and this one passed the test. No grays.

The steam from the shower billowed over the top of the glass doors, so he stepped inside. As he went through his routine, Debbie popped back into his thoughts and he pictured her in his favorite photo from their honeymoon in the Bahamas. She was sitting poolside in a bright yellow bikini with a strawberry daiquiri in her hand and a parrot on her shoulder. Her eyes were hidden behind big Versace sunglasses but her smile showed off the deep dimple in her left cheek, and her long, chestnut-brown hair glistened in the sunshine. They had met at a friend's Super Bowl party. She had recently moved to Milwaukee from Florida as a sales representative for a pharmaceutical company and was renting the small house next door to Viceroy's friend. Up to that point neither of them had ever come close to getting married, but now they were both in their mid-thirties and something seemed to click. Within six months Debbie had a ring on her finger, and before year's end they were married at a small local church with a few friends and family in attendance.

The honeymoon photo was the last one he recalled taking of her. It was their final day on the island. Six weeks later he came home one Monday evening to find an empty condo and a note saying only that being married to him had completely overwhelmed her. Viceroy felt the pain welling up once again as he whispered the word "Jesus" and stuck his head under the hot water and finished.

He grabbed his towel from the rack when he heard his cell phone. He hurriedly wrapped himself in it and grabbed the phone off the dresser just in time to miss the final ring. The missed call identifier said "Unknown," resulting in a fling of the phone to his bed and a realization that he'd spent more time in the shower than he'd intended. He finished drying off and shaved as quickly as he could without cutting himself. His hair naturally fell into place with just a few brush strokes. Dressing in the khakis, blue-striped button-down shirt and blue blazer he'd laid out the night before, and slipping into his brown loafers, he hit the power button on the remote and headed downstairs to the kitchen. His options were all lined up on the top shelf of the refrigerator and he settled on an energy drink. It was 7:30 a.m. when he climbed into his vehicle. Within ten minutes he was wheeling down the freeway to his office. 'No radio' was his mantra. The commute was his time to think. Streamline thoughts. Focus. Prioritize known tasks. Reaffirm the strategy for the day.

Rush hour traffic was unusually heavy this Tuesday morning, causing him to weave from one lane to another in an effort to make up some time.

His office occupied a renovated one-story red brick building in downtown Milwaukee that had been built in the 1930s and formerly housed a small law firm. He was a cop: Investigative. Director of the Wisconsin Division of the Midwest Region Special Crimes Unit (MRSCU), or Mrs. Cue as the other police divisions called it. The agency was born out of the investigation into a series of rape-murders in the elite suburbs of northern Milwaukee that crossed multiple jurisdictions. The individual city police departments as well as the county office and the state police were pulled into the fray, but in six months almost no progress had been made, mostly because of the unintended lack of coordination among the departments involved. At one point, the rapist had actually been held on a robbery charge just over the state line in Gurnee, Illinois.

But due to legislated limitations on police communications in Illinois, he had been released once the charges were dropped on a technicality and was back in Wisconsin a few days later, breaking into a home and raping then murdering a mother of four before he was recaptured. Had there been coordination and cooperation among neighboring states, the Gurnee Police Department would have known that the police in a suburb on Milwaukee's north side also had the guy as a top suspect in their investigation.

In the aftermath, a cooperative examination conducted by the Wisconsin and Illinois state police departments revealed the many flaws associated with the investigation of heinous crimes covering multiple jurisdictions. As a result, the governors of Illinois, Wisconsin, Minnesota, Iowa, and Indiana had come together to create MRSCU, which would henceforth take the lead in the investigation of crimes that were particularly serious, such as serial killings and acts of potential terrorism, or those that spiraled into multiple jurisdictions. At the behest of any one of the governors, MRSCU could be called upon to take precedence over state or local authorities. Each state housed a division of the agency, whose personnel reported directly to the governor of the state they served as well as to MRSCU Central Command in Chicago. There was also one person in each governor's office assigned to be the liaison with the local agency.

At the time MRSCU was formed five years before, Viceroy had been working as a lead investigator for the FBI in Milwaukee. His detective skills along with his vigorous determination had built him a reputation for excellence that was unmatched within the agency. A man who lived by one rule: answers to every mystery are in the molecules. Not sometimes, not by happenstance, not with weak fervor, and never on a macro level. Not ever in the matter. Always the molecules. *Always.* When MRSCU was formed, his superior recommended him to the governor and MRSCU headquarters for the Wisconsin director's position. It didn't hurt that Viceroy was also a Wisconsin native.

The MRSCU offices in Milwaukee were extraordinarily plain and small. Windows were at a premium. As head of the unit, Viceroy had two in his office and his six employees reminded him regularly and with good humor that he was the only one among them to enjoy such luxury. He believed his staff was absolutely the best in the MRSCU system and he sincerely cherished having each of them. They were involved in dangerous work, and what some lacked in experience they more than made up for in principle and values, which was far more important to him than having a lengthy resume.

His office was at the end of the narrow hallway that bisected the building. His two lead investigators had offices on either side of his assistant's desk just outside his door.

Regina Cortez was a short, muscular woman in her early forties with closely cropped, jet-black hair that accentuated her Latina heritage. The style was unique, but Viceroy thought her presentation was neat and crisp, just like her police work. She was by far his favorite; he tried not to show it, but it was hard at times since she had been with him from the beginning of the agency.

Trevor "Silk" Moreland was his safety valve. When all investigative roads seemed blocked, Viceroy could count on Silk to find a way around the barrier. He leaned towards coldness but was a monster for details and knew the streets. His nickname stemmed from his high school basketball days on Milwaukee's northwest side. At 6'5", his height was a gift that complemented his perfectly smooth jump shot, causing his high school gym to erupt with shouts of "Silk" at his every made basket. All-State honors and being named MVP of the state tournament his sophomore year had landed him a scholarship to Marquette University. Turning pro was in his sights until the summer before his senior year of high school when he got caught in the crossfire of a gang fight while walking to a basketball court two blocks from his home. A bullet ripped through his left leg, ending his basketball dream. His scholarship lost, he vowed that he would climb the ladder one way or the other, and he could think of no better way to do that than by stopping crime. It became his obsession. By the age of twenty-eight, Silk had risen rapidly through the police ranks and was noticed by Viceroy during a hostage case that MRSCU had worked on with the Milwaukee PD. When he'd needed to replace a lazy detective two years ago, Viceroy remembered Silk and hired him away. Now thirty, he was still smooth, efficient, and hungry.

His third deputy, Jerry King, was Viceroy's man in the governor's office. The two spoke daily, keeping each other informed of what the governor was doing and sharing information about current investigations.

Viceroy had just passed a delivery truck and cut into the right lane to catch his exit ramp when his cell phone rang. He saw the caller ID. Something important.

"Preacher," Silk barked in his nasal tenor the minute Viceroy answered the call. He had given Viceroy the pet name within a few months of his arrival out of playful respect for his new boss's Christian faith that occasionally made an appearance. Viceroy didn't mind and had embraced his new nickname in the spirit in which it was offered. "Preacher, are you there?" he repeated.

Viceroy said, "Yeah, Silk, I'm here. Just getting off I-94."

"Well, turn your ass around. I'm already out the door. There was a bombing at Pine Creek."

"What?"

"Turn on your radio. Milwaukee PD just got the call. A bomb went off at the golf club."

"What are you talking about?"

Viceroy exited the freeway and parked at the top of the ramp.

Silk shouted, pronouncing each word deliberately and slowly. "A bomb went off at Pine Creek!"

"Okay, I'm moving. Use the radio instead of our cells."

"Got it. I was talking to Regina when the news broke so she's already on her way. I told her I'd call you. She'll get there first. I'll see you there."

Still idling, he had a quick conversation with Regina. She informed him she was about five minutes from the club and would call him back as soon as she got there. He repeated his instructions to use the radio and then slapped his siren on the dashboard and swung onto the ramp, heading back the way he'd come. Flipping on his car radio, the media was off and running with the story. "Eyewitnesses report casualties. No one knows exactly what happened, but there is talk of an explosion on the course itself," the radio man said in a newsy cadence. Viceroy needed more information. Now.

"Regina, Silk, you guys there yet?"

"Almost, boss," Regina said. "I just turned down the approach road."

Silk said, "I've got pedal to the metal."

"Okay. This sounds bad. Real bad. I'm going to call DeWitt but radio in if you have anything I need to know."

They each confirmed as Viceroy frantically scrolled through the contacts on his phone for DeWitt's number. He hit the call button and prayed for a quick connection. Scott DeWitt had been the Milwaukee County sheriff for the past sixteen years. He and Viceroy had a strained relationship. So much so that Viceroy was counting the months until the sheriff's retirement. Ever since its inception he had been the one man to blatantly disregard MRSCU's authority, and on multiple occasions he had delayed, drawn out or circumvented communication, stopping just short of obstruction each time. His tenure and impending retirement were the only reasons he had not been removed from office. The last incident had occurred the month before, in the midst of a cooperative regional effort headed by MRSCU to hunt down a serial bank robbing operation that involved a distant cousin of Indiana's attorney general. The guy was on the run and got cornered inside a bar on Milwaukee's south side with the help of a tip from the bar's owner. DeWitt had demanded that, until there was absolute proof he was inside the place, jurisdiction reverted to his office. He simply wanted to take credit for the capture, but his shenanigans almost allowed the guy to escape out the back door while the law enforcement agencies clashed on the street. DeWitt answered on the first ring.

"DeWitt here," he said.

Viceroy said, "Scott, it's Roger."

"Hey there, Viceroy."

"You heard?"

"Yep. Who hasn't? Already got some of my boys on the way. I was just heading out the door myself."

Gee, how competent of you. "Okay, I'll see you there. I'm about fifteen minutes away."

"Now don't go pokin' around without us. I don't want a problem like last time."

"Scott, this isn't a traffic violation. There was a bomb."

"Whoa, slow down there. I know damn well it was a bomb. I wasn't born in Iowa, you know? Besides, until we know what the hell we got, you're just an official bystander."

Viceroy knew he had a point, but he hated hearing it from Scott DeWitt. "Look, just get there, okay?"

"I will," DeWitt snapped. "And make sure Mrs. Cue stays in the kitchen," he chuckled as he hung up the phone.

"Bastard," Viceroy said out loud as he clicked off. *Stay in the kitchen. Yeah, we'll stay in the kitchen until the whole house is ready to burn down and then we'll have to save it as usual.* At least that call was out of the way.

He veered around a school bus full of teenagers who had all jammed themselves to one side so they could see the speeding car coming up their rear with its red light flashing. He clipped by them and saw the sign indicating that his exit was still six miles ahead. A white minivan suddenly cut him off, and he had to swerve to the shoulder at 90 miles per hour, kicking up dust and spewing litter back across the interstate.

"Dammit," he shouted in response to both the idiot driver and the idiot DeWitt.

Regina radioed.

"Yeah, I'm close to Pine Creek," he said. "Are you there?"

"Yes, I'm here."

"And?"

"Just get here, Roger. Good God, just get here."

"I'm about five minutes away," he said as he pressed on the gas and hit the exit ramp. The streets were already swarming with cars and curiosity seekers. A TV-8 news crew was flying fast down Pine Creek Boulevard on its way to the club entrance and Viceroy just missed it as he turned. The driver slammed on the brakes and fishtailed into a light pole. *Media. Bane of the modern world.*

An ambulance sped out of the driveway as he approached the main gate. Local police guarding the entrance waved him through, and, as he turned in, the surreal impact of the crime scene hit him square in the forehead.

Pine Creek wasn't just any country club. It was Milwaukee's best and most elite. Its members were all "old money." The stately wrought-iron gates set in marble-clad walls, lush vegetation, and faux castle clubhouse took one back to an earlier, more elegant time. He parked amid the throng of police cars and EMS units. His immediate thought was how out of place those vehicles were in this setting—like a Rolls Royce sitting in a trailer park. He grabbed his cell phone and radio and threw open the door, all in one motion.

Police were crawling all over the place, like ants. A few recognized him and gave him a wave. Viceroy noticed the standard yellow tape just off the corner of the clubhouse where three officers were doing their best to keep the media at bay. On the other side of the walkway, a gently sloping lawn with a marble fountain had quickly become a holding area for what he guessed were club employees, members, and anyone else who needed to be detained. He could see the utter panic pasted on all their faces. The collective noise of the sirens just added to the chaos.

Viceroy spoke into his radio. "Regina, this is Roger. Where in this mess are you?"

"Go through the clubhouse, I'm out back."

Viceroy's unit crackled again as he hustled through the front door, "Preacher, they just closed the ramp to the exit. I'm weaving my way through but its hell gettin' to Pine Creek."

Viceroy said, "It appears hell *is* Pine Creek. How close are you?"

"Just about to the bottom of the ramp."

"Okay, step on it. And give that TV-8 news crew wrapped around the light pole a ticket on your way in."

"What?"

"Never mind. Just get here."

Viceroy wove his way through the main lobby. Two women were sitting on the floor, propped against the wall in the front foyer, being both consoled and questioned by police. The kitchen crew were all huddled in a corner of the grandiose lobby, heads bowed, some visibly distraught. Medical responders were sprinkled throughout the crowded lobby and dining area while a rogue reporter from some news outfit was being roughly escorted out a side door by a policewoman. Viceroy found the stately staircase leading to the back of the clubhouse and made his way to Regina.

When he opened the massive double doors he stopped dead in his tracks. The only place he'd ever seen this kind of carnage was on television footage of some distant country. The first thing that hit him was the partially collapsed balcony to his left. Tables, chairs, and chunks of cement were scattered on the brick pavers of the walkway. Shattered glass was everywhere. Viceroy noticed three people being attended to but couldn't tell if they were dead or alive. Two more were being strapped to gurneys by medical personnel. Police were taking photographs of everything, and three ambulances with lights flaring were parked around the perimeter of the devastation as one more approached from the service road adjacent to the fairway.

Further down to his left, Viceroy spied the lifeless body of a teenage boy in a caddie's apron sprawled next to a meticulously manicured bed of flowers. The pin with the number 6 flag still attached looked as if it was growing incongruously out of the petunias.

And there, straight in front of him, was the green, or what was left of it. Almost half of it was missing, having been replaced by a blown-out crater. Clearly the bomb had detonated somewhere on the green, itself; probably in the cup.

"Reg....Regina?" he said into his radio.

"Yeah, I see you. Look up to your right."

Viceroy turned his head and spotted her just off the green, standing next to a sand trap along with five or six others. She motioned for him to come over and then turned back to the trap. He stepped over the jagged remains of what once had been a window pane and made his way around the green. As he approached the edge of the sand trap, she looked up, shaking her head, before returning her gaze to the sand below. Viceroy stopped just behind her and peered over her left shoulder. There, in a twisted crumpled position, lay the body of a tall, athletic-looking woman who appeared to be in her early thirties. Her coffee-brown hair, pulled back in a ponytail, seemed as if it was the only part of her that was untouched by the bomb. Her left leg was twisted behind her at an awkward angle, and her right leg was missing from the calf down.

There were deep gashes and multiple shrapnel wounds on both arms. Her midsection had also sustained significant damage, and red sand gleamed beneath her torso.

"My God," Viceroy said.

"Yeah," Regina said. "Let's hope she's with Him."

"Who is she?"

One of the uniformed officers spoke up. "It's Mary Hale. Or... it was Mary Hale."

Viceroy spoke without looking up. "Mary Hale? The pro?"

"Yes, sir."

He swallowed hard and got down on one knee for a closer look, peering intently into her eyes. He remained in that position a few moments longer before standing up and walking towards the namesake creek cutting across the fairway. Regina knew to follow.

CHAPTER 2

Silk parked his vehicle in the police area and made his way to the blast zone along the same general route that Viceroy had taken just minutes prior. As he approached, Regina looked up and gave him a nod. Viceroy stood on a small stone bridge spanning the creek with his back to the green as he talked on his cell phone to Jerry King, his liaison in the governor's office.

"Look, Jerry, just tell the governor it's pandemonium and I don't have anything concrete to tell her at this time," he said, emphasizing 'concrete' to punctuate his statement.

Jerry must have been pushing back because the next thing Regina and Silk heard was, "I hear you, Jerry. Just do the best you can until I can make some sense of this chaos. I'll get back to you as soon as I know anything of substance."

Regina shook her head at Silk. The governor was tenacious when she wanted to be, and this one hit close to home. Mary Hale was known to be a good friend of the governor, the trophy wife of Howard Hale, one of Wisconsin's most influential business leaders and a childhood buddy of the governor's husband.

Viceroy said, "So I say again, I simply cannot provide her with anything more at this juncture. Talk to you soon," he added before clicking off the phone and turning toward Regina and Silk. "Mr. Moreland, glad you could join us today."

Silk said, "Beautiful day for golf," as he scanned the scene.

"You don't own clubs."

"Oh, yeah. Maybe I can borrow yours. Or hers," he added as he nodded back toward the sand trap. "I don't think she'll be swinging 'em anytime soon."

Regina looked down and grinned. She always got a charge out of the banter between her boss and Silk. He said things she would never think to speak out loud, but she admired his ability to be just irreverent enough to break the tension in even the most horrific of situations.

Viceroy said, "Silk, you are the most politically incorrect person I've ever met."

"Yeah, I know. Just messin' around. This scene sucks."

"Well, you two can start. You know what to do."

"We're on it," Regina said, tugging at Silk's elbow as the two of them headed toward the clubhouse. Regina was scanning the information she'd written down earlier when Silk stopped. She followed his gaze up the walk towards the corner of the clubhouse. "Yo, Roger," she called back to her boss.

Viceroy looked up to respond and, as he did, he saw Regina motion to her right with her head.

He shifted his eyes to the left and saw Scott DeWitt walking down the banked rough around the sixth green with two of his officers in tow. He was a large, out-of-shape man and seemed to be having difficulty keeping his balance on the hillside. Viceroy's tongue flicked his upper lip and, bowing his head, he made a beeline toward the sheriff. DeWitt could not get the upper hand in this. That was the goal. The crime was too big and catastrophic. Viceroy also knew that if the investigation got messed up the feds might grab it.

The sheriff talked first as Viceroy drew near. "Well, well, well, hello Viceroy. I hope you've kept your promise to stay in the kitchen."

Viceroy said, "Hello Scott. I was hoping you'd get out of your office today."

"Wouldn't miss it. Already gave a few words to the boys in the media; even spoke to CNN."

"You haven't even gone through the scene yet. How can you

27

talk to the media?"

"My boys briefed me on the way in. Besides, all I did was tell 'em 'no further comment.' They hate that, ya know."

Viceroy scratched the side of his head at the idiocy of the man in front of him. "Well, I'm glad you're taking care of the media. But there are a few other things going on here right now."

"I know, I know. Deputy Kemper here already has things in control," DeWitt said as he put his hand on the man's shoulder. "And the boys in the bomb squad are on top of their game, aren't they Bogert?" he added, nodding to the other one.

Bogert was the first to respond. Viceroy was standing slightly above all of them on the hillside, making Bogert appear even more subservient than he actually was. "Well, sir, Mr. Viceroy, it appears the bomb was inside the cup."

A rather obvious puzzle piece.

"We don't have it nailed yet, but our best guess is that it was a homemade job."

Viceroy said, "Why do you say that?"

"Our hunch. It was a little messier than what I would've expected if it were done by someone with experience. Plus, we can't find traces of any of the standard stuff one would normally find. The guy had to have made it out of household products, fertilizer, and materials like that. The container was possibly a simple thermos or some sort of jerry-rigged pressure cooker. The bomb must have been packed with BBs, small screws, and nails to maximize the damage. They're everywhere, and the woman's body was shredded by them."

"Why do you say 'guy'?"

"Oh, no reason."

"Well, it's a little early to be eliminating possibilities," Viceroy said. "Women are capable of blowing things up, too," he added with a sweeping gesture that took in the entirety of the war zone around them. As he scanned the scene once more, he noticed Regina standing near the walkway by the dead caddie in deep conversation with a member of the Milwaukee PD and two golf course groundskeepers. He also spied Silk out of the corner of his eye standing at the edge of the green and looking over the course.

From experience he knew that Silk must be onto something and that Regina always wound up wherever the action was hottest. *Good work.*

"So, as you can plainly see, we're jockeying the horses," DeWitt was saying. "No need for you to saddle up just yet."

Viceroy said, "Well, lame horses get put out to pasture. And also lame ponies," he added with a quick glance to Kemper. That comment sent Bogert back to the bomb squad.

"Hey, no need to get huffy now. I was just drawing up the lines of responsibility."

Viceroy's cell vibrated. "Hold that thought, would you?" he said and stepped away, out of DeWitt's earshot.

"Viceroy here."

"Roger, its Jerry. She wants to talk to you. Now."

"Fine, put her on."

Viceroy could hear muffled conversation in the background as he waited for the governor to speak. She was clearly issuing edicts to her staff, but he couldn't make out what she was saying. All he could do was picture Jerry King in his rumpled suit, waiting for everyone else to clear out. He was Viceroy's second hire years ago and held all the characteristics that went along with a self-deprecating man in his late fifties. Viceroy even knew where he was standing; against the west wall of the spacious office next to the grandfather clock, the customary on-deck circle.

"Okay, here she is."

"Roger?" the governor began in her elegant, throaty tone that anyone in Wisconsin would recognize.

Viceroy said, "Yes, Governor."

"What the hell is going on?"

He wasn't quite sure where to begin. Part of his hesitancy was the difficulty in talking to her about the details of Mary Hale's demise.

"Roger, are you there?"

"Yes, I'm here. I just don't know how to tell you about Mary Hale. I know she was a friend."

There was a long pause on the other end of the line before the governor continued. "I'm going to say something." Another

29

awkward pause. "I have to be the governor right now," she finally said, and then added in a measured tone, "I need you to tell me everything you know and what you think it might mean."

Her calm leadership immediately registered with him. He didn't know Kay Spurgeon as well as he'd like to, but he just experienced the qualities that had gotten her elected in an unprecedented landslide. The people simply loved her. He'd first met her in his final interview before being hired by MRSCU. She'd been warm but professional, and after the hour-long process he'd walked out knowing the job was going to be his. She was taller than most women, his height, with rich, auburn hair just beginning to be flecked with gray. She was a vocal vegetarian, and her eating habits kept her trim and fit, looking younger than her sixty years. Her style oozed experience, confidence, and clarity without being overbearing. Her husband, Roy Spurgeon, was a prominent lawyer and power-broker. Together they made a storybook couple, as close to Wisconsin royalty as the state would ever see.

In as matter-of-fact a tone as he could muster, he reeled off as much information as he had at that moment. "I don't have the whole picture yet, so bear with me. As of this moment we know the bomb went off inside the cup on a green near the clubhouse. The Milwaukee County bomb squad is working on it, and we need to determine if it was planted there last night or sometime this morning. Regina Cortez is questioning the grounds crew. I will make sure they are all talked to with individual interviews. It just stands to reason that they would have some knowledge of how this could have been pulled off. Mary Hale must have been right next to the cup at the moment of the explosion. She and her caddie took the brunt of the blast."

Viceroy paused and after an uncomfortable moment of silence continued. "The clubhouse is in shambles and Milwaukee PD is gathering all employees and guests into a holding area near the front gates. I'm sure they will not be allowed to leave until everyone is confident the bomber is not among them. The terrorism angle is a possibility, but as of now I have zero indication that was the motive, but we have a lot more digging to do in order to determine if some group was behind this. Also, the bomb was powerful enough to cause some significant damage to the building, resulting in a collapse of the balcony. There are other injuries and apparently additional deaths, probably among those who were on the balcony at the time, but we don't yet know exactly how many."

Viceroy heard some noise and turned to see a news helicopter coming into view high above the clubhouse roof. "The media are going crazy. For the most part they've been kept away, but I see a TV helicopter now, so if you're watching there might be some rather disturbing scenes on your screen in a few moments. Other than that, it's just general chaos and we'll continue to do our job to the extent we are able. DeWitt is here, as you've probably surmised, and I've had a conversation with him, but in all candor I'm afraid he'll muck up the process. Nevertheless, all we can do at this point is watch, investigate, and provide information if we come across anything. And, of course, I'll let you know should there be any further developments."

"Thank you," the governor said. "Stay in touch with Jerry. I'll be within reach at all times."

"Yes ma'am." Viceroy was thinking she would just say goodbye and hand the phone back to Jerry King, but when she said nothing, he didn't know if she was still on the line or if the next voice would be Jerry's.

"Roger?"

"I'm still here."

"So am I. I'm going to make an executive decision right now. I want you to handle the case."

Viceroy stopped pacing. "Pardon me?"

"You heard me right."

"But, Governor, Milwaukee PD and DeWitt…"

"I don't want DeWitt in charge of this," she shot back. "I'm pulling him off and putting you on. I will go through the proper channels to inform your folks in Chicago of my decision. It's a phone call and a signed form, which I will process when I hang up. You're my man, okay?"

"Okay, Governor. I'll speak with DeWitt right now. He's just a few yards away."

"No, I'll speak with DeWitt right now. Put him on."

31

Viceroy walked over to the sheriff and interrupted a conversation he was having with the club's general manager. DeWitt flashed a "can't this wait" look, but Viceroy didn't flinch. He knew the next minute of his life would very enjoyable. "You have a phone call, Scott."

DeWitt snatched the phone out of Viceroy's extended hand and turned his back to speak. "DeWitt," he snarled, walking away. Viceroy watched as the sheriff stopped, understood whom he was speaking with, became nervous, protest, hear the response, meekly protest again, let his shoulders slump in resignation, say goodbye, and stab his finger on the off button. After a moment, he turned back and tossed the phone to Viceroy with a glare. He opened his mouth to speak, but stopped before a word came out and stomped down the hillside to the clubhouse entrance.

Regina approached. "What's up with him?" she asked, having watched what had just transpired.

"It's ours."

"What?"

"You heard me. The governor gave us the steering wheel."

"Ooh, I wouldn't want to be around him tonight. I hope his staff has their hard hats within arm's reach."

"He'll come around. He has no choice."

Their radios crackled as Silk's voice told them to look down the fairway where they spotted him next to a fairway bunker, motioning with his arms for them to come. They took off at a jog and came to halt behind him just as he finished taking a photo.

Silk said, "I kidded you about not playing golf. I've actually played the game enough to know the dos and the don'ts."

Viceroy asked, "You found a don't?"

"A big one," he said, pointing toward the sand trap. In the middle lay a golf ball.

"I don't get it."

Regina said, "Me either."

"Look closer, Preacher," Silk said as he stood. "Look at the sand trail the ball made after it hit the trap. It leads back to the sixth green, not the tee box. And there ain't no other hole coming in this direction in case you're thinking some hack sliced one."

"But that ball could have been here for a while. Who knows how it got there?"

"No, Roger. Silk's right," Regina cut in.

"What are you two talking about?"

Silk bent down and grabbed the rake lying at the edge of the trap as he spoke. "The head groundskeeper said they were going to be short-handed today, so he had his crew do some work last night before they left, including raking all the traps on the front nine—something they would normally do in the morning." Silk reached out with the rake and gently pulled the golf ball towards them, flipping it onto the grass at their feet. "This ball ain't supposed to be here." The ball rolled a little and settled at Viceroy's left foot. There, on the face of the golf ball, were words handwritten in block letters.

Viceroy squatted for a closer look and softly repeated what he read. "Six. Start counting."

CHAPTER 3

CURWOOD, WISCONSIN – AUGUST 1964

A new family moves to Curwood. The town is two hours northwest of Green Bay along Highway 32, the main thoroughfare through Wisconsin's north woods. It is one of the many small enclaves that dot the region. Curwood is predominately German Catholic. The flowage between Pike and Magonset Lakes serves as the divider between the north and south parts of town. Sitting in a downtown park is a black steam engine from 1902, dedicated to the town by the area's World War I veterans to honor the legacy of the railroad's impact on the region. The locals call it "Molly," although no one living there knows why.

There is not much else notable about the town. The terrain is hilly on the north side of the flowage and flat on the south. The businesses, such as they are, line the south side of Highway 32. Side-by-side covered bridges—one designated for motorists, the other for pedestrians and bikes—span the heart of downtown. The high school sits some four blocks up, atop the highest hill overlooking the south side of town.

St. Mary's Catholic Church is there as well. It is the only church in Curwood. No other churches are needed. No other churches are wanted. Each Sunday morning most of the people dutifully gather at St. Mary's to hear Father Freitag's homily.

The majority of families have lived there since the late 1800s. Paper mills, logging companies, and fisheries are the region's prime commerce. Occasional tourists pass through; some on guided fishing tours, some by sheer accident. Curwood does not rely on the tourists. Curwood feeds itself. A small hospital clinic headed by Dr. Edgar Spurgeon is conveniently located on the outskirts of town and serves the whole county. Dr. Spurgeon is also the parish deacon and unofficial mayor. His status grants him unquestioned power.

Juniper Street, home to all wealthy families, is three blocks east of Curwood High School. The houses are all faced with local fieldstone and sit on acre parcels. Neatly trimmed hedges, tall evergreens and old oaks frame their yards. Dr. Spurgeon and his family live there. He has just one living child, Roy. His other sons, identical twins, both died serving in Vietnam and are buried in the town's cemetery.

Roy is five when the new family moves into the old Hombarger residence two doors down, also with one son. The scuttlebutt is the buyer is a chemical engineer from Chicago and has accepted a job at the American Papers mill in nearby Antigo. Everyone on the street is anxious to meet them. Not many people move into Curwood. Most of the young people leave after high school never to return. New families need guidance. It is understood that they will not know the ways of Curwood, its traditions or its values.

One Saturday afternoon, a rented moving van driven by the man of the family, glides down Highway 32 and turns left onto the bridge headed for Juniper Street. A station wagon driven by the newcomer's wife follows the van. Curwood residents stare as both vehicles pass by. At Pat's Place, even the pancake flipper pauses to look out the front door, flicking the cigarette he had tucked into the left corner of his mouth with his free hand. The vehicles climb the steep hill and pull into the driveway of their new home. Two doors down, the Spurgeons watch from their wrap-around porch as the new people get out and stretch. The woman opens the rear door and a little boy hops out. The Spurgeons stare. The new family is Asian.

"Come along, Bennett. This is our new house," Mom calls over her shoulder in a foreign-sounding accent as she disappears inside the home. The boy stops playing with his yoyo and darts to the front door.

Two doors down, standing behind his son, Dr. Spurgeon unconsciously grabs Roy's shoulders and gives them an icy squeeze. Mrs. Spurgeon wipes her hands on her apron, quickly turns on her heel, and heads inside. Dr. Spurgeon heads to the telephone in his den. He calls his chief lieutenant to gather the inner council for a 7:00 p.m. meeting at the VFW Post. Curwood must know what has just descended upon it.

CHAPTER 4

Sitting in a corner booth at Jimmy's Café, Viceroy was engrossed in the media coverage of Mary Hale's murder. The headlines would have been laughable if it weren't for the seriousness of the crime. "MARY HALE BURIED IN HER OWN BUNKER," screamed the *Milwaukee Times*. The *Wisconsin Lantern*, trying to outdo its competitor had, "HOWARD LOOKING NOT SO HALE," plastered across the front page above a picture of the ashen widower leaving the church after the funeral. The accompanying article mentioned Howard Hale was still at the top of the suspect list. *Yes*, Viceroy thought, *but not for long*.

"Here's your coffee, darlin," the waitress said, putting down two cups along with his usual two creams and one sugar.

"Thanks, Lydia," he said, barely looking up.

"That's horrible. You got the guy yet?" she asked, pointing at the paper on the table in front of him.

"No, we don't, assuming it's even a guy."

"You mean a woman did that Pine Creek thing?"

"No, I don't mean a woman did it. I just mean we're working on it and we don't have a suspect yet. As far as we know, it could be anybody."

"Okay then. You'll get 'em, Roger, you'll get 'em," she said as she patted his shoulder and moved on with her coffee pot.

It was 6:30 a.m. Friday morning and Viceroy was waiting for Pastor Greg Oxenhaus to arrive. It had been five days since the bombing and this morning was literally his first opportunity to catch his breath. He was, quite simply, dead tired and wanted nothing more than to be back in bed. The past four nights he'd awakened in the wee hours, unable to fall back to sleep. His instinct this morning had been to go right to the office but, ultimately, he concluded that keeping his appointment with his pastor and friend was a priority.

They'd met almost a year ago following the emotional wreckage created by Debbie's exit of the marriage and subsequent communication void. Broken by the ordeal, Viceroy had taken to lonely rides on the weekends to avoid long stretches of time alone in their condo. One Sunday morning he drove past a huge church called Bread of Life and saw the cars streaming in, felt an ethereal tug, made a U-turn, and found himself in a back pew. Two thousand people. Amazing music. Spiritual joy on full display. Stirring message by a blond-haired guy who looked like he should be playing professional football for a living. That guy was Pastor Greg Oxenhaus. Viceroy filled out a guest card and received a phone call the next day from a pleasant-sounding woman who arranged for a pastoral visit. Over the next few months "Ox," as Viceroy came to call him, provided the counsel he sorely needed, becoming a great friend and confidant in the process.

Viceroy finished the first story and spread open the Metro section of the *Lantern* to read the feature article on the police investigation into the bombing. He was quoted numerous times and wanted to see if they'd got it right. All of the information came from the press conference he and the Milwaukee PD had held late the previous day. As he scanned the piece he felt comfortable that nothing had been misrepresented. The media's questions and opinions regarding the bombing being part of a terrorist act had subsided and the press conference he held had put it to rest.

Silk and Regina had already verified the whereabouts of both Hale and his ex-wife, Ellen Murphy, in the days prior and the morning of the tragedy. Both had come up clean. The two deputies were now going through their phone records, mail, and other potential indicators, but it looked like they were once again going to come up empty. Howard Hale was clearly shaken to his core, while Ellen Murphy had been vacationing on Martha's Vineyard at the time of the bombing.

As he flipped to the next page, a big human mitt with blond-haired knuckles grabbed the top of the paper and gave it a soft yank. Viceroy half-smiled as he looked up into the grinning face of Greg Oxenhaus.

"Hey, Ox," he said. The big man slid onto the bench across from him.

The pastor was dressed in his normal everyday attire: blue jeans, faded red polo shirt, and tennis shoes that had lost their tread some time ago.

Ox said, "How you holding up?"

Viceroy simply shrugged in response.

"Saw you on TV last night. You don't look too bad on the tube. In fact, I think you might want to start your own show. You could call it 'The Roger Viceroy Police Files,'" adding with a smile, "with special guest Greg Oxenhaus of the Bread of Life Church."

That gave Viceroy his first real laugh of the week. "Well, I think it may sound better simply as 'Ox Tales.'"

Ox let out one of his signature guffaws. Other diners turned to look, but neither man paid them any notice. Lydia swung by with her coffee pot, put down a cup for the new arrival and refilled Viceroy's. They each ordered the "usual"—two eggs, side of bacon, and, of course, a Jimmy's Famous Blueberry Scone. She gave them her patented wink as they settled back into their benches.

"I find it a hoot that I'm having breakfast with Milwaukee's biggest celebrity. You're looking alright."

"Celebrity by default. I'm just doing my job."

"Yeah, I know. Truthfully, you are looking a little bit on the ragged side."

"I don't doubt that. I've barely slept since Monday, so forgive me if I'm a bit slow today. This one cut deep, all the way to the governor, so I've got that to contend with on top of the normal roller coaster of an investigation. I'm just simply wiped out."

"Keep the faith."

"This line of work can make that challenging. At least at times. Like this."

"So how can I help?"

"You can't. I'm bound not to tell you very much."

"Bound by what?"

"By duty, that's all."

"Duty? That's got nothing do with it. You know whatever we talk about stays between us. Look, don't misunderstand me. I'm not going to ask you anything about the investigation, but if you want to talk about any of it, I'm here to listen."

"You mean you don't want to know who did it?" Viceroy asked, feigning shocked disbelief.

"You already know?"

"No, we don't know. We haven't got a clue. Well, actually, we have a few clues, but none that point in any particular direction."

"To answer your question then, I'm as interested as anyone would be." Ox sat back as Lydia reappeared with their food. He said a quick blessing and swallowed his first bite before continuing. "So?"

"Alright, listen. I'm probably breaking a few rules by talking about it, but after a week of hell I would appreciate just letting me vent. So, here goes." Viceroy leaned forward and lowered his voice. "We've eliminated terrorism. No group or individual has claimed responsibility and we'd have that by now. I've consulted the FBI on that angle and they agreed with me the night before last that it's not pointing in that direction. Other than that, we don't know who or what we're dealing with yet, and that bothers me a great deal. Normally, after the first week or so, I've got some sense about the direction we need to take. But this one has me completely in the dark. And if the public had a clue that we're still barely out of the starting gate…well, I don't even want to go there."

Taking a forkful of eggs and gulping his coffee, he continued, "So we don't know if we're dealing with a love triangle, a psycho, a disgruntled golf course employee, a stalker, or something even uglier. Five people have now died and the only thing they did wrong was go to Pine Creek for breakfast that morning, or be a caddie for Mary Hale, or be a twenty-year-old waitress serving coffee on the balcony."

"Yeah, it's brutal."

"And, I can't tell you about the one clue we discovered, but it carried a message and I'm afraid there might be more to come."

Ox paused in mid-bite, gently setting his fork down and then sitting back as the reality of his words sank in. "And that's the burden of your moment. Another attack may happen."

"Yeah," Viceroy said in a whisper.

A long silence hung over the booth. Viceroy held his hands together on the table contemplating what else to say, if anything. A busboy a few tables over dropped some silverware, breaking the moment for them. As Ox's attention returned to the tabletop, he noticed for the first time that Viceroy wasn't wearing his wedding ring.

"So prayers will continue for the investigation, but it looks like there might be other developments," he said with a nod to Viceroy's hand. "You're not wearing it?"

Viceroy looked out the window. "I know I told you I wasn't going to take it off, but I just can't handle having it on anymore. I'm resigned to simply checking my mailbox every day for the papers."

"Well, where does that stand? Does she have them?"

"Yeah, I think she does. I signed them like I told you I was going to and sent them down to her sister in Orlando so she could deliver them to Debbie. But nothing's come back yet."

"Did Donna say she got them?"

"Yeah, she texted me a month ago that she'd received them and that she'd get them to Debbie. Donna's been great through this whole thing. I can sense she's torn whenever I've talked to her. Debbie's lucky to have her as a sister."

"Do you still think she's living with her?"

"I really don't know. I guess I believe that's where she is, but Donna won't say. I think she wants to tell me, but she's honoring Debbie's wishes. I stopped asking four months ago. The divorce papers list Donna's address as the residence so it's not much of a reach to surmise that's probably where she is. I guess she could be anywhere, though, and just using Donna's home as her address."

"Look, as hard as this may be, don't return to that place you were in when I met you. I know the note she left didn't give you much, but someday down the road she'll realize that she owes you more than 'being married to you just completely overwhelmed me.' Maybe someday she'll stop running and realize that what she had was something very special."

"Maybe. But it's been so long I'm out of hope. If God's talking to me, I can't hear Him."

"He usually never strikes up direct conversation, but I understand how you may feel."

"Just some sort of sign isn't too much to ask, is it?"

"I suppose not. But then again things go unseen without light. The two of you have been looking for answers for over a year, but you're looking into darkness to find them. Light brings visibility. The stronger the light, the clearer the understanding. And light is always strongest at its center. That's where God lives and shines. I guess I'm telling you to shift your gaze. The eyes of your heart may simply need enlightenment. Return to the center. And I think that goes for all of life's challenges. Do you understand what I'm saying?"

Viceroy stared into his coffee for a long while before answering. "I need time." He reached into his coat pocket and pulled something out. "In the meanwhile, I ask for a favor." Ox nodded. "I was wondering if you'd hold onto this for me until such time as, well...." He pushed his wedding ring across the table.

Ox let it sit there for a moment while he contemplated the request. Taking the ring would seem that he was supportive of the possibility of their divorce, but not taking it would devastate his friend. In slow motion he pulled it closer to him but didn't pick it up.

"It would be appreciated if you held it in safe-keeping for me. Having it anywhere near me is just too demoralizing right now."

Ox scratched his chin, wrestling with an appropriate response. "Then I'll hold onto it for you. Not out of agreement, but just because you're my friend," he said as he took the ring, adding with a smile, "although, my Roger Viceroy prayer requests are getting numerous."

"Well, of all the prayer warriors He has to listen to each day, the Ox has to rank pretty high."

Ox chuckled and raised his coffee cup in a toast.

"I think I'm just behind the Pope," he said as he set his cup down.

Viceroy held up his hand and scrunched together his thumb and forefinger to signify how little distance there was between Ox and the Pope. Lydia whisked by to pick up their empty plates and slap their bill on the table.

"I've got this," Viceroy said.

"You got it last time."

Before he could respond, his cell phone rang. After a brief conversation, with the person on the other end doing most of the talking, he clicked off, pulled a twenty out of his wallet, and flung it on the table as he scooted out of the booth.

"Roger?"

"Gotta go. I think Howard Hale just committed suicide." Before Ox could even comment, Viceroy was at the door. With one hand on the knob he turned back towards the booth. "Ox?"

The big man twisted around. "Yeah?"

"Thanks."

"Always."

"And one more thing. This is going to consume me until we get whoever did it. I don't know how long that's going to take, but until then you shouldn't expect to see me on Sunday mornings. I hope you understand." He hurried out the door to his vehicle and drove off.

Pastor Oxenhaus watched him through the window and turned back to his coffee, cradling the cup with one large hand as he stared ahead. *May the Lord guide your steps...and your heart.*

CHAPTER 5

What a dump, the assassin observed as he turned off the Interstate on the outskirts of Buchanan, North Dakota. The sun was descending towards evening on this western outpost; a woodsman's paradise with rolling hills, farms, tracts of forest land, and the occasional stream along the fifteen-minute drive into town. Buchanan was an echo of Curwood, feeding his rage. The downtown area, a four-block-long strip, included a couple of restaurants, a country gift store, the offices of the town's only lawyer and doctor, two gas stations, three churches, one grocery store called Wolski's, and the obligatory two bars per block. One traffic light controlled the only intersection of significance.

He had been here five times before; most recently two months ago when he'd had to spend three days completing his arrangements. Wanting to stay out of sight, he had avoided the Green Gables Inn, the town's only motel, and spent the first night in his car at the Interstate's rest stop one mile east of the Buchanan exit. There were a few truckers and one other vehicle, but nothing to cause him alarm. On the second night he drove an extra twenty miles west to stay at the Holiday Inn in Jamestown. This time, however, he had no need to hide. He'd be in and out before anyone even noticed.

He made sure to stay at the posted speed limit as he drove north towards the Green Gables on the southern edge of town, a few blocks from Williams Street, the road that would take him east in the morning to Spiritwood Lake and his appointment with Mrs. Wanda Schmitt.

The motel's neon VACANCY sign lit up just as he pulled in to join the other two cars in the gravel parking area. The Green Gables was a simple strip with an office at the south end and eighteen single-bed units stretching to the north. He parked the Maverick some distance from the office and shut off the engine. There he sat for a moment, contemplating his next twelve hours. The engine pinged for a few minutes as it cooled down. His rear was aching; the three day drive from Milwaukee in a less-than-smooth car had taken its toll. The Maverick was serving its purpose, but he longed for the comfort of driving his well-appointed pick-up. *My own bed as well,* his mind screamed at him, *instead of this rat-infested flea bag motel.* He forced himself to concentrate on tomorrow morning's events. The venom began to stir once again, and his eyes narrowed as he stared through his windshield at the darkening North Dakota sky. Unconsciously, he gripped the steering wheel ever tighter and his upper arms went taut. The vengeful rage that had consumed his life was once again bubbling to the surface. *There will be an accounting.* The motel sign flickered for a moment in his peripheral vision, and he relaxed his grip on the wheel.

As he stepped out into a surprisingly warm evening, a dog somewhere down the road barked its welcome. He walked to the back of the car and opened the trunk to retrieve the duffel bag he had packed with enough clothes to last him a week. Enough, he had figured, to take him to Buchanan and back, with his next scheduled stop in-between.

He slung the strap over his shoulder, slammed the trunk shut, and entered the office to register. Inside, it was everything he had expected—crappy wood paneling, beat-up orange carpet pocked with a free-form pattern of cigarette burns and stains from a thousand spills. Straight ahead was a desk in desperate need of refinishing. He walked up to the counter and hit the bell. After a minute, he hit it again.

A young woman no more than twenty years old came through the door behind the desk. Her blonde hair was cropped short,

45

just covering her ears with bangs that barely grazed the top of her eyebrows. Her face was as plain as he'd ever seen, and he thought, but didn't say, "Hello, Jane," the moment he saw her.

"Good evening, sir. Can I help you?" she asked.

"Yes, I'd like a room for the night please. Non-smoking."

The young lady giggled. "We don't have none of those."

"Then whatever you have will do," he said, noticing that she was staring at the Star of David pendant hanging from his neck, a prop for his assumed identity. After ten seconds of silence he leaned forward and repeated, "Miss, I said any room will do."

"Oh, I'm sorry. Sure. If you'll just fill out this here sheet," she apologized as she finally tore her eyes away and handed him a slip of paper. "Will that be cash tonight?"

He took the paper from her and gave her a nod. She simply smiled and stared while he stood at the desk filling out the paperwork. Under the line for NAME he put in his working alias and made up an address in Wisconsin to match the plates on his car. Factually, the Maverick was registered in the Upper Peninsula of Michigan, where he'd bought it for $5,000 cash. So long as he stayed within the speed limit and didn't get into an accident the discrepancy would never be noticed.

He handed the slip back to the girl, who looked down at the name and then back up to him. She continued to stare, finally forcing him to speak.

"Is there a problem?"

"No, no, I'm sorry, sir," she stuttered as she put the slip down and turned to grab a room key. "It's just that, well...we don't see your kind around here much."

"Well Miss, I could take offense at that comment, but I think you're a nice young girl and you didn't mean anything by it."

"Oh, no, no," she stammered as she handed him the key. "It's three doors down. Room sixteen."

"Thank you...?"

"Oh, the name's Karen."

"Thanks, Karen. Have a delightful evening." He picked up his duffel and headed to the door.

"You're welcome, Mr. Goldberg," she shouted as the door shut behind him.

Outside in the falling shadows he felt more at home. Alone. Nothing but him, his thoughts, and his glorious purpose. The neighborhood dog began its noise again, causing him to long once more for his black Labrador, Raven, and the comforts of home. He inserted the room key and disappeared from sight, never to be seen in Buchanan again.

The bed creaked as he sat to untie his shoes and begin the long, slow wait until the appointed hour. One of the first things he did was pull the travel alarm clock out of his bag and set it for 4:00 a.m., then duplicate the wake-up time on his phone. *Two alarms always.* He unpacked a few more things and gazed around at his sorry surroundings. The water had a slight whiff of iron and the walls were cinder block, adding to the misery.

He undressed and put on a pair of silk shorts and a well-worn t-shirt. Settling onto the bed, he propped two pillows behind his head and relaxed as best he could against the hard mattress and thin pillows. Even though he had many hours to wait, he began mentally rehearsing the next morning's protocol. It took all his willpower to stop and tell himself to slow down and stop worrying.

Mary Hale's death went exactly as planned, and this one should be just as smooth. Not wanting to focus on the potential hazards in his strategy, he reached for the TV remote on the nightstand and pushed the power button.

Clicking through the channels he found CNN and decided to catch up on what the pundits were saying about the Pine Creek Country Club bombing. Except for the last day in North Dakota, when all he could get was static-filled country music, he'd been listening to all the news talk radio stations—so far, he hadn't heard any mention of the golf ball. *Either they haven't found it, or the inept grounds crew unknowingly raked it away. Or else they're just keeping that little piece of information to themselves. It doesn't really matter. They'll do the math and figure it out eventually.*

He leaned forward as the woman at the anchor desk began her update. Two minutes in, however, a crawl at the bottom of the screen had him on his feet. HOWARD HALE'S DEATH RULED A SUICIDE. Pacing furiously, he screamed in silent rage at the dead man. *You son-of-a-bitch! You coward! Five days is all you could last? You're more pathetic than I thought. Was it the photo? Wish I could make the funeral. Seeing you permanently horizontal would be a blessing. That's if they can make you presentable after blowing your brains out. At least your last days were spent in hell.*

He took a deep breath, let go of his fury, and lay back on the bed exhausted. He kept a fuzzy eye on the television as the segment concluded with a prerecorded interview with the lead investigator. *Well, well, well. My enemies have a white knight, eh? Roger Viceroy of the Midwest Region Special Crimes Unit. A name I must remember. I knew Mary Hale would bring out the cavalry. Wanda won't. But then again, I'm not in control of the order or the method. They decided both of those all those years ago. So many, many years...*he mused as he finally nodded off.

CHAPTER 6

Sixteen-year-old Bennett Wang falls in love for the first and only time. It had been a decade since the Wang's arrival in Curwood. The elementary and middle school years were, in hindsight, a difficult but smoother walk. Children tend to be less hardened than their parents. Yet, as the years passed, the bias and the vitriol grew ever thicker, save for a few of his classmates. One of those was a girl who was always ready with a tender smile or an unspoken aura that she was not in the prejudice camp.

Every-other generation or so, a small town in a remote place produces a daughter with looks that transcend her environment; a girl straight out of a Hollywood love story who lands in their lap to bless them with her beauty and grace. Someone the locals recognize as special, the town's treasure—until the next one comes along sometime in the distant future. In this generation, her name is Greta Zumwald, the girl with the vibrant red hair that falls around her face and shoulders like soft waves on the shore. A few freckles, perfectly placed, accent her cheeks and the bridge of her flawlessly molded nose. Her posture is faultless; her shoulders at just the right width, blending to her torso, which flows down to legs that are both long and elegant. She has the demeanor to match the grace with which she carries herself. Truly she is a treasure in the Zumwald family. In all of Curwood, for that matter.

It is a snowy Saturday afternoon a few days before Christmas when Bennett finally finds the courage to proactively say hello to her. School let out the day before and will not resume for two weeks. The wealthier families are already leaving for warmer destinations, while many of the remaining residents are heading south to Green Bay for last minute shopping or to other places where they have family. Those left behind will revel in their Christmas traditions, attend St. Mary's on Christmas morning, and more or less hunker down for a couple of weeks of relaxation. The paper mills are on shut-down and ice fishing season is officially beginning.

The Wangs decided to stay put for this year's holiday, the first time they do so in the ten long years they have lived in Curwood, despite being mostly outcasts since the moment they drove into town all those years ago. Many of Curwood's citizens had fought the Japanese in World War II. A few were veterans of the Korean War, and the two Spurgeon boys were killed in Vietnam. The locals hold fast to the belief that those young men's days were cut short fighting the yellow peril. Never mind that Tao Wang is from China.

Equally important to the Curwood faithful, the Wangs aren't Catholic. The Wangs aren't even Lutheran. The Wangs don't believe. The Wangs are not to be associated with except when absolutely necessary. Within a week of their moving in, Father Freitag had paid them a visit on behalf of the town elders, asking them to leave. They politely declined. In the aftermath of that moment the Wangs had established a surface-level accommodation; a sort of truce between perceived enemies that would never allow for complete acceptance, but would provide a modicum of livability in the face of a strong undercurrent of blind hatred.

Tao's job at American Papers is the anchor that keeps the Wangs in Curwood. He makes extremely good money and has been assigned a project that excites him. His intellect and talent in the field is not lost on the mill's owners, and they soon realized having him on board trumped any other considerations. Ethnicity be damned. Profits be exalted. Tao has an equity stake in the project's outcome. He is on the cusp of something major, and leaving Curwood is not an option. Moving to any other town in the area would just be a repeat of what they are experiencing, so the Wangs decide to ride out this storm, no matter the cost, while trying to shield Bennett as best they can.

As the snow falls that December afternoon, Bennett sleds at Bullwinkle Hill on the eastern outskirts of town where no one else ever goes. Except today.

He rides his snowmobile over from Juniper Street with sled in tow. As usual the spot is deserted and he is able to sled without having to share the hill. When he climbs back up after his third run, he hears the soft hum of another snowmobile followed by the distinctive noise of a troubled motor. He knows the person is just over the top of the hill, so he picks up his pace a little to see who it is. Upon reaching the crest, Bennett spots the machine. The rider, whose back is to him, is standing with hands on hips, obviously annoyed. She pulls off her helmet and long, red hair tumbles out.

Bennett has a choice: get on his machine and go back home, or help out the girl. Not just any girl. *The* girl. Her. The one. Roy Spurgeon's girlfriend. His heart pounds so hard in his chest that he thinks he is having a heart attack.

Responding to the little voice whispering in his ear, Bennett sticks his sled in a snow pile, takes a deep breath, and descends the hill to Greta Zumwald.

CHAPTER 7

David Green was sitting comfortably in one of the interview rooms at Milwaukee PD headquarters when Viceroy, Regina, and Silk arrived. A detective from the force met them at the door and informed Viceroy that the gentleman's home was across the street from Pine Creek and he had come down to the station about an hour ago because he had witnessed something he wanted to share. But, having seen Roger Viceroy on television, Mr. Green had stated in no uncertain terms that he would speak only to him.

Viceroy extended his hand and the man took it with a surprisingly firm grasp. He was older and mostly bald. Viceroy guessed he was in his mid-eighties and, based on the fact that he was wearing a neat blue suit, white dress shirt, and red and white striped bow tie, it appeared that he considered this an important occasion. Viceroy introduced his deputies, and all three took seats across from the man at the interview table. Another police officer entered and passed out bottles of water and mugs of fresh coffee. Viceroy nodded his thanks and turned his attention to the man across from him. Thick glasses covered almost half his face and Viceroy's first thought was that his eyesight might have an impact on the accuracy of what he was about to tell them.

Viceroy started with an encouraging smile. "First, Mr. Green, we want to thank you for coming down here this morning. It's a brave thing to do and it must have been a tough decision for you."

"Tough?" Green exclaimed in a raspy tone. "Hell, Mr. Viceroy, I'd have been here sooner if my mind wasn't so addled. I've been watching you on TV all week and I finally remembered something from that morning."

"Well, regardless, we want to thank you. Any bit of information you have will be helpful."

"Just doin' my part. I'm an Army man, ya know? Thirty-seven years in the service. It's my duty. Been retired for twenty-five years and me and Lucy just sit at home nowadays."

"Well, your wife must be very proud of you," Viceroy said, noticing the man's wedding ring.

The man leaned forward a bit and drew his eyebrows together. "Mildred? Hell, man, she's been dead for nine years. Lucy's my dog." Silk and Regina tried to hold back their grins and Viceroy looked embarrassed at his gaffe. The man leaned back again and continued, "Now don't be feelin' weird or nothin'. Hell, how were you supposed to know about Mildred? Good thing my cat died too, 'cause his name was Ricky. If I'd a said I was home with Lucy and Ricky you'd a thought I was some kinda *I Love Lucy* freak. Truth of it is, Lucy was my dog's name when I was a kid, so we named her the same, and Ricky is short for Rickaroo, the cat's real name. Mildred's choice, not mine. Anyway, I'm just doin' my part and figgered you were the man to talk to."

Viceroy said, "You came to the right place. My understanding is that you saw or heard something the morning of the bombing?"

"Both."

"Please share what's on your mind then."

"Well, my house is four doors down from the top of the street on Talbot Lane. It's a quiet little dead-end street with not much traffic. Lucy occasionally gets into a barkin' match with Shadow in the next yard, but besides that it's like bein' on a private road most a the time. Anyway, I bring that up because you notice things when they're out of place, ya know?" All three looked at one another. Something "out of place" is exactly what they had been hunting for the whole week.

Green continued, "Look, I'm not tryin' to sound uppity here, but let's just say Talbot Lane doesn't have a car on it with a motor that you can hear. Hell, the only reason Mildred and I moved there was because of the inheritance she got. That, and because I love to play golf. Used to belong to Pine Creek, but when my driver couldn't go farther than my grandson's wedge, I gave up the game." Scratching his forehead, he continued, "Anyway, what I'm tryin' to say is that it's not a neighborhood people come home to after shoppin' at Walmart, if you get my meaning."

"I get your meaning. It's a very upscale street, as are most of them around Pine Creek," Viceroy said.

"Yeah, detective, but Talbot doesn't have anyone under the age of sixty on it unless the relatives are visiting. You won't find that in any other neighborhood around the golf course."

"Mr. Green," Viceroy said, impatient to get to the information he was hoping the man might possess, "clearly you think you know something connected to what happened at Pine Creek. Something 'out of place' as you said?"

"Yes, sir."

"Well then, could you please tell us what you think you saw?" Regina piped in.

"Well, ma'am, I was just gettin' to it. I thought you should know about the street because that was what the weird thing was." He paused and took a large gulp of his coffee. The three were like children at a storybook reading, waiting for the page to be turned. When he finally resumed, he spoke in a more determined manner as if to convey that what he was going to tell them was the crux of his reason for coming in. "I take Lucy for a little walk at 7:30 a.m. every morning. She enjoys that. I usually let her pee in Barsamian's yard because I can't stand that bastard. Anyway, we were just gettin' home around 8:00 a.m. when I heard the bomb go off at the club. Of course, I didn't know at the time that it was a bomb and I sure as hell didn't know where it came from. I stood on my front porch for a minute or so tryin' to figger out what was goin' on, and I was just about to go back inside when I heard the sound that brought me down here today." He paused again and took another drink of coffee. "Can I have some more of this? Since Mildred died I'm afraid I'm just no good at makin' a cup of good coffee, and this stuff's great."

Silk took the cup, went to the door, and handed it to a detective who had been watching the proceedings through a two-way mirror. He took the empty cup and handed a new one to Silk, who delivered it to Green with a soft pat on the man's shoulder.

"Thanks, son."

"No problem. But you have us on the edge of our seats."

"Sorry. Don't mean to be all dramatic but, hell, all I have to look forward to is goin' back home, so I guess I'm stretchin' it out a little."

"No problem," Viceroy said.

The old man took off his glasses, wiped them with a hanky from his back pocket, then put them back on, adjusting the angle just so. "As I was sayin', I was about to go inside when I heard a sound—a car. It had a very loud motor on it and it was comin' from up the street by the fence near the golf course. Sounded like a teenager's car or somethin'. Very noisy. After it started, it revved once and I could tell whoever was drivin' it took off real quick. You remember what I told you about the cars on Talbot Lane? Cadillacs, Mercedes, and Lincolns are all that you'll find. Not one of 'em in a color other than black, white or silver. I mention that because the sound from the motor made me look up the street and I caught the rear end of the car that was peelin' away. It was yellow, Mr. Viceroy." He then put his hands on the table and leaned straight forward for added emphasis. "Yellow's not a color you'll find on anyone's cars on Talbot Lane."

The three snapped to attention. "You sound like you know your cars, so do you know what make it was?" Viceroy asked.

"'Fraid not, Mr. Viceroy. But it was older. Had that look to it that you don't see on cars today. Don't know what that may mean, but if I were you three I'd be lookin' for an older model yellow car with a loud engine. Can't be many of those around town." The old man took one last gulp of coffee, wiped his mouth, leaned back into his chair, and crossed his arms; a grin lit up his face.

Silk was out the door before Viceroy could thank the gentleman.

CHAPTER 8

The Maverick was pinging once again next to a willow tree about ten feet from a small river which could've been classified a stream, but the assassin didn't care to know the difference. All he knew was that it was roughly two miles away from the nearest road and, as far as he could tell, probably ten miles from the nearest human being. The flat land and scrubby terrain of North Dakota made for an easy off-road excursion. He needed to burn a half a day and thought some target practice wouldn't hurt.

He pissed away his morning coffee into the slow-moving water, then retrieved the two exact guns he needed from the trunk and began walking. A rocky hill on the other side was perfect and he soon found a narrowing point where he could jump across, then walked back to the hill.

Using it as a backdrop, he picked out a red-colored rock about five feet off the ground and paced out twenty steps, the maximum range he would possibly need and that accuracy could handle. The dart gun was different. A dart's arc was more variant than a bullet. He dropped both bags and knelt to prep.

He inserted the ballistic syringe into one of the practice darts; a collared one to ensure retention of the needle and syringe once he removed it from the target, and that the full dose would be administered. Essential point. He knew he would need the full twenty minutes before it wore off. He fired off twelve rounds standing and another twelve while bent on one knee. All two dozen were bullseyes.

Satisfied, he restored the dart gun and pulled out the rifle, admiring the black beauty as he held it. An aluminum Barrett M98B Tactical. *Probably too much weapon for the task, but what the hell.* Grabbing the tripod, he climbed to the top of the hill which he determined would be approximately the same height as his perch for the kill shot. Using the scope, the assassin found a lone tree on the plain below him, also approximately the appropriate distance. Tripod next. Thirty shots to follow, all with him squatting. Each crack of the rifle firing was music.

After thirty minutes and the first twenty-eight hitting, he picked out a more specific target other than the main trunk five feet off the ground. A knot of wood on the first main branch about the size of a baseball. Repositioning, he knelt, scoped and fired, then saw wood chips splinter off the branch dead to target. A self-congratulatory feeling surged through him and he loaded the final bullet. Number thirty.

Let's repeat. Same routine, same target: the knot. The crack of the rifle pierced the air. He stood up and stared. *Fuck.* Missed it. His mind raced with what-ifs and he sat down to think. This only happened once in the last two years, but his inability to calculate the wind impact was the culprit that time. No wind now, at least not enough to make a difference on top of this hill. He gathered his rifle and tripod into the bag and descended.

Can't happen...

It won't.

CHAPTER 9

Silk sounded like he'd been running as his voice came over the speakerphone in Viceroy's office. "Ford Maverick," he repeated, taking a deep breath.

"You're absolutely sure?" Regina asked. "There's lots of yellow cars."

"Yeah, but Sandy Holden would know."

Regina said, "Sandy who?"

Silk took another breath, "Holden. As in Holden Ford."

"Where does she fit into this?" Viceroy asked, hoping for an express version of the story. Both he and Regina recognized the name, of course, but that didn't answer the question.

"Sandy Holden lives on Talbot Lane. Her house is the first one on the left when you come onto the street. I came out here as soon as I left and spoke to half a dozen residents on the street to verify or add to Green's story, but no one had a clue. I was about to give up and come back downtown when I noticed her pulling into her driveway. I ran and caught her on her front porch. Nice lady. I introduced myself and she was very accommodating. When she told me who she was, I couldn't believe my luck. We're looking for a type of vehicle and Milwaukee's largest Ford dealer pulls into her driveway."

"That's a gift," Viceroy said.

"Yeah, Preacher, I hear you. So I explain the situation and she tells me that she wasn't home when the bomb went off. She left for the dealership at around 7:45 a.m. But then she tells me that when she got to the end of the street she saw what looked like a yellow car in the grove of oaks at the corner, and she gives me the nugget of all nuggets. When she completed her turn off the street, she glanced toward the trees one more time and saw the car almost in its entirety. A Ford Maverick. She said her son used to drive one when he was a teenager and she still has one on display in her showroom's retro section."

Viceroy said, "Bingo."

"Then she asks if that helps," Silk added. "All I could do was give her a huge smile and tell her my next car is going to be a Ford."

"Mine too. Check out the oak grove and see if you can get a tread mold for testing," Viceroy said.

"Will do," Silk replied and rang off.

Viceroy turned to Regina. "Get in touch with Wisconsin DMV and let's see what records they've got on a yellow Ford Maverick."

"Should we notify DeWitt?" Regina asked. "To put out an APB?"

"Not yet. Let's see if we can get a better handle on what we're dealing with first."

Regina hurried out of the office and Viceroy pushed himself away from his desk, spun his chair around to face the wall, and drew a deep breath.

Hanging on the wall was a bulletin board with pictures of the only two pieces of evidence they had. One was of the golf ball with the writing on it. The ball itself had been cut in half by whoever planted it there, core removed, and glued back together; surmised by Viceroy after he had it x-rayed by forensics. The other picture was of the one item that had been placed inside the hollowed-out ball: a penny from 1982.

CHAPTER 10

The car was packed to the brim with her entire wardrobe and other material needs. The trip had taken three days, with one stop in northern Georgia and another in Indiana before arriving in Milwaukee. Debbie steered into the hotel parking lot as she and her sister quickly checked-in. The appointment with the apartment rental agent was in a mere forty-five minutes and the two wanted to freshen up after the six hour final leg of the journey.

Debbie had selected a five square mile radius in which to search; a place that would be near enough to her husband's condo, yet removed enough to ensure a random chance meeting would be extremely low risk. She just felt better if she was in the area, hoping to find a way to connect with him when the time was right. For the moment, her first step was to reestablish a basic semblance of a life in Milwaukee.

Five months prior, with the tatters of her marriage having consumed her ability to fully function, she reached the end of the trail. During a long tearful weekend of introspection, and with Donna's help, she looked in her wake and saw the self-inflicted pain and anguish wrought on her, Roger, and what should have been the beginning of a newly fulfilled life. With eyes wide open, the rush of unconditional love and unquenchable thirst to repair the damage became a tsunami of raw emotion and spiritual hunger. She knew what she had to do. Within a few weeks she found a position as a regional franchise sales manager for a Florida-based pizza chain that was expanding into Wisconsin. It was half the money, but that didn't matter. It was her ticket to return.

The sisters gobbled down a grab-and-go sandwich from the hotel's convenience store as they hopped into the car. Within ten minutes they met up with the leasing agent at the first apartment stop. Four hours and five apartments later Debbie was exhausted and sullen. Not one was what she was hoping for and the only one that was close to acceptable was twice the rent she was willing to pay. The agent took her to one final place; a smaller, one-bedroom apartment in a new complex, fully furnished as she needed. The moment they pulled into the parking lot Debbie knew it would be the winner. Not too pricey, quality furnishings, good-looking building, and a private entry to boot. But the clincher was its location. It was within walking distance of a really nice looking church called Bread of Life that she saw on the way in.

Debbie took her sister to the airport to catch the late night flight back to Orlando. They had an emotional goodbye on the sidewalk of the departing gate area. Donna grabbed her suitcase and disappeared into the terminal. Debbie watched her go, then drove in the dark back to the hotel; a half hour of being suddenly very lonely.

When she got to her room, she quickly got ready for bed and flicked on the TV to finish the night, flipping to the local newscast. There, on her screen, she saw him. Roger. He had just finished a taped interview and was exiting the shot as the reporter gave her wrap-up of the status of the Pine Creek bombing. She sat at end of the bed and reached out a hand to the screen, as if in some way it would connect her to him. At the end of the report, Debbie flicked off the TV, sitting in the stillness with the image of her husband fresh in her mind. She scooted herself back to her pillow and laid down. The last thing she saw before turning off the light was her briefcase sitting on the edge of the desk in the corner. Inside was the lease agreement for the apartment and a stack of paperwork for her new job which was to begin the following week. Buried at the bottom was a clasped manila envelope with the divorce papers awaiting their fate.

CHAPTER 11

Cub Foods in Appleton, Wisconsin, was almost deserted. Clare Kittleton always shopped late on Thursday nights because the store was a ghost town. It was midnight and she'd just finished her nursing shift. She was pleased to find the parking lot wide open, as expected, as she found a front row parking space. Even though it was still mid-September, a cold wind was blowing, and she hurried inside, grabbing a cart on the way. With all three daughters coming home from college to celebrate their father's birthday this weekend, she knew she would have a houseful. Her oldest was bringing her fiancé and the other two were bringing their roommates.

The assassin had followed her from the hospital where she worked and pulled the Maverick into a space a few rows over. Once he'd seen her enter the store he got out, checking his mustache in the side view mirror to make doubly sure it was glued on correctly; he was pleased to see that the wound on his forehead had almost completely healed. He touched it gently. *Wanda got me with that paddle. Damn, that hurt. Didn't expect any fight from that little thing.* He straightened up and locked the door, then put on a baseball cap over his recently dyed black hair and pulled down the brim to hide his face as much as possible. Finally, he slid a wedding band onto his finger and headed inside.

He had been monitoring Clare's shopping habits and had

followed her here many times over the last two years. The aisles were long, wide, well stocked, and devoid of customers. He also knew that she was a slow and picky shopper, so there was no reason to hurry. He let his fingers find their way into the front right pocket of his jeans and unconsciously began playing with the penny. Grabbing a cart, he headed over to aisle four and surveyed the products in order to choose just the right one. He'd intended to do this when he first arrived in town a few days earlier, but he was tired after his trip to North Dakota and, with two now under his belt, his confidence level was high. He rewarded himself by taking some time to relax in his hotel. But now, to ensure a flawless execution, he would have to make just the right product selection. Once he'd made his decision, he turned and began hunting for Clare Kittleton. Along the way he randomly grabbed an assortment of items to use as props.

He found her in aisle seven as she was deciding which oatmeal flavors her daughters would like best. He looked up and down the aisle and saw that they were alone. Pulling out the shopping list he'd prepared in advance, he began moving toward her, looking as if he were lost. He pushed his cart steadily in her direction, keeping his head turned to the shelves on his right. After nine paces, his cart bumped rather hard into hers.

"Oh my gosh, I am so sorry," he said, feigning embarrassment.

Clare had her back turned when the carts bumped. Startled, she pivoted and saw a man with a mustache awkwardly apologizing.

She put her hand out to indicate that it was no big deal. "Oh, no worries. I bought cart insurance at the front desk," she cracked.

He smiled and gave a self-conscious chuckle. "I'm afraid I'm just useless in supermarkets. My wife usually does our shopping so I'm never sure where anything is, and I just wasn't paying attention."

"Well," she said, examining the items in her cart, "no dents or broken glass, so I guess you were within the speed limit."

He laughed again. "Please, I'm really sorry. But now that I'm talking to a friendly face, maybe you can help me…?"

"Sure. I'd be glad to. What are you looking for?"

"Well, I would call my wife but I left my cell phone in the car. She's looking for cream of tartar. I'm not even sure what that is."

"Cream of tartar? Hmm…"

"She wrote down that it should be the McCormick brand only," he added, as if to help clarify the situation.

"Well, cream of tartar is used in baking, so it's either in the spice section or near one of the bakery items, like flour."

"And that would be…?"

"Probably aisle four or five."

"Okay, thanks." He turned to go and then stopped and sheepishly addressed her once more. "Miss, I don't mean to be a bother, but I've already been here far longer than I should and if you could help me locate this tartar thing I would really be very grateful." He helped seal the deal with the best smile he could muster.

Clare Kittleton grinned in return. "Sure," she said, "no problem. I'm actually headed there myself to get some flour." She quickly grabbed a couple of boxes of oatmeal and indicated that he should follow her. As they walked, she explained about her daughters coming home for her husband's birthday. He asked about the girls' ages and where they all went to college. By the time she got through her explanation, they had reached the baking aisle. There was just one other shopper, a young woman at the far end, but she was finishing up as they arrived.

"Ah, here you go," Clare said with satisfaction. "A whole shelf of spices and baking goods." She scanned the items and spotted cream of tartar on the bottom shelf. "Down here." She grabbed a can, straightened up, and was just turning to hand it to him when she felt a sharp stab of pain in the middle of her chest. The man was smiling again, but instead of reaching for the can, he swiftly shoved a handkerchief in her mouth. Clare's eyes widened as she looked down to see the handle of a small knife protruding from her pink nurse's scrub top, which was quickly turning red with blood. For the first time, she noticed that the man was wearing surgical gloves. As the pain registered with her brain, she tried to react, but the life was already leaving her body. Gently, he laid her down on her back in the aisle next to the spice shelf.

He pulled the penny from his jeans and placed it in her mouth, then removed the gloves and stuffed them in his left-hand pocket. Bending down, he softly whispered in her ear. "Thank you, Clare. On second thought, I don't need the cream of tartar after all."

With dying eyes she saw him get up and walk away before the darkness descended forever.

The assassin hustled to the back of the store as quickly as he could without drawing attention to himself, and heard a woman scream as he pushed himself through the stockroom doors and out the rear of the store. In the darkness of the parking lot, he threw his mustache into a drain a few feet from the Maverick. A block down the road he pulled into a gas station for a fill-up, and a few minutes later was humming along I-43 on his way to Green Bay.

CHAPTER 12

Curwood's varsity basketball team wins the state title, beating the South Milwaukee Eagles in overtime. Most amazing about the feat is that there are only seven players on the team. The whole class of '77 number only sixty-eight kids, but somehow they pull off the impossible. The upset makes national headlines and earns a small feature in *Sports Illustrated*. The Curwood Bears become state heroes and high school basketball legends. Bennett Wang is on the team but sees only a few minutes of play that entire season and absolutely none during the state tournament.

Three months earlier, Dr. Spurgeon had held a meeting with Curwood's athletic director and boys' head coach, Marlin Butters, a man in his early fifties with outrageously bushy eyebrows and a closetful of pants that stop at his ankles. Dr. Spurgeon informed Butters that should the Asian kid try out for the team, as was the rumor, the coach was to ensure that he didn't make the cut. Coach Butters dutifully acknowledged that he would make certain Bennett Wang was left off the roster, but on the night of the final cuts, with only nine boys trying out, two juniors get tangled up during a scrimmage and suffer season-ending knee injuries. Doing the math, Coach Butters knows that he must keep Bennett Wang; what's more, after witnessing the years of bullying Bennett has endured, he secretly holds a soft spot for the boy. He calls Dr. Spurgeon the next day and informs him of the situation, pleads his case, and hopes the good doctor will relent. Dr. Spurgeon remains silent for a long minute and then gives Butters new instructions. He is to make it so miserable for the boy that he will quit of his own accord. Coach Butters begins to object, knowing that he will need a minimum of seven players on the team in order to hold meaningful practices. Dr. Spurgeon threatens his job, and Coach Butters relents.

The coach informs Bennett that he's made the team and brings him into his office before the first practice. He outlines Bennett's role and shows the boy where to find all the bench towels, water coolers, shower towels, and soap. He instructs him on how to pump up a basketball to the correct air pressure. The team will need any and all of these items, and Bennett's main duty is to provide them to any player at any time. Other than that, he is not to touch anything else, *ever*, or he's off the team. Coach Butters then makes him run twenty laps around the gym while he addresses the other six players at mid-court.

During the next two weeks, Bennett never misses a practice. He also never touches a basketball except when he's pumping one up. He gets involved in physical activity when the tenth practice ends in a locker room towel-whipping by the other six players while Coach Butters finishes reading his paper before breaking it up. That night Bennett has to run only five laps before Coach shuts off the lights and locks up.

During the twelfth practice, Coach finally allows Bennett on the court during a particularly aggressive drill designed to teach the other six how a player can plow through a pick set by an opponent. Bennett lasts through three players before succumbing to dizziness from hitting his head repeatedly against the hardwood floor. Coach pretends to be indignant that Bennett can't finish the drill. Twenty-five laps are assigned before he can ice his head.

At the final practice, before the first game of the season, the players all receive their uniforms and warm-ups, which they will wear with great Curwood pride. The same uniforms have been handed down and used by Curwood basketball players for more than fifteen years, ever since Coach Marlin Butters came and changed the colors. The jerseys are numbered sequentially, and Bennett Wang is assigned number seven. Coach hands out the jerseys at the end of the practice. The other six slap hands, and they all put on their uniforms to pose for the team photo. The picture is snapped with the help of a student photographer, after which Bennett takes off for the stairs and his usual twenty-five laps. Once he's left, Coach tells the remaining six to put on their warm-ups and repositions them at center court for the official team photo, as per Dr. Spurgeon's instructions.

Even after his twenty-five laps, Bennett has enough energy to run all the way home. He has made it. He got his jersey. He has not allowed them to break him. He is on the Curwood Bears varsity basketball team. His parents weep with joy. Bennett never tells them the truth about what's happening at practices, but he does tell Greta during one of their secret meetings. She consoles him and comforts him. He feels better about the abuse.

Bennett never gets into a game, and every practice is a repeat of the last until Coach Butters and the six other team members figure out he isn't going to quit. Then they just ignore him. However, one of Coach's long-standing rules is that every team member gets to play at some point during the season, and he is not about to break with that tradition under any circumstances. Bennett gets into one minute of one game, an easy blow-out victory towards the end of the season. He doesn't score, rebound or record any statistic. After the game, Coach tells him he didn't contribute when he was on the court so he shouldn't expect to play again. He doesn't.

The season ends with an incredible run during the state tournament and the stunning victory over the Milwaukee team in the finals in front of five thousand fans at the Field House on the campus of the University of Wisconsin-Madison. Roy Spurgeon leads the team with twenty-seven points. Howard Hale adds twenty-two. The other four players knock in a few points as well. Bennett sits at the end of the bench. When the final buzzer sounds the Field House in Madison erupts as media, fans, parents, siblings, and other well-wishers swarm the floor to congratulate the Bears. The Spurgeon family rushes to Roy at center court and Dr.

Spurgeon, along with Howard Hale, lift Roy onto their shoulders. They spin slowly around while the media feverishly snap one picture after another. The noise is deafening as the Curwood fans revel to the tune of the Curwood fight song played by the school band assembled on the massive bleachers at one end of the court.

From his perch, Roy Spurgeon scans the ecstatic crowd searching for Greta. When he spots her, she is embracing Bennett Wang. He reaches down and taps his dad to get his attention, pointing toward the trysting couple. Dr. Spurgeon stops turning and follows the finger to see what his son sees. Their eyes alight on the abomination. The secret is no longer such.

CHAPTER 13

"I've never seen her like this before," Jerry King said as he turned toward Viceroy. "She's been unusually short-tempered. It's all just a little weird, like there's something in the air, but I can't put my finger on it. Wish I could tell you why she wanted this emergency meeting, but I don't have a clue."

Behind the wheel, Viceroy was regretting the Spanish omelet he'd eaten before picking Jerry up at his apartment in Madison on their way to meet with the governor at the Capitol. "Unfortunately, she isn't going to get any happier with the news I have for her," Viceroy said as he steered the car into a slot in the authorized security parking lot. "As you know, we haven't made much progress other than identifying the vehicle we think may have been involved in the bombing. That's the good news. But the bad news is that Wisconsin DMV gave us their final report at the close of business yesterday. Absolutely zero registered yellow Ford Mavericks. We've expanded the search to the surrounding states as of this morning. Regina's down at the office now coordinating."

"And Silk?" Jerry asked.

"He's on his way to MRSCU headquarters in Chicago. Strongsmith wants an in-depth report face-to-face. I was going to go myself, but when I got Governor Spurgeon's email last night saying that she wanted to meet at ten this morning, I sent Silk to cover for me."

"Silk and Strongsmith? Ha!" Jerry laughed out loud as he pictured Silk, six-and-a-half feet tall, sitting across the desk from the infamous Anthony Strongsmith at MRSCU, legs crossed, calmly sipping his coffee. Strongsmith was Silk's exact opposite, a short man with a taste for power suits and extravagant gestures. "I'd pay to see that one," he added.

Viceroy chuckled as he conjured his own images of the meeting. "My money would be on Silk."

"Mine too, except Strongsmith can outrank him to the finish line."

"Outrank, yeah, but I've never seen Silk outflanked. If Strongsmith tries to corner him he'll find the slickest detective he's ever run across. Strongsmith doesn't stand a chance." The two men looked at each other one more time and started cackling like drunken chickens as they imagined the two going toe-to-toe. It was the first release of tension either one of them had enjoyed in many days. "Okay, okay. Enough." Viceroy nearly shouted, biting his lip as he turned off the ignition. "It's almost time and we have a very serious meeting ahead of us."

It was a few minutes before ten when they reached the main entrance and stood waiting outside as they'd been instructed. Both men pulled their coats a little tighter against fall's bite in the morning air. With a little time to kill, Jerry lobbed a question. "So how're things going with Debbie, if you don't mind my asking?"

"I don't know what to tell you. We're nowhere. I'd say I'm managing, but that'd be a lie. I've gone over it about four thousand times in my head and I still can't figure out what happened. What did I do? What did I not do?"

"She's still AWOL?"

"Yeah. Look, I appreciate you asking, but I'd rather not talk about it. Maybe someday."

Jerry nodded and gave Viceroy a friendly pat. "No problem. For now, let's just focus on finding the bomber. It's been two weeks as of today and I think the governor wants more answers than we've been able to give her, which is why we're standing out here this morning."

At precisely 10:00 a.m., a black limousine pulled around the west end of the building and crawled towards them. Viceroy gave Jerry a nudge and both men unconsciously straightened their ties as the limo pulled up. Nick, the governor's long-time driver, got out and greeted them both. "Morning, Mr. King. Hello, Mr. Viceroy, good to see you again."

Viceroy nodded his head in acknowledgment. Nick opened the rear passenger door and gestured for them to get in. The governor was already seated, and the two men took up positions on the bucket seats facing her.

"Gentlemen," she started. "Good morning and thanks for coming on such short notice. As unusual as this is," she added, gesturing to the limo, "I sometimes find it convenient to hold important meetings while driving. I'm due to appear at an energy conference down in Janesville at 11:00. You'll be driven back to Madison once we arrive, so you won't have to sit through a laborious session on the negative effects of wind turbines." She smiled, putting both men at ease.

"Governor, you know I would drop almost anything to meet with you," Viceroy began. Nodding to Jerry, he added, "We're here—"

"You're here because I'm the governor and that's the way it works. Now, enough silly pleasantries. You both know I'm very fond of each of you and you have my trust. Agreed?" Both men nodded. "Good. Then let's keep this conversation real and not try to dress up a dirty pig. If you have something unpleasant or politically incorrect to say, just say it. That's why I like this limo. It gives me a space to drop the pretenses. Fair enough?" Both men nodded again. "Alright then."

Kay Spurgeon toggled the button and told Nick he could pull out. A police escort appeared with one car taking the lead and the other bringing up the rear. The limo began rolling and Kay settled back in her seat as she studied the two men before speaking again.

"So, Roger, Jerry tells me you've made some progress in the bombing investigation, but I've perceived a bit of reluctance on his part about divulging too much information to me," she said with a friendly glance to Jerry.

Viceroy cleared his throat and leaned forward to begin

the explanation. "Jerry was just protecting the integrity of the investigation, but yes, we've made some progress. We firmly believe that someone connected to the incident was driving a yellow Ford Maverick that morning. We have two witnesses who can place the vehicle near the golf course in a spot where a Ford Maverick wouldn't normally be parked. We also know that the vehicle took off rather quickly, shortly after the bomb went off. It's a lead that we hope will bear some fruit."

"Has the DMV come up with anything?"

"Unfortunately not. But we didn't get their report until late yesterday, and as of this morning we've expanded the search to the surrounding states. Regina's coordinating."

"I like her. I like her very much."

"I do as well. She's a fantastic detective with a very bright future."

She paused for a moment and turned to look out the tinted window. They were just entering the freeway headed south and the scenery was already transitioning from urban to rural. The outlying suburbs provided glimpses of green spaces and bigger homes on larger lots. Soon they would be in the middle of gently rolling stretches of farmland and forests.

"I assume you're going to let the public know about this vehicle? Perhaps someone will come forward with information once they know we're looking for it."

Viceroy said, "Well, to be honest, I'm not sure who or what we're dealing with yet. The thought has crossed my mind, but I talked with Randi Richards, our head of communications down at HQ in Chicago, and we both think an announcement might just work against us at this time. We think it would be better to make it seem like a leak, which could be just enough to alert the public without sending our perpetrator into hiding, and it might even cause him or her to make a mistake. Randi's figuring out what would be the best time to leak it and to whom."

"And Randi's good, Governor," Jerry chimed in. "She's a pro."

The governor said, "I want you to keep me posted on any progress. And now I also want to give you both a clearer picture of where I am on this entire tragedy." Viceroy and Jerry looked at each other. Viceroy raised one eyebrow ever so slightly. The reason for the limo meeting was about to be revealed. "Ten days ago Roy and I attended Mary Hale's funeral. A short while after that it was Howard's, Roy's best friend from childhood. In between, I also attended funerals for the others who were killed at Pine Creek. It's all been extremely difficult and has taken a deep personal toll. We're now also in the national spotlight for a reason I'd rather not be. And as much as I want to stay strong for my constituents and staff, there have been times over these last two weeks when I've had to shut my office door and take a few moments to gather myself together."

Viceroy brushed a piece of lint off his thigh to eat up the moment, not knowing what to say.

"My emotions have gone from rage to tears and everything in between. My husband is beyond distraught and has had to take time off from his law practice. This single, horrendous event has altered the landscape, changed the psyche of our citizens, and pushed our collective emotions to a very raw and unsavory place. Do you understand?"

"Of course," Viceroy said. "It's the single most terrible crime I've ever been involved with, and I can't take my emotions out of the equation either. You can rest assured that all my waking moments are completely focused on bringing whoever is behind it to justice. My staff will not rest until we get him or her or whatever group is responsible. I promise you that we will find them."

She held his eyes for a moment, and Viceroy sensed her gentle acknowledgement of his dedication. "Thank you. To a degree, we're all in your hands. DeWitt isn't getting in your way at all, is he?"

"No, not at all."

"Good. If he does, just let me know and I'll arrange for his early retirement."

"Understood."

"Thank you both for hearing me out. It was important for me to know you understand the full scope of this thing for a variety of reasons. Our state has suffered a deep wound. Your efforts will help heal it if you can find the bad guys. And one more thing...." She pulled herself forward and clasped her hands in front of her for emphasis. "Today is September fourteenth. In a little more than a month we will be putting on the single biggest musical extravaganza in the history of our state in front of our Capitol and in the streets of Madison. Ticket sales project more than one hundred thousand people attending the inaugural Badger Fest. Families, kids, grandparents, our young people, and every music lover in Wisconsin will be on hand the last weekend of October. Country, jazz, rock-n-roll, techno—it's all going to be there. There will be twelve music stages scattered on the streets surrounding the Capitol, and a giant plaza with a huge ice rink is already under construction. The whole thing has been two years in the making and it's going to be a signature event for years to come. It will be the legacy I leave behind." She shifted in her seat and leaned even closer to the two of them. "But now we have a bombing that needs to be solved, and quickly. Anyone who could pull this off at a country club sure as hell might be bold enough to target the festival. This is something I cannot allow. So you can see why this tragedy has been so upsetting and why I'm counting on you to right the wrong. Several people, my husband among them, are seriously pressing me to cancel the event if we don't find the bomber. I will not do that. As reasonable as I think I am about most things, on this one I am admittedly irrational, but with good intention. Do not fail me, please. While I know you will always do your best, I ask that you find a way to ensure we are congratulating each other well before October twenty-eighth. You have my full faith and nothing you need will be withheld from you. *Nothing.* If you find a statute or law or protocol you would otherwise not violate, you have my blessing to do so. Is there anything about what I've just said that you do not understand?"

Viceroy sat in contemplative silence. Jerry just looked down at the floor between his legs and waited for his boss to respond. Viceroy saw a woman utterly bound by her conviction. Governor Kay Spurgeon stared unflinchingly back at him. "No, ma'am, I understand perfectly," he said.

She held his gaze for one more moment before settling back in her seat and instructing Nick to pull over. Within a minute they had exited the freeway and were at the top of the off-ramp. Before either men could say anything, Nick had opened the door and was inviting them to step into the black sedan that had appeared out of nowhere to take them back to Madison. Not knowing what else to do, they each shook the governor's hand, exited the limo, and climbed into the sedan. Before Viceroy could sort out his thoughts, they were already cruising back to the Capitol at seventy miles per hour.

"Don't get too comfortable," the driver said. "We got one more stop."

"I beg your pardon?" Viceroy asked, leaning forward to address the driver, who half-turned his head while keeping one eye on the road.

"Mr. Viceroy, I don't mean to alarm you. Same for you, Mr. King. Things will be clear very soon, and I think you'll be pleasantly surprised."

"I'm sorry, but I need to know what's going on."

"I'm sorry, sir, but we need to turn off right up here. Everything will be clear in just a minute." The car turned into the next rest stop and pulled into the furthest parking spot available. "Please get out. It's just a short walk from here."

The two men got out and followed the driver to a secluded spot with a few picnic tables adjacent to the parking lot. The surrounding trees were beginning to turn color and a light breeze chilled the air. A man was sitting with his back toward them at one of the tables. Even seated, Viceroy could tell from the way he held himself that he was just over six-feet tall. His coat was rich, black leather, and a shock of finely groomed silver hair spilled out from under his tweed cap. His white silk scarf stirred slightly in the breeze. This was a man of means, to be sure.

The driver gestured for them to continue on before turning back towards the car. They walked around the table to face the man, who reached up and removed his sunglasses. There, in front of them, sat Roy Spurgeon.

CHAPTER 14

Ox's favorite place to jog was Lojo Community Park, a fairly large tract of land a half mile from Bread of Life Church. The park's trails wove through patches of forest and alongside an occasional pond, providing him with a peaceful hour to listen to music or just converse with God. The full loop was a four mile route which Ox had just completed, ending near the parking lot next to the trailhead. He sat on a park bench in the shade letting his body cool down. The sweat that had soaked his t-shirt acted as a cooling agent with the slight breeze. He removed the earbuds and let the sound of nature take over as he turned his thoughts to the many things that needed his attention—mostly church business and forward planning, big picture stuff.

Two young men got out of a car, stretched, and then approached the trail Ox had just run. He tried not to listen in on their conversation but they were loud and it was hard to avoid eavesdropping. All he caught was something to do with their plans for the coming weekend and, as they passed, the really skinny one said to the other, "Roger that," before disappearing into the woods.

Roger that. His thoughts instantly pivoted from the upcoming sermon series to his friend.

I'm failing with helping him. His marriage is probably over. His life in dangerous territory. His faith weakening. I'm walking along beside him but...

The thought trailed off into a fog; the thick kind where every form was a blobby outline of something unknown. Each idea he contemplated appeared like a faint grayish wisp of possibility only to dispel. He sat for a good hour longer in prayer and conversation, then returned to his car and exited the lot. When he arrived at the church he had an extra bounce in his step with the answer still fresh and warm inside him.

Stay the course.

CHAPTER 15

The two detectives could only sit there and wait while Spurgeon held his hands against his lips—palm to palm, finger to finger—and stared down at the picnic table. They had gone through the introductory pleasantries and he had begged their pardon for the awkwardness and political sensitivities involved in meeting with him about a case in which he normally would not and should not be involved. He told them that Kay knew nothing about this and that he hoped the meeting would remain confidential amongst the three of them. After they nodded their agreement, he asked that they simply view it as a very unofficial discussion but worth the improprieties. And so, now they waited.

Finally, as if he had just made a decision, Spurgeon lowered his hands, raised his eyes, and began to talk, all the while staring into the distance over their heads.

"It's been an awfully difficult time," he started. "Mary and Howard's deaths are still fresh, and I've been trying to manage Ellen's emotions as well. Ellen was Howard's high school sweetheart and I've stayed close to her through the years, even after their divorce. My wife is holding herself together and she isn't going to crack, but…well, I'm sure you know it's been rough."

Viceroy said, "We understand. I completely appreciate the toll these deaths have taken on you and the governor. That said, I have

80

to tell you this meeting takes me over a line I'd have preferred not to cross."

A moment passed as Spurgeon looked up the hill behind the picnic grove as if to gather himself for a brave attempt at an explanation. "Look, you're here because I need you to be. You need to know something. I'm sure you've heard about the woman who was killed at the grocery store in Appleton yesterday. It's been all over the news."

"Of course," Jerry said.

"Her name was Clare Kittleton."

"Yes, we know that from the news reports."

Spurgeon adjusted his scarf and raised his voice just enough so that Viceroy and Jerry felt the impact, but still did not look directly at them. "You need to look into it."

Viceroy stiffened. "With all due respect, unless my boss at MRSCU or your wife tells me to do that, it's absolutely not something we would do. It's a local crime and, awful as it might be, it's in the hands of the Appleton authorities. The real question is, why would you ask us to do this?"

Spurgeon looked Viceroy in the eye, holding his gaze for a long moment. He rose slowly to his feet, adjusted his cap, put his sunglasses back on, and leaned in with his full height and hands resting on the table. "Kay would never ask you to," he said in a hoarse whisper, "because she doesn't know what I know. And this isn't a request. Consider it an unofficial mandate." He turned and began walking back toward the car, saying over his shoulder, "Look into it." As if on cue, a second car emerged from a few spaces down.

Viceroy stood and shouted at Spurgeon's retreating back, "I won't do that. Not without cause."

The driver had opened the back door and Spurgeon stopped just before getting in. "When I was growing up, I knew her as Clare Hahn." He lowered himself into the back seat, and the driver hurriedly shut the door.

As the car pulled onto the freeway, the two detectives just stared at each other, not knowing what to say. Viceroy had no idea who Clare Hahn was, but it seemed clear that the investigation had just taken a bizarre turn.

CHAPTER 16

Curwood High School's class of '77 holds their five-year reunion. The brief years since their high school graduation had been a combination of maintaining small-town traditions coupled with the advent of new economic advances impacting the region. The Indian tribe had opened a casino on their reservation just on the outskirts of Curwood two years prior that was drawing in tourists, and American Papers had launched an invention to the logging industry with smashing success. The region was experiencing a moderate influx of workers and money was becoming more fluid. New homes were going up; something that hadn't occurred since the 1950's following World War II. Curwood's traditions and values were just beginning to be tested. Some responded in stride. Pat's Place bought out the struggling furniture store next door and expanded, becoming a sports bar catering to the tourists. Other businesses either were in the process of folding or making their own adjustments and renovations to accommodate the new landscape. On the personal side, many of Curwood's residents were faced with change and were sifting through their attitudes towards it all. The "old way" still held the majority but the new forces were starting to make some progress. In the midst of this dynamic,

Bennett Wang married Greta Zumwald three years after graduation to much resistance, other than their families and the few friends who were willing to stand alongside the new couple. The bias and hatred that permeated the town's feelings toward the Wangs had never abated, it just went deeper underground. And now that the town's treasure was "one of them," the battle lines had become even more entrenched. Against this backdrop, the reunion of the Class Reunion of '77 was underway.

It's late in the evening and almost everyone is heavy headed from booze, smoke, storytelling, and dancing. Earlier, the evening had gotten ugly when "the six" showed up about an hour into the event, coming only for the ceremony honoring their basketball championship. Everyone on the team, including Bennett, was given a commemorative jersey. They all put them on and were introduced one by one. Bennett received a courtesy round of applause that reminded him of his and Greta's daily existence in Curwood.

Bennett understands that he will never truly be a part of the community. He is tolerated only because of his marriage to the town's treasure, who smiled at him from the floor as he was the last one introduced on stage.

Marlin Butters said a few words and then passed the microphone to the captain of the team. Roy Spurgeon, already plied with three shots and a few beers, recounted the championship season and acknowledged each player's contributions. Bennett was not acknowledged. Spurgeon then tripped over the microphone stand, eliciting loud sloppy laughter from five of his former teammates. His words were becoming more slurred and salty by the moment. Howard Hale and Kenny Kittleton chimed in to sing the Curwood fight song. The entire gym joined in halfway through. Roy Spurgeon ended his speech with "...and Bennett Wang, go back to your hole."

For a moment, everyone in the gym stood in stunned silence until someone yelled out an encouraging refrain to Spurgeon's comment. The school administrators quickly took back the microphone and gestured to the band to restart the music. Spurgeon high-fived his teammates as he exited the stage, falling halfway down the steps and bringing the rest of the five with him in a drunken pile-up at the bottom. Hoots and laughter ensued while

Bennett quietly walked to the front of the stage and jumped down. Grabbing Greta's hand, he headed to the bar. A few sympathetic classmates gave the couple a pat on their shoulders as they passed and joined them for a drink.

The six got up, still laughing, and headed for the back door with a bottle of vodka in hand. Marlin Butters watched from the stage and shook his head in disgust before exiting behind the curtain.

As the clock hits midnight, Bennett tells Greta he's had enough and would like to leave. He throws the jersey over his shoulder as she puts her arm in his and they exit the gym. They walk back to Bennett's childhood home, a gift from his parents when he and Greta got married two years before.

Greta's family had insisted that the couple stay in town and convinced them that attitudes would change over time. Truthfully, Greta's parents were afraid they would lose their daughter for good if she moved, and she and Bennett had agreed to stay for their sake. The Wangs also stayed, building themselves a luxurious new home nearby, if for no other reason than to keep a protective eye on their son and new daughter-in-law. In addition, they used part of the fortune Mr. Wang had made from the launch of the successful project at American Papers to establish a trust fund that has allowed Greta and Bennett to live very comfortably.

The couple's walk takes them past the cemetery where Bennett's mother was buried when a heart attack claimed her life the year before. She was offered a plot in the far northwest corner, away from the front entrance and the military burials. Bennett and Tao accepted the deal.

As they walk arm-in-arm in the moonlight, Bennett's thoughts turn to his mother, the illness that claimed her life, and the year that has passed since her death. He decides this would be a good time to tell Greta about the wise investments he has made over the past two years using part of their income from the trust fund, investments that will ensure they live prosperously for the rest of their lives. And he will also tell her about the house he's having built on the beach in the Cayman Islands, so that they will have a place to go when it comes time to leave Curwood behind. He begins to speak, but she immediately interrupts him. Greta, too, has a secret to share. She stops her husband on the sidewalk two blocks from their house. She makes him face her as she wraps her arms around his neck and gives him a slow, wet kiss. He pulls her close, and for a few moments they lose themselves in the moonlight. When she pulls back and smiles at him, her absolute, pure beauty is not lost on Bennett Wang. He smiles back at her in awe. This goddess is his wife. Standing on tiptoes, she whispers something in his ear. He jerks back in surprise and she rests her head on his chest as he caresses her red hair with his fingertips before letting out a joyful shout in the darkness.

Bennett Wang is going to be a father.

CHAPTER 17

Viceroy, Regina, and Silk were escorted to the lower level of the Appleton Police Department's crime lab by the portly chief, Kurt Wiese. It was clear that the lime green halls hadn't been painted since the building opened a few decades ago. Silk had to bend every eight feet to avoid banging his head on a light. Their destination was the last door on the left, and Silk once again had to lower his head just to get through. Wiese held the door open as they all squeezed into a rather small and dimly lit room lined with industrial metal shelving. The only other furniture was an old metal desk with a green shaded lamp, behind which sat an elderly woman wearing a lab coat; she rose as they all entered, letting her glasses hang from her neck as she said hello.

"Hi Constance," Chief Wiese said, introducing them all around.

"I'm Roger, the head of this rascally gang," Viceroy offered, sticking out his hand.

She clasped both her hands around his, saying, "Good to meet you. I'm Constance, Constance Ovesen. I manage the evidence room here and I'm not head of anything rascally except my grandkids."

Viceroy said, "Well, we appreciate the opportunity to talk to you and Chief Wiese."

"Of course. We're all in this together, aren't we?"

"I agree, but not everyone feels that way about MRSCU. Your

cooperation is much appreciated."

"Our pleasure," the Chief said, clearly ready to cut to the chase. "So what is it exactly you want to look at? If you can tell me what you're sniffing around this case for, we might be able to help you."

"We're not one hundred percent sure. We received a tip concerning the Kittleton murder. Nothing specific, but we thought we should see the evidence you have in case it somehow shines a light on something we're looking into."

Chief Wiese nodded to Constance, who put on her glasses, pulled a box off a shelf towards the front of the room, and invited them to follow her through a door into an even smaller room. Once inside, the light was infinitely better, but barely room for the five of them to squeeze around the six-foot-long, stainless steel table that took up most of the space. Constance carefully removed one item after another from the box. An envelope full of pictures first, followed by Clare Kittleton's clothing, the knife in a Ziploc bag, and a sheet of paper diagramming the position of the body and the two shopping carts, along with a large schematic of the store that someone in the police department had drawn up for reference.

She placed the empty box on a shelf behind her as they put on gloves and began their examination of the items now laid out in front of them.

Regina started with Clare's clothing, Silk grabbed the Ziploc to inspect the knife, and Viceroy opened the envelope to pore through the grisly crime scene photos, pulling the dozen or so pictures out of the envelope.

"Pretty ugly," Chief Wiese finally commented. "The last time we had one this ruthless was 2006, when that lunatic from Green Bay Federal Penitentiary escaped and landed here in Appleton. Don't know if you recall, but he ended up murdering a pizza delivery boy for the few bucks he was carrying. It happened just across the street. The kid didn't stand a chance. We got the S.O.B. though. He's back in the pen."

Viceroy said, "You know, Chief, I've never been able to get used to these scenes no matter how long I've been on the job."

Chief Wiese nodded his agreement as Viceroy backed away from the photos and Silk took his place. Viceroy moved down the table to examine the clothing and knife, while Regina joined Silk looking at the photos. "Any fingerprints on this?" he asked while holding up the knife.

Wiese said, "No. Must've been wearing gloves when he or she stabbed her."

Viceroy said, "Well team, I don't see anything here that's going to help us. I'm not sure what the tipster was getting at."

"Can I ask who or what the tipster said?" the chief asked.

"I can't tell you who, but the 'what' part was simply a tip to look into the Clare Kittleton murder. So we called and came on up here."

"Well, I'm sorry if you wasted your time." Wiese paused, looked over the evidence laid out on the table, then turned to Constance and asked, "Where's that small black case?"

Constance looked down at the table, "Oh, my goodness." She whirled around and reached into the box she'd placed on the shelf. "Uh, it's not in here. Check that photo envelope. It must've been dropped in there. I'm very sorry, Roger. I thought I'd pulled everything out."

Viceroy said, "No worries," as he tilted the photo envelope upside down and a small hinged black case, about the size of a business card, dropped onto the table.

Chief Wiese offered the explanation. "This was one more item we found at the scene. It's a little weird, so maybe it's what your tipster was referring to. It's not often a murderer leaves a signature item, but we think that's what this perpetrator was doing. We put it in that case to keep it secure."

The deputies gathered around Viceroy as he opened it. Nestled on a patch of velvet was a penny.

"Holy shit," Silk said.

"Oh, my God," Regina said, almost in a whisper.

Viceroy lowered his face to within six inches of it. "May I have tweezers, please?" he asked. Constance pulled one out of her lab coat pocket. Viceroy carefully grabbed the item with the tweezers and flipped it over. He took a close look and then very slowly lifted his head. "It's from 1982."

"I'll be damned," Silk said.

Viceroy switched into investigative mode. "Where was this

item found?"

Chief Wiese looked at each of them and then down at the table. "We found it in her mouth, under her tongue. I told you it was weird. Who the hell leaves their calling card in someone's mouth?"

"Have you shared this evidence with anyone outside the department?" Viceroy asked.

"No. Well, wait…let me think." He paused for a moment, then said, "The day after the crime I got a strange call from that big law firm down in Milwaukee. Some guy had me on speakerphone. He said he was representing the governor and wanted to know what we knew. I, of course, thought he was a crackpot or maybe someone from the media, and I wasn't giving him anything. That's when a second gentleman chimed in. It was Roy Spurgeon, believe it or not. I met him when they stopped here in Appleton during the governor's campaign. You can't mistake his voice. Anyway, I told him everything, being he's the governor's husband and all. He was polite, said thanks, and told me that the governor just wanted to be sure everything was going alright with our investigation. I thought at the time it was a nice gesture."

Viceroy quickly said goodbye to Chief Wiese and Constance, and herded his crew back down the hall and out of the building "Alright. This has gone from an interesting moment in a rest stop picnic area to a walk down an eerie dark alley. Regina, get back to the office and check on the status of the DMV reports. Hopefully Michigan and Ohio have finally responded. If they haven't, we'll get Strongsmith to apply some muscle. You can take my car. Silk and I are going to pay a little visit to Mr. Kittleton. I have a feeling he's got some info we need."

Viceroy jumped into Silk's car hitting the speed dial on his cell for Jerry King. "Jerry, listen up. Things are getting stranger by the hour." He proceeded to tell him what had just occurred and concluded with a directive. "I need you to meet with the governor as early as possible tomorrow. I want you to talk to her about that phone call her husband made, and it has to be in person so you can see her reaction."

Jerry said, "Alright. She likes to keep her first hour open, so I'll try to get to her then."

"Great. Keep it straight and on point and make sure you watch her carefully. My guess is she doesn't know anything because I have a creepy feeling about her husband right now. But I want the full report when you're done. I want to know if she fidgets, plays with her hair, looks away when talking, or anything that might indicate she's not telling you the whole truth. I'll come to Madison tomorrow, if need be." Jerry clicked off and Viceroy called Chief Wiese to thank him again for his time. He also said that he wanted to talk to Kenny Kittleton and asked for his address. The chief obliged, and Silk plugged the information into his cell phone's GPS.

After a long minute of silence, Viceroy looked over to Silk. "This smells."

Silk slowed down as he steered into a right hand turn lane. "Yeah. Sure does, Preacher. The dots aren't connecting yet, but they're looking at one another."

"Well put. Two murders, both women connected to Spurgeon. Why the hell would he ask us to look into this case? I don't get it. I've got an ugly thought starting to take form and I'm hoping that it's just a fleeting wild notion regarding Roy Spurgeon. Let's pray Kittleton can shed some light."

"The pennies are a brain-buster right now. Gotta be the clue to the whole damn thing. If we can just figure that out."

Viceroy said, "1982. What the hell is with 1982?" He was so lost in his own thoughts that he didn't say a word for the next two miles.

CHAPTER 18

Ox nodded every so often as he listened to the woman tell her story. She was sitting across from him in a comfortable chair, her chestnut-brown bangs dancing across her eyebrows as she spoke. Her cheekbones were high and sharp, and he noticed the hint of a dimple on her left cheek when she forced a soft smile. Her green-flecked, brown eyes contributed to an overall homespun prettiness. She was neither fit nor out-of-shape.

They were sitting in Bread of Life's Prayer Room, a place he liked to take first-time guests seeking counsel. Situated down the corridor from the church offices, the room was designed to impart a sense of tranquility and encourage visitors to listen to God's voice or that of a pastor or prayer leader. Paintings of serene landscapes hung on the neutral-colored walls. Strategically positioned in the center of the longest wall was a large-framed parchment with the words: *"Be still, and know that I am God." —Psalm 46:10*, written in calligraphy.

Ox had been listening to her for a while now. She was describing her emotional turmoil and asking for guidance. He sipped organic tea as he listened. She hadn't filled out a visitor's card, but the previous Sunday evening she had emailed a request for a meeting with the head pastor. And now here they sat on a Friday morning. She said she had recently moved back to the Milwaukee area to pick up the pieces of her life that she had left behind. The name on the appointment sheet was Debbie Giralte, which she explained was her maiden name. She disclosed that her true married name was a unique one, and with her husband leading an investigation into a big crime, the name 'Viceroy' might've drawn unwanted attention to herself. Ox wanted to do nothing more than stand and leap for joy; instead, he offered up a silent thanks to God for answering his unceasing prayer.

Debbie took his guiding words to heart and assured Pastor Oxenhaus that she was recommitting herself to her faith and to straightening out the mess she had made of her life, specifically her decision to flee. She confessed that she had abruptly bolted from the marriage when she realized that he could be killed on any given day. She said she thought she was prepared to handle it all knowing that her husband was a detective involved in dangerous circumstances at times, but the reality was far more powerful than she could've possibly imagined. That mindset overtook her, she acknowledged, on the heels of her new husband coming home one night about two weeks into the marriage with a bandage on his abdomen; a wound he sustained from a grazed bullet. She also confessed that much of her motivation to marry was that she wanted to start a family, and the very possibility that she might be left a single mother had driven her to do what she did.

As she spoke, Ox understood that this was a woman whose decision making was driven by her extreme fear of the unknown. She believed her decision was justified because she knew that her husband would never give up his career. She admitted that she had panicked, but once she'd started running, she didn't know how to stop.

She finished her explanation by asking for grace and telling Ox that she had returned having worked through her fears and understood that she was allowing her life to be dictated by "what-ifs" that might never come to pass. She said that she still held out the slim hope of salvaging her broken marriage.

They ended the meeting with Ox leading a prayer for continued guidance and for God to guard her thoughts. Ox said, "Amen," and gave her a tissue as she welled up.

They chatted as he escorted her out of the prayer room and walked her to the front door. Before they parted, he reassured her that she had done the right thing, and said he hoped she would come again on Sunday. She attempted to smile back but guaranteed him that the meeting had been very powerful and would be the first step in her effort to rebuild her life. They agreed to meet as often as she desired for counsel. Ox went back to his office, asking his assistant to hold all his calls. After closing his office door, he knelt by the chair at his desk and prayed for Roger Viceroy, unable to contain his joy.

CHAPTER 19

Silk slowed down as he neared the entrance to the Kittletons' subdivision and turned onto the second street on the left. "Alright, we're looking for five ten Marigold." Six houses down on the right, they found it—an ultra-modern, two-story brick house with an attached three car garage. Silk pulled into the driveway and angled his SUV to block anyone from driving out, a habit he'd picked up as a cop on the streets of Milwaukee.

Viceroy looked at him sideways.

"If Kittleton wants to shoot us and make a run for it, he'll have to tear up his beautiful lawn I guess," Silk said.

"What if he's not home and wants to come up his driveway while we're here?"

"Didn't think of that. Same deal, though." Pointing, Silk continued, "He can drive around that spruce and still be able to get to the garage."

"You're nuts."

Silk just smiled and opened his door. The two men got out and proceeded up the brick walkway to the front door. Viceroy was beginning to dread what he knew was going to be a difficult and emotional conversation. With a deep breath and a sideways glance toward Silk, he rang the bell. When there was no answer after about a minute, he pressed the bell again and peered through window to the right of the door. Still no answer and no sign of life inside. He flicked his head sideways to indicate that they should go around back.

They continued around the side of the house, peering in windows as they went.

"Not looking good, Preacher."

"The Kittletons aren't hurting. Maybe there's money involved in this mess," Viceroy said as he rounded an artfully placed boulder and started down the stone stairs leading to the back patio. An in-ground pool was gated off and covered for the winter. On the far side of the patio was a sizeable tiki bar and lounge area.

"Nice," was all Silk could say.

Viceroy moved towards the bay window on the ground floor, while Silk climbed another flight of stairs to the cedar deck that stretched along the back of the house and looked through the sliding glass doors leading to the main living area. Below him, Viceroy cupped his hands around his face to cut the glare and peered into a finished basement. A huge flat-screen TV hung on the wall to the left. Straight ahead was a full wet bar, and what looked like a gaming area was to the right. He squinted but couldn't see anyone inside.

"You got anything?" he heard from above.

"No go," Viceroy said.

"Same here. I think we struck out."

Viceroy stepped back from the window and started up the stairs to join Silk on the deck above. "Yeah, well, we'll just have to camp out down the street and wait for him to come home."

They crossed the deck together, heading for a second flight of stairs leading down to the other side of the house. Viceroy stopped to sneeze and Silk took one more look through a small circular window at what appeared to be a den area with a desk and computer. Viceroy started down the stairs.

"Preacher, hold on."

"What?"

"Come here," Silk said as he stepped closer to the window.

Peering over his shoulder, Viceroy said, "I don't see anything."

"See the desk?"

"Yeah."

"Look at the computer. Is that what I think it is?" Silk asked, stepping aside to give Viceroy more room.

Taking Silk's place, he pressed his head against the window. "What the…?"

Reflected in the laptop screen was a pair of shoes, attached to legs, hanging from something above. Viceroy banged on the glass and shouted to see if the person would respond.

When there was no movement, Silk reacted with lightning speed and grabbed a deck chair, stepped as far back as he could, and hurled it at the sliding glass doors. The chair bounced off the glass without making as much as a crack.

"Silk, let's try this," Viceroy shouted as he went for the wrought iron table at the far end of the deck.

Together they grabbed it and, on the count of three, launched it at the door. This time the glass fractured. Silk wasted zero time yanking the table away and kicking at the cracked glass. The pane crashed inward and the two men made their way inside, careful not to cut themselves on the sharp edges left around the door frame. Viceroy was through first, with Silk at his heels. When they reached the desk with the computer on it, they looked up. Kenny Kittleton stared back. The noose around his neck was thick and tied to the railing of the second floor balcony.

CHAPTER 20

The assassin made his way down the ladder of the fire watchtower after spotting the Udells arrive in their RV through his high-powered binoculars. He had been waiting since noon, not quite sure when to expect them. With each arriving vehicle he zoomed in on the driver and was pleased to finally exit the tower around 3:00 p.m. Dressed in camouflage, he picked his way through the woods towards the annual Udell Family Bash underway at Starling Park on the outskirts of Curwood. A crisp autumn day provided the perfect blend of sunshine and cool temperatures. The campground was situated on Lake-On-One, the smallest of the three lakes in the massive park, which he kept in his periphery while approaching his next station, being sure not to get too close to the shore and risk being seen. He hiked with purpose; a predator stalking his prey.

For the Udells, this day was a joyous occasion. The Bash was always held at Starling, and always on the first weekend in October as a means of gathering a family that seemed to get larger and more dispersed as time went by. Larry and Emily Udell never missed it, even though they had moved to Phoenix, Arizona, more than thirty years before. Larry had never let on to Emily or anyone else that he had actually fled. They had cut ties to Curwood at Larry's insistence and simply never looked back. Their only remaining bond to anything remotely connected to their hometown was their return each October for the family get-together. They and their two daughters had arrived at Green Bay's airport on Friday afternoon, taxied to the RV rental shop, and then continued up to Starling through the spectacular north woods of Wisconsin. En route they pointed out various memories from their childhood to the girls, who had been hearing the same stories ever since they were old enough to understand. Larry was able to muster an upbeat disposition to seem like a man fondly returning to his childhood home. What he didn't express were his feelings of relief that the gathering was held in the park and they didn't have to stay in Curwood itself. When he spotted the ancient sign indicating that Starling was one mile away, he had finally relaxed and allowed himself to focus on the fun he would have over the next two days.

Cheered on by relatives, they drove to their assigned position at the far corner of the east camper lot. The girls spilled out of the vehicle as soon as they stopped and ran to hug the cousins they hadn't seen since the previous Bash; Emily joined the women, while Larry finished parking the RV.

In less than an hour the Udells had a campfire going, with a spread of munchies and deli sandwiches on an adjacent picnic table. Larry settled into a fireside lounge chair within arm's reach of a cooler for easy access to beer. Emily poured herself a cranberry juice and vodka and settled in next to him. His parents were the first to pull up chairs, and the evening's campfire party just grew from that point on. At 2:00 a.m., they finally called it a night.

The assassin, crouched behind a patch of large bushes, watched their silhouettes retire into the RV from the glow of the dying campfire, and then quietly picked his way to the hammock he had rigged up in a particularly dense grove of pines next to a small stream. He pulled two blankets from his backpack and let the sounds of the forest sing him to sleep.

The next morning was a leisurely pace. Larry and Emily strolled to the lake and back while the girls slept in, finally awakened by the smell of bacon wafting from the small stove inside the RV. Around mid-day someone grabbed a whistle and blew hard, indicating that it was time for the annual softball game. All those who wanted to participate grabbed their gloves and favorite bats, and headed over to the field.

Most of the wives and teenage girls took up positions in the bleachers or on lawn chairs lining the first and third base lines. Emily Udell and her daughters took a spot in the third row of the small wooden bleachers and watched as the game began.

From behind a tall pine tree, eighty yards behind centerfield, the assassin watched her through his binoculars. He was anxious, but he told himself that all he had to do was be patient and the plan would go off without a hitch. It had been almost three weeks since the Kittleton murder and he hated having to wait so long, but he knew this was the best opportunity he'd have. His extensive planning had included heavy surveillance of all the targets to figure out the precise place, means, and connectivity to their numerical order. He was elated when he figured out that the Udell's annual family reunion fit in chronologically and provided a perfect location.

At the top of the fourth inning, his opportunity presented itself. Emily got up, said a few words to the woman on her left, and headed down the steps toward the campground's bathroom facilities. One of the daughters also got up and quickly ran to catch up with her mother. *Damn!* Mom and daughter locked arms as they strolled. The assassin followed, tree-to-tree, moving only when he was sure he would not be noticed.

The two entered the building. He crouched behind a pile of firewood close to the exit and with a good angle to the open space. He froze when two more women showed up to go to the bathroom, but just when he thought he might have lost this chance, Emily came back out. Her daughter was not with her. He wasted no time.

Grabbing the dart gun from the holster on his hip, he took quick aim and fired, striking Emily in her neck. She grabbed at it, thinking it was some kind of insect, but before she could react further she began to fall. He sprang from the wood pile, scooped her up before she hit the ground, and ran back into the woods. The stolen four-wheeler was ten minutes away at a brisk walking pace, and then another ten on the vehicle to the site he had predetermined for the murder.

When Emily's daughter emerged from the restroom a few minutes later and didn't see her mother, she decided that her mom must have gone back to the bleachers. When she wasn't there either, and no one had seen her return, both daughters determined that she must have went to the camper and thought no more about it.

Upon completion of the game, the sisters decided to go looking for her. When they arrived at the camper their mom was nowhere to be found. Fifteen minutes later, their dad showed up, dripping with sweat and in high spirits from the win. The girls explained their mom's disappearance with a hint of worry in their voices. Larry changed clothes and the three of them went on a casual search mission, certain they would find her at someone else's camper, having a glass of wine or helping with the barbecue preparations. After an hour, their casual search turned frantic, with the entire clan scouring the park and yelling Emily's name. The authorities were called, and three deputies from the county sheriff's office joined the search party.

As the sun was setting, Larry's third cousin, along with his two boys, rounded a bend in a remote trail abutting Lake-On-Three and came to an abrupt halt. Thirty paces ahead, on a small rocky outcropping overhanging a river feeding into the lake, they found her. She was tied with chains, legs and arms spread-eagled to two posts. Her body was still smoldering as the fire that had consumed her slowly died. The acrid smell was overwhelming as the man tried to shield his boys from the horrific sight. Screaming uncontrollably, all three of them turned and ran back the way they had come. A pack of cigarettes with a penny taped to it rested against a crook in the lone birch tree that stood at the first bend. A half minute after the three ran past, a strong gust of wind dislodged the pack and carried it over the outcropping into the river below.

CHAPTER 21

The ball whizzed past Viceroy's head and he instinctively moved forward to await the rebound. The angle wasn't the greatest, and he had to drop to one knee in order to get his racquet on it just inches from the ground. The resulting volley was no more than a soft flip that barely got the ball to the front wall but made it seemingly impossible for Ox to respond. Ox's body hurled past him in a blind stretch of blond hair and sweat-soaked gray t-shirt. He caught it a second before it hit the floor; his diving maneuver, along with a full backhand swing, were enough to carom it off the front wall and arc it back to the right corner. Viceroy jumped up, took two quick strides to the back, and leapt. Fully horizontal, he landed in a thud about half a foot from victory. The ball came down and buried itself in the corner. He simply looked at it bouncing gently a time or two just in front of his outstretched racquet. He let his head drop to the floor in complete exhaustion.

Ox righted himself at the front of the court and sat up against the wall with his legs stretched towards Viceroy. He unwound the racquet cord from his wrist, pushed his goggles up, and wiped his face with the only dry spot he could find on the bottom of his t-shirt. He glanced at his friend, who was still laid out in the far corner breathing heavily. Ox began to laugh.

"I think I would have preferred a scone," Viceroy said when he was able to speak again, but the comment came out sounding funny because he said it with his cheek still mashed against the floor. Ox laughed even harder. A minute passed before he was able to stop, but eventually they got to their feet and headed to the showers. With several people in the locker room, they kept their conversation light as they dressed.

Once they were out the door Viceroy thanked Ox again. "Much needed," he added, his breath visible in the early morning cold.

"Anytime."

"And same for you."

They began the walk to their cars. Ox said, "This state's going nuts. Something is out of whack. Did you hear about that woman up north in that park?"

"Oh yeah. Talk about a nut job. Who burns another person at the stake? Some sort of witchcraft?" Because the park was so close to Curwood, he had asked Regina to talk with both the Department of Natural Resources and the county police from the area to find out what she could. He knew it might simply be a coincidence, especially since the victim and her husband had moved away from Curwood decades ago and no penny had been found at the scene; nevertheless, he figured it couldn't hurt to check it out. In the end, the only remotely interesting piece of information she came up with was that the dead woman's husband had been a classmate of Roy Spurgeon. Viceroy parked that fact in his "too coincidental for coincidence" mental file to have Regina follow up in the near future.

Ox stopped at his car and tossed his gym bag onto the back seat. "Witchcraft? Don't know about that, but certainly rather chilling. Look, just keep the faith and know that prayers are covering you daily, and not just mine." He put his hand out to say goodbye.

Viceroy clasped it hard, pulled the big pastor towards him, and gave him a brief hug. "I hope they're working," he said softly.

Ox nodded and climbed behind the wheel. "One more thing. After all this is over, there's someone I want you to meet."

"I'd be happy to."

"There's a woman I've come to know a little. She's fallen away from her faith and wants to turn that around. I think your own journey might be useful in helping her down the path."

"No problem. You know I'm a good Bread of Life welcome wagon." With that, Ox gave him a wink of acknowledgment and closed the door.

Viceroy headed toward his SUV as he scrolled through the emails on his cell phone. Without looking up, he hit the remote to unlock the car, tossed in his gym bag and heaved himself into the driver's seat. He turned on the ignition while scanning the last two emails and finished, putting the phone in one of the beverage holders on the armrest. He was about to put the car in reverse and back out of his parking space when he noticed a note stuck under the wiper blade on his windshield.

"What the…?"

He put the car back in park, opened the door, and leaned out just far enough to grab the note. "What car cleaning special do we have today?" he muttered as he opened the sheet of paper that had been folded over and secured with Scotch tape, and began to read.

MR. VICEROY,
I BELIEVE THIS IS THE CAR YOU ARE
SEEKING.
HAPPY TO BE RID OF IT.
I GOT A DIFFERENT ONE!
HAVE A NICE DAY.

Ever so slowly he raised his head and looked through the windshield. For the first time in the early morning light he saw the yellow car parked in front of him. Moving his head as little as possible, he looked left, then scanned all the way across to his far right, skimming over the roof of the yellow car in the process. He gave a long look in his rear and side view mirrors. Only then, relatively certain that he was in no immediate danger, did he pick up his phone and place a call to Silk.

"Yo, Preacher, good morning. I'm at a Starbucks. You want any?"

"Silk, listen," Viceroy said.

"What's happening?"

Viceroy looked left and right, continuing to scan his surroundings as he spoke. "I'm in the parking lot at the Brookfield Athletic Club.

I'm staring at a yellow Ford Maverick about six feet in front of me."

"Holy shit!"

"Yeah. I'm also staring at a note that was left on my windshield. He left it there, Silk. The guy just left it there."

"What the hell's it say?"

"Not much."

"Well, how the hell…?"

"The tidbit we leaked to the media a few days ago about the possibility of a yellow car being involved, that's how. Look, get over here. I'm calling the Milwaukee and Brookfield PDs. We'll need a crime unit to go over the car. Call Regina on your way so she knows. I'm going back inside to see if they have any security cameras on the lot."

"Got it."

Silk's phone clicked off and Viceroy killed his engine, put the note on the dashboard, and slowly opened the door. After searching the area around both cars, he called the two police departments, told them what had happened, and asked them to meet him at the club in unmarked cars to avoid calling too much attention to the scene. Looking around one last time, he headed inside to speak with the manager about security cameras.

Across the street another man set his binoculars down on the passenger seat of his black Jeep 4X4, gulped down the last ounce of his Speedy Stop coffee, and tossed the cup out the window.

The assassin had experienced a moment of panic when he heard the yellow car mentioned in the media. *How in damn hell did they figure that out?* He'd been on the road towards Madison when he heard about it on the morning news report. Pulling off the interstate at the next exit, he'd found himself near the town of Plover and drove into a wooded area near a farm to think. His plan quickly developed as the panic subsided. He drove a bit further down a forestry road and chanced upon a thicket of wild raspberry bushes where he parked the Maverick out of sight. Grabbing his duffel bag, he hiked the mile back to the road and was able to hitch a ride from a friendly trucker heading into town. Without much difficulty, he found a used car lot, bought the Jeep, and drove the two hours to Milwaukee to track down the detective.

He'd parked within view of the small parking lot adjacent to the MRSCU offices and waited until he spotted Roger Viceroy, having recognized him from all the TV reports, leaving the building in the early afternoon. He followed the detective the few blocks to a small restaurant, taking careful note of his vehicle. The assassin took the booth behind Viceroy positioning himself so their backs were facing each other, hoping to overhear something useful. Initially, he was annoyed to find that the detective was apparently dining on his own when Viceroy's cell phone buzzed and he answered. Viceroy did more listening than talking but he ended the conversation by saying he would see the other person at 5:30 the next morning at the Brookfield Athletic Club.

Trap set.

The assassin left the restaurant, parked the Jeep at the bus station, and bought a ticket to Plover. When he arrived, he stole a bicycle and pedaled out to the thicket where he'd left the Maverick. He entered the athletic club into the GPS and got back on the interstate after sunset, heading for Brookfield. He arrived around 11:00 p.m. and found a parking space at the edge of the lot away from the lights. The bar across the street made it easy to call a cab, and he was back at the Milwaukee bus station retrieving the Jeep within a half hour.

Now relaxed, he took a leisurely drive back to Brookfield and finished the night by closing down the bar. He grabbed a few hours of sleep in his Jeep in the bar's parking lot and set his cell phone for a wake-up alarm at 5:00 a.m. When it went off, all he had to do was wait for Viceroy to appear. A few minutes before the bottom of the hour he spied what looked like Viceroy's SUV entering the lot. Dawn was still an hour away as he glanced over to where he'd parked the Maverick. He could make out the general outline of the vehicle, but the color wasn't visible in the dark. He turned the binoculars back onto Viceroy. Once the detective had entered the club, he ran across the street and moved the Maverick to the space in front of Viceroy's vehicle, left the note he'd already prepared, and hustled back to the Jeep where he repositioned it at the Speedy Stop for a better angle.

As he watched Viceroy leave his friend and find the note on

his windshield, the assassin allowed himself a satisfied smile. *So, white knight, what do you think of that?* He put the Jeep in drive and turned out of the lot. By late afternoon he would be back in the Upper Peninsula to take care of some unforeseen business created by the discovery of the Maverick.

CHAPTER 22

Viceroy pulled into his reserved space at the condominium complex and shut off the vehicle. It was just past midnight and the day's events and activities had finally caught up to him. He sat, exhausted, and let the darkness envelop him as the interior lights faded out.

The Maverick's presence had rattled him more than he let on to his staff. Instead of being the hunter, he had now become the hunted. The car's appearance and the note meant only one thing—he was being watched. The feeling of paranoia was like a thin sheen on his thoughts. *They could be parked here right now watching me.* He shook his head as if to dislodge the idea from his brain and turned to something more positive. Knowing the Milwaukee PD had agreed to send a roving patrolman every hour while he slept gave him at least a shred of added security.

He'd just given a report to the press that was broadcast on the eleven o'clock news, and he hoped his brief comments would at least provide some small level of comfort to the people he was pledged to protect. He hadn't said anything about the Maverick, but just knowing that MRSCU had the vehicle in their possession kindled a small ember of hope that it would provide some new piece of evidence to propel the investigation forward.

He got out of the car and scanned the parking area as he crossed to his front door. Before entering, he opened the mailbox, dreading, as he did every day, that he would find the divorce papers Debbie had not yet returned. He didn't know whether to be relieved or not when he saw nothing inside but a bill and a magazine.

Once through his door he dropped his key and the mail on the table in the front hall and headed to the kitchen to pour himself a glass of merlot. Wine in hand, he sank into his favorite chair. Relaxation took a foothold after a couple of sips.

As he considered flipping on the television, his eyes wandered to the two pieces of mail on the hall table, which reminded him again of mail that wasn't there.

He finished the last swallow of wine and headed upstairs to bed.

Outside, Debbie stared at the condo's front door from her position across the parking lot behind the wheel of her car; her mascara smudged from wiping away the few tears that had escaped. After all the lights went out in the condo, she pulled herself together and headed back to her apartment.

CHAPTER 23

The assassin crossed the Michigan state line back into Wisconsin an hour or so before dawn, eventually stopping in Oshkosh for a quick bite at a truck stop. He hated that he'd had to do what he did, but circumstances demanded it. Sitting in a booth by the window, he picked at the remains of the cinnamon roll stuck in his teeth as a bright orange semi let out its air brake, reminding him that it was time to get his ass in gear and back on the road.

Saturday morning seemed like an ideal time to make one more site visit to ensure that there had been no alterations to the streets and buildings around the Capitol since he was last there. His protocol did not allow for any major adjustments, particularly this close to completion. The vacant and decaying building he had selected would provide a perfect sightline to the Capitol steps a quarter mile away, but now that the weather had turned colder he wanted to ensure no homeless people were going to be using it as a crash pad. A squatter inside the building would just mess things up, and that would be an unnecessary murder.

Two to go.

As he drove, he twisted his neck back and forth, trying to get a kink out. The perfection of his grand plan thus far made him swell with pride. *Six years.* Once he'd hatched the scheme, it had taken him that long to work out every excruciatingly intricate detail and make sure that he was completely familiar with his targets' patterns and the opportunities they offered within the framework of the chronology, as well as the applicable weapons and methods. During that time, he'd also took the photo that would make everything clear.

He flicked the radio on and turned the dial to WOWL-AM 710, the only all-news station with a clear signal throughout the region. So far he'd lost it only once, on the trip to North Dakota.

Three days had passed since he left the Maverick in the athletic club parking lot, and six since he took care of Emily Udell. *I wonder if they ever found the cigarette pack?* He turned the volume up for the national report at the top of the hour. Most of it focused on politics, with a brief reference to an international story from the Mideast, and a sports segment covering the afternoon's college football match-ups and Sunday's NFL schedule. When the story was announced of breaking news coming out of Phoenix, he turned the volume up as he passed a noisy tanker trying to retain its speed on the slow incline they were traveling. "Larry Udell, husband of Emily Udell, who was murdered at Starling Park in Wisconsin last week, was found dead in his garage this morning. His oldest daughter discovered him with the motor running and the garage door closed. He died of carbon monoxide poisoning. It has yet to be determined whether his death was a suicide or an accident. Emily Udell's murder is still under investigation and no arrests have been made."

What? He steered his car onto the next exit ramp and pulled into a gas station to think. *Another suicide. Are these assholes that weak? What the hell is going on? Is it the pennies? The pictures?* Reaching into the back seat, he grabbed one of the photos. There were just three left; two to be delivered to specific individuals at the correct moment, with an extra one "just in case." He looked at the black and white photo of the burnt-out house on Juniper Street as he had done a thousand times before, touching it as a reminder of the place, the people, and the event that had changed everything.

CHAPTER 24

Greta Wang is awakened by a sudden noise. It had been a swift eight months since she broke the news to her husband that she was pregnant, with the birth occurring in mid-October. The joy and unification that the arrival of her son brought to her marriage and, in some ways, the town itself, was part of the completely wondrous ride that she hoped would never stop. Sure, there were still plenty of prejudicial forces at work, but she could feel them beginning to ebb. Perhaps her status as the treasure of Curwood and the choices she had made would ultimately rule the day, she thinks.

This particular evening was a quiet one. She and Bennett had enjoyed dinner at her parent's house and, despite her brother's continued coldness towards her husband, the baby's presence was enough to make for a delightful two hours across town. After they got home, her tiredness kicked in and sent her to bed within twenty minutes. Bennett assured her the baby would find his crib. She never even heard him slide under the sheets an hour later. The house, the wife, the husband, the baby are all in peaceful sleep by 10:00 p.m.

At some point after midnight, she picks her head up and listens intently for what she thought was a strange sound, but hears nothing further. Still, her maternal instincts kick-in. She gets up and walks down the hallway to check on her one-month-old son. Bennett awakens just in time to see her back disappear through the bedroom door. He lifts himself up on his elbow and is about to follow her when Greta returns. She tells him that everything is alright. She thought she heard a noise, but baby John is doing just fine. She climbs into bed and they fall back to sleep.

Forty-five minutes later there is another noise. This time it is in their bedroom. The sound cracks the night air like a thunder bolt. Bennett startles awake and turns to his wife, who is bleeding from her right ear. An M-80 firecracker lies smoldering between them. Before he can do anything, a slurred voice slices through the darkness.

"Hello Mr. and Mrs. Wang." It is Howard Hale. He is standing at the foot of their bed, a wild grin on his face. Raw alcohol permeates the very oxygen in the room. Oddly, he is wearing the commemorative jersey from the high school reunion. "I wouldn't move," he adds as he pulls a handgun from his pants pocket and points it in Bennett and Greta's general direction.

Greta, blood dripping and tears now streaming, makes a lunge for Hale. Bennett reflexively does the same. Out of the gloom two figures emerge to intercept the Wangs and drag them to opposite sides of the room. "My team plays a heckuva defense, don't you remember?" asks another figure from the bedroom door. As the light switches on, Bennett looks up, squinting, and sees a jersey with a "1" on it. Roy Spurgeon. Glancing at his wife, he sees Kenny Kittleton, eyes blazing and a wide smile on his face, holding her against the wall. Greta struggles, but is only making Kittleton laugh. Bennett hears a hoarse whisper in his ear. "Good to see you again, Wang." The alcohol fumes are so thick he almost gags, but he recognizes the voice of Archie Schmitt, who tightens down even harder so Bennett can't move.

Two more figures stumble through the bedroom door. Bennett looks up to see jersey numbers "2" and "3" almost collide as they land on the floor at the foot of the bed laughing hysterically.

"Well?" asks Spurgeon as he kicks one of them.

Bruce Wink speaks up, "Ow! That hurt, Roy." Spurgeon shoots him a look, prompting Wink to continue. "The kid's okay. The little Wingle Wangle hasn't moved." That brings another whoop of laughter from Larry Udell as he attempts to stand up but falls face-first onto the Wangs' bed. All six hoot it up until Spurgeon shouts for them to shut up.

"Get off the bed, Larry," Spurgeon says. "It's time to play." Howard Hale passes the gun to Spurgeon, who motions for Larry Udell to move it. Spurgeon proceeds to the bed and sits. Hale closes the door. Spurgeon motions for Kittleton and Schmitt to bring Greta and Bennett to the foot of the bed and make them kneel.

"So, Mr. and Mrs. Wang, you have a little boy," Spurgeon begins. Greta struggles to get up but Kittleton grabs her hair and forces her back down to her knees. Bennett is frozen, knowing there is nothing he and Greta can do except ride this out. "Now, now, Greta, no reason to get edgy. We didn't come here for him. We came here to straighten out the wrong that's been perpelated…er… perpentecrated…um…perpetrated, that's it!" The other five snicker again. "Perpetrated on our town. Namely…you." Spurgeon points the gun directly at Bennett and jabs the barrel into his forehead.

Bennett remains frozen. "What do you want, Roy?"

"To rid this town of you. See…you stole my girlfriend and made her your wife. You're now having babies, I mean…abominations, which means you've been sleeping with the one girl in town who should have become Mrs. Spurgeon. Simply put, you're an Asian… um…boys?" he asks the rest of the team.

"Toilet," blurts Kittleton.

"No, he's an Asian vomit," says Udell.

"Feces," Hale counters.

Spurgeon turns to Schmitt and asks, "Archie?"

Schmitt presses down harder on Bennett and says, "An Asian virus."

"Yes. Precisely," slurs Spurgeon. "A virus on this town. You and your kind killed my brothers. And now, you piece of turd, you actually believe you belong here. Don't you get it, Wangle? You're a fucking virus. And you've infected my should-a-been wife." He takes the gun and backhands it across Bennett's right temple with a force that sends him sprawling to the floor. The blow cracks his skull and penetrates Bennett's brain. He goes limp, but remains conscious. Hale picks him up and slams him against the far wall. Bennett crumples to the floor once again as Greta shouts her husband's name.

"Roy, whoa…" Roy looks up to see Bruce Wink backtracking a few steps toward the door. "You said we was just gonna scare 'em."

"Indeed, Brucie. We're just scaring 'em. Now get your ass back over here," Roy says, pointing the gun at him.

Larry Udell moves between his best friend and Roy, holding his hands up to bring some immediate calm. "Hey, hey, hey, Roy. Let's take it down a notch, buddy."

Roy stares at him, then lowers the gun and stands. He places the gun in his belt and reaches into his jacket, pulling out a small bottle of whiskey. He takes a few gulps, then smashes the bottle against the bed post and holds onto the neck. He points the sharp jagged edges at Larry. "How's this for a notch down, buddy?" All five stare at Larry, who gulps and lowers his head to stare at the floor. "You and Brucie are gonna play along tonight, just like you agreed." Spurgeon reaches for the gun and again points it at Bruce Wink. "Understood?"

Wink and Udell look at each other. Larry replies first. "Understood."

"Brucie?" Roy asks.

Wink takes a moment but then nods his assent.

"Stop this, Roy!" Greta shouts, as Kittleton tightens his grip on her hair.

"No, Greta. I won't." He throws the remains of the whiskey bottle to the far corner of the bedroom. "This should have been done a long time ago. Pick him up!" he screams, pointing at Bennett.

Howard Hale hauls him up from the floor while Schmitt yanks his head back so he can see the room. They prop him up against the far wall as Bennett hangs loosely in their arms. Greta begins screaming and crying.

"You should have thought about this before you shared your bed with that animal," screams Spurgeon. "No more, Greta. We're here to cure your virus. Bruce, take the bastard," he shouts, motioning Wink to take over holding Bennett against the wall. Wink walks over and looks into the paralyzed eyes of Bennett Wang. Archie Schmitt

114

practically throws him at Wink as the two exchange positions. "Tie her up, Archie," Spurgeon says.

Archie Schmitt approaches Greta while Kenny Kittleton puts her in a full nelson. She begins kicking, but Kittleton wraps his legs around her to stop her struggle. Archie Schmitt pulls a reel of fishing wire and a hunting knife from his pocket. "It's okay, Greta. I'm only gonna tie ya up." Hale and Kittleton begin chanting, "Archie, Archie, Archie…" First he jams a handkerchief in her mouth to prevent further screaming. Kittleton and Schmitt haul her to the bed and Schmitt ties her arms to the posts. They then move down to her right leg and Schmitt begins to tie a loop, but before he can, Spurgeon speaks. "Wait, Arch. We forgot a step." He comes to the bed and grabs the knife from Archie Schmitt while Greta looks up in terror, unable to make a sound. Spurgeon smiles and cuts open her pajama top, exposing her beautifully rounded nipples and perfectly formed breasts. "These should have been mine," he says to no one in particular, giving the left one a squeeze. Greta kicks violently, sending Spurgeon flying off the bed. Kittleton and Hale immediately grab her legs and hold them down. Spurgeon gets up, beet red and frothing at the mouth. "Archie lied to you Greta. We ain't just gonna tie ya up." Spurgeon approaches and swiftly knifes through her pajama bottoms, revealing Greta's glorious naked body. All the men can do is stare in awe at her beauty. There is a flicker in Bennett's eyes, but his brain can't tell his muscles to react. "Finish the legs," Spurgeon orders. Archie and Kenny spread her legs and finish the job.

Spurgeon jumps onto the bed and straddles Greta. Her eyes are glazed as she looks up at him. Sweat pours down her temples, mixing with the blood dripping from her ear. Spurgeon's eyes soften as he looks down at the one woman he can't have, and for a moment they connect. Greta shakes her head back and forth, silently pleading with him to stop this madness. Before he can speak, Bennett lets out a grunt. Spurgeon whirls, jumps off the bed and in one rush kicks Bennett in the stomach while Wink holds him upright. He lets go and Bennett falls to the floor. Bruce Wink sits on the ground behind him and pulls him back up so Bennett's head rests against his chest. He grabs his hair and makes him look straight at the bed where Greta now lies whimpering—the rag in her mouth and her limbs tied to the posts. Bennett can only sit there and stare.

"And now, my dear Wangs," Spurgeon announces, "let us finish." He turns and sits down next to him. "She was mine. No, allow me to restate that. She was Curwood's best. The treasure of the whole town. And now I must take you back to that championship season. Remember that, Wang? No? Well, let me refresh your memory. We won. Ring a bell? And...if I recall...we all scored." Then, leaning over to within an inch of Bennett's face, he adds, "Except for you. So tonight we're going to recreate that special moment."

Spurgeon gets up, fumbles in his pocket, and pulls out a whistle. Leaning down to Bennett, he blows as hard as he can right in his face. "Game on," he says, and then turns to the bed. "Brucie, make sure he sees all of this."

"Gotcha, Roy," Bruce responds, adding with a hint of self-loathing, "just like we agreed."

Spurgeon continues, "In reverse numerical order just to keep it fun, would you all please welcome the starting forward on the Curwood team: Howard Hale." They all break out in applause and laughter as Hale moves to the foot of the bed. He takes off all his clothes except for the basketball jersey. Looking at Greta, he hardens. Hale leers over at Bennett and says simply, "Number six. Start counting." He climbs onto Greta and rapes her. After Hale finishes, Spurgeon assumes the announcer role again and goes through the same ritual with each of them. The rest of the "fun order" was Schmitt #5, Kittleton #4, Udell #3, and then Wink #2. Both Udell and Wink need peer pressure, along with the force of Roy's gun, to summon the ability to participate. Greta Wang goes limp during the ordeal. Knowing that nothing is going to stop this assault, she closes her eyes and focuses her mind on Bennett and her son. Bennett's brain is registering what's happening, but that is all.

At the end of Wink's session, Roy Spurgeon steps to the foot of the bed and blows the whistle once again. Greta can hear her baby down the hall. She is bleeding from the assaults. Spurgeon speaks. "And now, Mr. and Mrs. Wang, it comes to me, number one. Look at me, Wang!" he orders. "Greta, I'm afraid you won't get the privilege of my love in you. After China boy, you are not worthy of a Spurgeon seed. No, instead I've allowed my team to cleanse the viral infection he's been injecting you with. The problem is, once we're gone, that Asian virus over there can begin once more. At this moment you're Curwood's again, thanks to the boys on my team. Only thing is, the Wang virus can never really be eradicated. And so, Mr. and Mrs. Wang, our only solution is a final solution. Kenny..."

Kenny Kittleton stumbles to the bed and grabs the knife from Spurgeon. "Looky here, Wangle," he says to Bennett. "Final solution." He turns and, straddling Greta, uses the knife to carve a small "C" just above her breasts. She arches her back in pain. A muffled scream escapes from behind the rag still stuffed in her mouth. "Cee is for Curwood."

"Enough, KK," says Spurgeon. "Time to move on. Brucie's got a little something to contribute to tonight's effort." Kittleton moves away as Spurgeon walks over to Greta's make-up table. He picks up the small bench and snaps off a leg. Wink, now terrified of Spurgeon's madness, approaches to get his instructions. Roy leans down and whispers in his ear, then hands him the bench leg. Wink walks across the room and faces Bennett, standing over him and robotically repeating what Roy has just said.

"No more babies, Wangle." He turns and, with a giant stride, whips the bench leg over his head and brings it down with full force on Greta's stomach, as per Spurgeon's instructions.

"That oughta do it, Brucie," Roy says. Greta can only lie there and try to survive the torture. She passes out for a brief moment but awakens to see Larry Udell straddling her.

An unlit cigarette dangles from his mouth as he peers down at her. "Roy says my final solution is to remake your beauty to match that animal over there." He pulls out a lighter and fires up his cigarette. Then, without hesitation, he touches the lit end to her forehead. Udell can't hold back a tear, and he jumps off the bed as quickly as possible to end his involvement in the nightmare. Sidling up to his best friend, Bruce, who is standing against the wall by the door, Larry flings the cigarette to the far corner of the room. Greta is completely passed out. Bennett can only stare from the floor.

"And now, Wang," Spurgeon says to Bennett, "it's my turn." He pulls out the gun. "Her graceful stride cannot be allowed to walk the streets of Curwood. She needs to walk as the wife of a virus for all to see." He points the gun at Greta's right foot and fires a bullet through it. "And that, Bennie Boy, completes the final solution." He shoves the gun back in his belt and motions to his cohorts, "Let's get the hell out of here."

All six men move swiftly out of the bedroom, down the stairs, and out the back door. Tripping and sweating, they hustle the half mile down the road to where they left their cars. Roy gathers them together one last time; using his gun for emphasis, he reiterates that "the events of tonight are to forever remain between us." Howard Hale, Archie Schmitt, and Kenny Kittleton all laugh and agree. Larry Udell and Bruce Wink need the added threat of death should any of this ever come out. Once agreement is reached, Roy takes the knife and cuts a small slit in his thumb, then instructs each of the others to do the same. After the knife is passed around the circle, they lift their hands to the center and touch thumbs. Roy tells them not to worry, because his dad is going to make sure they are never held accountable. With that, Schmitt gets into his car with Kittleton and Hale, while Udell gets into his with Wink. Spurgeon watches them drive off, then gets behind the wheel of his own car and heads home. He passes the Wang house and smiles, pulling into his driveway.

Two houses down, Greta lies tied-up and unconscious on the bed. Bennett sits against the wall, awake but unable to move. The cigarette Larry Udell flicked into the corner burns down to a nub and ignites a small spot of splattered whiskey near the curtain by the front bedroom window.

Little John Wang cries in his crib. No one will care for him tonight.

CHAPTER 25

Regina put down the phone and sat back in her chair. It was 4:00 p.m. and for the past forty-eight hours she'd been trying to track down the owner of the Ford Maverick. The VIN number made it traceable, and she was hoping it would lead to a crack in the case, but this last phone call had knocked her for a loop. Her back ached and she desperately wanted to scream. She closed her eyes for half a minute just to gain a respite from the pressure everyone on the team was feeling to come up with some small bit of information that would put them closer to a solution. The governor's insistence that they have the killer behind bars before the festival was an added burden that grew heavier with each passing day. Added to the pile was the apparent disappearance of Roy Spurgeon.

When Jerry spoke to the governor about her husband's phone call to the Appleton PD, she seemed honestly surprised, and Jerry reported her reaction was authentic. In addition, she had confided that her marriage had been strained in recent weeks, but she said she would ask him about it when she got home that evening. The next day she confessed that when she'd confronted him, Roy had simply walked out of the house. That in itself wasn't so surprising because he'd done the same thing on several occasions in moments of marital strife. Since they owned a home in Palm Springs and had apartments in Milwaukee and Manhattan, she suggested that he could be sulking in one of those places—or just about anywhere. She'd learned over time that the best thing to do during one of these silent storms was simply to wait him out. He usually resurfaced within a few days.

Viceroy and Silk were trying to manage their pressure levels as well and, along with Regina, had been up half the night trying to piece together what they knew in the hope that one of them would come up with some detail they'd overlooked. As it had turned out, neither the grocery store in Appleton nor the Brookfield Athletic Club's security cameras had been positioned to capture any video of the two areas Viceroy wanted to see, thus closing out those potential avenues. No body type to go on, no grainy face from a videotape, no peculiar walk. Nothing.

Regina opened her eyes and made her way into Viceroy's office to pass along the information she'd just received. Silk's crossed leg was visible through the office door. Viceroy was sitting at his desk talking on the phone, and behind him she could see the wall covered in evidence from the investigation: photos of the golf course scene, the oak grove where the Maverick had been spotted, the Appleton murder, the note left on Viceroy's windshield, the Maverick itself, the Kittleton murder and suicide scenes, the pennies, and the golf ball. Newly added were the horrible crime-scene photos of the Udell murder in Starling Park sent by the county sheriff's office. Taped around the edges of the whole grisly collection were random notes, rudimentary timelines, and flow charts with arrows attempting to provide some sense of direction. Regina let out a sigh as she stared at the puzzle pieces. Viceroy was just hanging up the phone, and she thought briefly about keeping the bad news until morning.

"Hey," Viceroy said as he leaned back with his hands behind his head. "Got any news?"

She took the chair next to Silk, who scooted over a bit to make more room for his legs. "Yes, unfortunately."

Viceroy said, "Let me have it. We'll just add it to the pile."

"Good first or bad first?"

"Wow. We have a shred of good?"

"A shred."

"Okay then, let's have that."

"Well, the Maverick is definitely the one that was in the grove by Pine Creek. The tread matches. Nice of him to deliver it to you so we could look at it," she added. "However, there was nothing found in the car that's going to help us. The last state to comply with the registration search was Michigan. Their DMV was adamant that the delay was due to our inquiries having come in just as they were switching to a new computer system. Anyway, they finally got their act together, and I was able to check the VIN against their database. So what do you know? I found the guy who originally owned it; a guy named Lou Mancini from Daggett, Michigan. The DMV also has a record of a sale to a Jackie Robinson on June twenty-eighth. The address Mr. Robinson used was a fake. There is no such street in Iron Mountain, Michigan." Viceroy and Silk looked at each other and shook their heads in amazement. "Mancini has a small rap sheet for minor theft, which allowed me to have the PD check the fingerprints in the car against his. His prints are all over it as you might imagine. There are also some other prints, but so far none that match any of the databases."

Viceroy almost jumped out of his chair. "And that's the good news?"

"Hold on, boss. I'm not through. Clearly our perpetrator has an odd sense of humor, using Jackie Robinson as an alias, and Mancini wasn't quick enough to pick up on it or didn't care. But the other piece of good news is that the miles recorded at the sale and the miles currently on the vehicle show that our Mr. Robinson was well traveled. He's put an awful lot of miles on that Maverick."

"Where in the hell is Daggett?" Silk said.

"Daggett's in the UP, across the state line but not too far. Let me finish. Mancini lived alone in a mobile home deep in the woods about a mile from town. Never married, no children. Basically a loner. I think our Mr. Robinson knew exactly what he was doing when he purchased that car. If you're as smart as this person seems to be and you need a vehicle to move yourself around, you'd probably buy one from a remote small town just to make it that much harder to trace."

Viceroy eased back in his chair. "Or you're a person from that general area. Good work. Now what's the bad news, and why isn't

Lou Mancini sitting in the police station in Daggett so we can talk to him?"

"Ah...the bad news," Regina said. "I just hung up ten minutes ago with the Menominee County Sheriff's Office up there. I've been talking to them most of the afternoon. Not news you're going to like. Lou Mancini was found dead on his property with a bullet in his head three days ago. He was evidently outside chopping wood when he was killed. Could have been a stray bullet from a deer hunter, but I'm guessing Mr. Robinson returned to Daggett."

Viceroy pounded his fist on the desk and let out an, "Aaaggghhhh!" Silk and Regina looked at each other, and Silk patted her arm to let her know he understood how much she hated being the bearer of bad tidings. Viceroy stared at his desk. "That press leak." He rested his head in his hands and let the news sink in.

When he resumed eye contact with his deputies, Viceroy saw them both slumped in their chairs; the strain they'd been under for several weeks now evident on their faces and posture. *They need a shot in the arm.* "Regina, fabulous job. Your attitude and pursuit of the facts have been outstanding. I commend both of you, really, and I hope you know how much I appreciate everything you're doing, even though I don't say it enough. This is by far the toughest investigation we've ever been involved in. I'll continue to handle the governor, so don't let her pressure dissuade you from doing your job the right way and for however long it takes. Stay steady and stay focused. I'll be calling Jerry tonight to tell him the same thing."

"Sure thing, Preacher," Silk said.

"Ditto," Regina said.

"So let's review what we do and don't have," Viceroy said, slapping his hands on his desk. "What we do have is at least two murders that appear to be connected, three if you count Emily Udell," he said with a nod to his side wall. "We don't have a penny connected to her but my sixth sense is telling me that it's too close to Curwood and Spurgeon to be coincidental, and there's also the brutality involved in all three. All three were women, and we also have three husbands who committed suicide following their wife's murder. More than strange and, frankly, something's weird there." He paused and looked directly at the big man in the chair across from him. "Silk, I want you to start sniffing around those suicides. Howard Hale checked out as a very overwrought husband and was quickly eliminated as a suspect. We never had a chance to speak to either Kittleton or Udell prior to their suicides." Silk gave him a thumbs-up.

"We have a penny inside a golf ball with some words on it, and a penny from Clare Kittleton's mouth. We have a yellow Ford Maverick connected circumstantially to the Pine Creek bombing. We have a dead man in Daggett, Michigan, who used to own the vehicle. We have the knife that killed Clare Kittleton without any fingerprints. And to top it all off, we have a murderer who was brazen enough to communicate with me directly."

Silk and Regina simply nodded agreement. "What we do not have is any surveillance or security tapes, a motive, and, most importantly, Curwood itself is seemingly the only thread we have connecting the crimes." Viceroy got up, closed his door, and returned to his desk.

"For this room only, Roy Spurgeon is far too close and connected to this for my liking. We know that all three husbands were high school classmates of his and that two of the wives—Mary Hale being the exception—also grew up in Curwood, but that still doesn't seem to account for why he was so determined to keep his interest in the investigation a secret. That said, I do believe that the governor had no knowledge of her husband's phone call after the Kittleton murder, or of his roadside meeting with me and Jerry. Let's just say I think something about Roy Spurgeon smells and the odor's getting stronger."

Silk said, "I agree. It's gotta have something to do with him. Some connection, that's clear."

"You both have my vote as well. But if this is going all the way up to the governor's husband, we're in some deep waters," Regina said.

"And what does a 1982 penny have to do with it?" Viceroy asked, thinking out loud.

"Don't know, Preacher."

"Look," Viceroy said, studying the wall, "this may be a long night. We've got to take a break to clear our heads. Then I want to go over every little fact again, while it's still fresh. This person has been two or three steps ahead of us since we left the gate. It's time to catch up. We're missing something, so right now seems like a good time for some pizza. Hunger is a distraction." He pulled out a small wad of bills and tossed them to Silk. "Will you please have one of the staff run down to Santino's and get enough for everyone? I'd appreciate it."

"No problem. I'm taking a walk around the block." Silk grabbed the cash and headed out.

"I was planning on lobster with wine, but I'll settle for the pepperoni and a Pepsi." Regina grinned. "I've got a few calls to make anyway, and a Happy Birthday to sing to my niece on the phone, so this will give me some time to be a good aunt." Regina got up and left to settle in at her desk until Silk's return.

Viceroy walked to the window. Staring out at nothing in particular, he conjured up a mental image of the man they now knew as Jackie Robinson silently stalking him from the shadows. The darkness infiltrated everything in view except for the streetlights at the intersections; the nearest ones emanating large swaths of light then diminishing to just dots with each further block. *Dots of light. The further from center, the more encompassing the darkness. Darkness is merely the absence of light. On its own darkness is nothing. It is dead. Light is alive. Darkness can only appear when light is removed. Light. Have I turned if off? Debbie. Love. Absence. Darkness.* He could almost hear Ox whispering at his side, *"Return to the center."* He sat down in the chair Silk had vacated, leaned back, and put his feet up on his desk. He rubbed his eyes and clasped his hands behind his head then switched gears back to the investigation. He stared at the materials taped to the wall across from him, hoping something would miraculously click. The wall stared back. *The molecules. Always. They're dark. Shine a light.* His eyes wandered to the blown up picture of the golf ball and the words #6 START COUNTING. He remembered the chill they all felt when they rolled it out of the bunker and saw the scribbled message. Mentally scrolling through the images of what came next: checking around the trap for further evidence, interrogating the head greenskeeper and his staff along with the general manager, same with the caddy master, and finally walking through the wreckage around the green on the way back to their cars. He recalled turning for a final look and the odd picture of the flag, blown by the bomb but still standing upright in the flower bed. And then…*I don't believe it.* His eyes darted to the photo of the woman on the floor in the grocery store, and then to the Udell murder site. In the background was the grainy image of a sign posting the rules and regulations of the campsite and identifying the lake. His heart was racing as he got up and leaned across his desk to look more intently at the photo. Without turning around, he shouted, "Regina, get in here. Call Silk. Forget the food. We've got work to do."

"What?" Regina yelled back, pulling the phone away from her ear. "What did you say?"

Viceroy took two long strides to his office doorway. "I said get in here. I might be crazy but you aren't going to believe this. Where the hell is Silk?"

"Here," Silk shouted down the hallway having just reentered, then joined them.

"Look," Viceroy said, pointing at the wall. "Okay, I may be crazy, but follow me. The first murder gave us the golf ball with the 'number six, start counting,' right?" The two nodded assent. "Where were we?"

"What do you mean where were we?" Regina asked.

"I mean…yes, we were at Pine Creek, but where at Pine Creek?"

Silk looked at Regina and then back at Viceroy before speaking. "On the golf course. Where are you going with this?"

"I said follow me. Think…we were on the sixth hole. Get it? The SIXTH hole."

Viceroy saw they had connected the dots and continued. Next, he pointed at the photo of Clare Kittleton. "Now look here, what does that sign say?"

Regina said, "It says spices and baking needs."

"No, no, no. What aisle?"

"Aisle four."

"Exactly. Now look at this." Viceroy took a step and pointed at the Udell photo. "It's grainy, but…."

There, without any doubt, were the words LAKE-ON-THREE. Viceroy pulled his hand away from the photo and slowly turned to his deputies. Regina's mouth hung open, and Silk shifted his gaze from the photo to Viceroy, then back to the wall.

"I told you I might be crazy," Viceroy said, "but the damn guy told us to start counting. Six, four, three. We're missing five, and I'm afraid to think about what that might mean, but the Lord can strike me down now if I'm not onto something."

Silk stepped around Viceroy's desk and put his hands on the images. "That's genius."

"Maybe. We started with six and we're down to three, so there must be two more to go. If we can figure this out, we *just* might be able to save two lives. But what the hell is the countdown tied to? Hale was six, Kittleton four, and Udell three. So who are five, two, and one? If I'm right about this, it seems to me that whomever we're looking for is from Spurgeon's hometown. We need to get to Curwood right away, like tonight."

Viceroy quickly gave the staffers a few marching orders and all three of them flew out the door. An hour later they reconvened at the police station in Whitefish Bay on Milwaukee's north side and jumped into Viceroy's vehicle with their luggage. They headed north into the darkness as Viceroy firmly gripped the steering wheel, lost in his own thoughts; his headlights piercing a forward path. *Maybe I found the light switch.*

CHAPTER 26

The three detectives sat in the lobby restaurant at the Black Hawk Casino & Hotel overlooking Magonset Lake. It was Tuesday morning and they'd all been up since 6:30 a.m. for their breakfast meeting with the county sheriff, Joe Vogl, a slightly built man in his late forties with a permanent hitch in his stride. Despite the influx of new residents over the years, Curwood, like many other towns, was still too small to support its own police department, so law enforcement services were provided by the county.

Although he was completely professional, Vogl was not originally from the area and, therefore, didn't really have all the information they'd been counting on him to provide. He knew that all the Spurgeons in the county except for Roy had moved away about twenty years before, back to the east coast, but he could tell them virtually nothing about Roy Spurgeon's childhood or his possible connection to the murders. As for the Udell murder, just down the road at Starling, the only new piece of information he had to deliver was that they'd found some interesting boot tracks two days before, but since Starling was a park that allowed small game hunting, they did not put much stock in the find. Viceroy asked to have the file on the tracks sent over to the hotel, nonetheless.

Viceroy didn't doubt Vogl's sincerity and believed he was doing his best to fill in the blanks, but conjecture was all he could provide, putting him in the same place as the three of them.

The meeting was winding down when Vogl excused himself to use the restroom. Regina and Viceroy got up too, leaving Silk alone at the table. They'd been there for two hours at that point, and he was glad they were almost finished. The session was proving fruitless. Looking around, he saw the restaurant filling up with patrons ranging from guys eating a hearty breakfast for a day on the snowmobile trails or hunting; to elderly folks, mostly women, preparing for a long day at the gaming tables. None of them seemed to be in much of a hurry. He let his fork move the remains of his scrambled eggs around his plate as he looked out the window at the stunning view of the lake and the fresh snow that had fallen the previous evening. *Different pace. Guess I'm just a city kid.*

The other three returned to the table at almost the same time, and the conversation immediately shifted back to the investigation. Vogl said he'd be happy to provide whatever additional assistance he could, and Viceroy jumped on the offer by asking if they could borrow a couple of cars. Vogl called his brother-in-law, who ran a used car lot a few blocks away, and arranged for two vehicles to be delivered to the hotel. Finally, after shaking hands all around and once again stating his willingness to help, Vogl went on his way.

The bright outlook they'd had the night before was now somewhat dimmed. Vogl's lack of information was disappointing, and Viceroy knew that the next few days were going to require a deeper dive into Curwood's culture and people.

When the vehicles arrived, they thanked the brother-in-law, who said that he knew the Udell family from way back and lending the vehicles made him feel good about helping. He was proud to say that he'd brought them two gently used pick-up trucks, and that there weren't any snow problems his vehicles couldn't handle. As he left the lobby, Viceroy flipped the keys to Regina and Silk, who already knew their assignments, and reminded them to stay in touch on their cell phones as things progressed.

Regina climbed into the red pick-up and headed for Emily Udell's parents' house on the west edge of town. Silk was heading for Starling. Viceroy saw them off, placed a brief call to Jerry King, and took off for Clare Hahn's father's house before returning to the hotel for an interview with Kenny Kittleton's sister later in the day. *One of them has to know something. Keep shining a light. The molecules.*

CHAPTER 27

The pick-up truck was louder than Silk had thought it would be, and it coughed out smoke on the steeper uphill climbs. He looked in his rearview mirror following one particularly noisy chug from the engine and saw a black cloud escaping from the exhaust and apparently chasing him up the hill. When he'd put some space between himself and the cloud, he turned back to the road ahead just in time to crest the hill and slam on his brakes to avoid hitting a small buck that came out of nowhere. He swore, swerved, and spun in a circle all the way down the other side until his back end hit a snow bank and jerked him to a hard stop facing the wrong way. *Son of a bitch, that was close.* He saw the deer leap across the road at the top of the hill and disappear into the forest heading west. Pretending to get a bead on the buck with an imaginary rifle, he shouted, "Bam! Next time, Bambi."

He'd just spent three hours traipsing through the campground and combing through the site at Lake-On-Three where Emily Udell had met her fate. Having discovered absolutely nothing of value, he was not in the best of moods. He usually came up with some detail most others would have overlooked, but today was not one of those days. He chalked it up to the snow on the ground and the fact that he was freezing. Around 2:30 p.m., he'd had enough and was heading back to town when he had his encounter with Wisconsin wildlife.

With the pick-up now facing back up the hill, he saw a road sign indicating that Curwood was a half mile west. It was still only mid-afternoon and he had nothing to bring back from Starling. *A little small town charm might be just the ticket*, he thought, as he put the truck in drive. *I guess I should see it since I'm here.* He called Viceroy on the cell to let him know what he was doing.

"Yo, Preacher."

"Hey. Where are you?"

"I just tried to run over a deer, but I missed him. I was hoping for some venison tonight, but I'm afraid we'll have to settle for the casino buffet. I'm somewhere east of town and heading back toward Curwood for a little look-see."

The cell signal was sketchy and Viceroy's reply was breaking up, but Silk got the gist. "Alrig..t then. I t..ke it you ha..e n..th..ng to rep...rt?"

"Nada. I'll fill you in when I see you. Beautiful place, but no dice."

"Okay.. I'm abo..t to in..ervi..w Ki.t..eton. sis..er."

Silk slowed and talked as he steered the pick-up around a branch that had fallen across the highway. "Gotcha. I'll see you and Regina when I get back, probably around dinner time."

"Be c..r.ful."

"Always." He clicked off and drove a little more cautiously down Highway 32 toward Curwood. The afternoon shadows seemed to grow with each turn he made, but he remained in awe of the beauty of it all. In the fading light, the evergreens and snow appeared to be painted into the landscape. The snow that had begun when they left the casino that morning had abated around noon, but as he neared town it was starting again, more heavily than before. As he rounded a bend in the road he saw a sign stating that he was approaching Curwood. He slowed way down for his final approach and was welcomed to town by a giant man with a beard and an axe holding a large sign. *Only up here.* The man, who was obviously meant to represent Paul Bunyan, held a sign that read: 'WELCOME TO CURWOOD. HOME OF THE 1977 BOYS STATE BASKETBALL CHAMPIONS.' *Holy shit. I forgot about that.* Silk was only an infant when the Curwood Bears pulled off their miracle, but it was part of

Wisconsin high school basketball lore. *I gotta see this school.* Roy Spurgeon's name suddenly registered as well. *Damn. He was on that team. I knew Curwood sounded familiar all along.*

With the pick-up now slowed to a crawl, Silk passed a few one-story buildings on his right and, about a block and half in, came across an ancient steam engine set in a small park on his left. There was a plaque on the engine, but he couldn't make out the words. A few locals looked at the pick-up as he passed and most gave a nod. He took an immediate liking to the place and found himself registering the shop names as he passed. Granny's Goodies and Spunkerdoodle's Bar got his vote for the best. Approaching ahead were two covered bridges, side-by-side, icicles hanging off their roofs. A block before the first bridge he saw a sign for the high school with an arrow pointing to the right. He hit the brakes, but not quite in time, so he had to back up. A car coming the other way through the bridge passed him on the left as he spun the wheel for the turn onto Church Street and began an uphill climb. At the top was a Catholic church and two more signs—one providing further directions to the high school; the other once again commemorating the 1977 team.

Silk's basketball juices started to flow as the school came into sight. The dismissal bell rang as he reached the red-brick building, and a minute later kids started to pour out the front door. In a couple of minutes they were gone, by bus, by car, and on foot. Silk pulled in and headed for the door.

Underneath the front entry's overhang, he stomped his boots to shake off the small amount of snow that clung to them. An older woman hurriedly exited, backside first, and collided with him, spilling a few files. Silk caught her as she lost her balance and then bent down to pick up the spillage. The woman stared, clearly surprised to see the extremely tall, black man who was about to enter the school. Gathering her senses, she said, "Why thank you, young man. Most kind," as Silk handed over her files, which were now a bit grimy and damp from the snow.

"My pleasure," Silk said.

The woman tucked the files under one arm, pulled her coat collar tightly around her neck, and was about to move on when she stopped, turned, and asked, "Is there something I can help you with?"

"Very kind of you, ma'am," Silk said. "I'm in town on some police business from Milwaukee and just wanted to see the school," he added as he showed her his badge. "I played basketball in high school and couldn't resist taking a look at the home of the champion Curwood Bears."

"Yes, we're proud of those boys. Local heroes, you know?" the woman smiled.

"I can imagine."

"Our star player is now married to the governor. Did you know that?"

Silk nodded. "Yes, ma'am. I'm aware."

"Well, you're a tall one yourself," she said, leaning back to look him in the eye. "You must've been pretty good too."

"Oh, I had my moments." A hint of pain shot through the old bullet wound in his leg, but it was gone in a heartbeat. He could see the woman getting colder as they chatted, so he asked for directions to the gym.

"Check in at the front office and tell Ruth you talked to me, Dawn Neely, and you're just checking out the gym. I'm the principal," she said, putting her left hand to her chest with pride. "Once you're in, go down the main hallway, turn left at the end, then take the second right, and go all the way to the end again. The main gym will be down the hall to your left. The gym from the 'seventy-seven Bears' day will be to the right. It used to be in a separate building, but we've grown a little since then, so we had to build an addition that now connects it to the main part of the school," she explained, as she turned and headed to the parking lot.

"Thank you," he shouted as she walked away at a surprisingly swift pace. Once through the door, he was hit by the familiar smells of high schools everywhere, calling up memories of his glory days on Milwaukee's west side and the sound of fans screaming, "Silk!" He shook his head as the memories faded almost as quickly as they'd arrived. Stepping through a second set of doors, he entered a small lobby. At its center was a glass case with a trophy. *I'll be damned.* He walked right up to the glass and peered at the plain, not-very-

133

large gold trophy whose plaque read, CURWOOD BEARS – 1977 BOYS BASKETBALL STATE CHAMPIONS. Silk put out his hand and gave the glass a congratulatory pat.

Two passing students caught his attention as they seemed purposefully to steer clear of him. They appeared to be headed into the office, and he followed them. There, seated behind a sliding glass window, was another older woman with curly, brown hair whom Silk assumed must be Ruth. When she saw Silk, she opened the window and he gave his explanation. After receiving yet another set of directions, he thanked her and started down the main hall. The few students he passed seemed as wary of him as the two he'd seen in the lobby. A teacher drinking at a water fountain looked at him as if to ask, "And what might you be doing here?"

"Just going to look at the gym," Silk replied to the unasked question. *No black man's been through these halls before.* The teacher nodded and went back into his classroom.

The hallways were extremely narrow and lined with lockers that looked as if they hadn't been upgraded since the 1950s. Once he made the second turn, he recognized he was in a newer addition to the school. This hallway was wider, brighter, cleaner, and more colorful. The floor was carpeted and the lockers were larger. Even the air seemed to be fresher. At the far end were two signs with arrows pointing in opposite directions, one for the main gym and the other for the memorial gym. He also heard the faint sound of a bouncing basketball.

At the end of the hallway, he turned to follow the sound emanating from the main gym. Poking his head through the open door, he saw a lanky teenager with a crew cut shooting free throws alone. The kid paused, resting the ball on his hip, when he became aware of Silk standing in the doorway.

"Don't let me stop you," Silk said.

"That's okay," the boy shrugged. "I just didn't expect to see someone like you. I mean…I'm sorry, that didn't come out…."

Silk walked forward and lifted his hands, gesturing for the kid to throw him the ball. "No problem, my man. I'm just visiting around here and I wanted to see your school." The boy skipped him a bounce pass, which Silk took on one hop, pivoted towards the basket a good thirty feet away, and grooved his smooth jumper. The ball swished through, cracking the net as only a perfect shot will do.

"Wow," the boy said.

"Not bad for an old man, hey?" Silk smiled as he walked over to the kid. "Even with a jacket on."

The boy gulped and extended his hand. "Hi, I'm Todd. Todd Schneider."

Silk gave him a firm shake. "Trevor Moreland," he said. "But most people call me Silk." The boy looked at him inquisitively. "A nickname I picked up for making shots like that," he explained, cocking his head toward the basket.

"I can see why."

"Well, I'm just glad to see I still got it."

The boy looked over at the basket. "Yes, Mr. Moreland, you've definitely still got it. I've never seen anything like that before."

"You can call me Trevor."

"Yes sir, Mr. Trevor."

Silk picked up another ball from the cart at the free throw line and started to dribble as he spoke. "So, Todd, you just in here figuring out your free throws?"

The boy looked down and away a little as he mumbled, "Yeah. We lost the game on Saturday because I missed half of them. Coach told me to find some extra time to work on them. We've got practice in an hour, so that's what I'm doing."

"Let's see what you got."

"Really?" the boy asked, perking up as he watched Silk take off his jacket and throw it to the sidelines.

"Really."

Silk spent the next thirty minutes working with Todd on his free throw form, retrieving missed shots, coaching him in his mindset, and tweaking his mechanics. Completely focused, he was genuinely in his element with the smell and the echo of the basketball bouncing in the empty gymnasium. Todd was like a dry sponge, soaking in every bit of direction Silk provided. By the end, he couldn't miss.

"Thanks, Mr. Trevor. That was awesome."

"You're welcome. Just remember to get that ball up to just above your eyebrows and hold it there for a beat before you go into your motion. That little extra bend in your knees will help too, okay?"

"Absolutely," he said as he rested the ball on his hip. "Wait 'til I show Coach."

"Lights out, Todd. You'll be lights out."

The boy smiled and dribbled the ball as the two headed for the door. "I can't thank you enough. Is there anything I can do for you?"

"No, I'm good. Would it be alright if I took a peek at the memorial gym?"

"Sure. It's just down the hall. Come on, I'll show you."

Both sides of the hallway leading to the memorial gym were lined with trophy cases and photos of Curwood's athletic teams. The majority were from recent years, and the football teams took up most of the space, but Silk also saw a few nods to some apparently good wrestling teams and the previous year's women's volleyball team. The closer they got to the memorial gym, the older trophies and photos covered the wall spaces, many of which were in black-and-white.

The gym itself was dimly lit, with only two overhead lights on minimal power, and it gave off the musty smell of age. Todd stepped inside and Silk followed.

Silk asked, "Got any more lights?"

"No sir, Mr. Trevor. Only Verne the janitor has the keys to turn this place on."

"Is he around?"

"Probably, but I wouldn't know where to find him."

"No problem," Silk said as he headed for center court. He could almost hear the echoes of screams and cheers as the gym welcomed him inside. When his eyes adjusted to the dim light he began to make out the bleachers, only six rows high, on both sides and one end of the court. Banners from years past covered every bit of wall space. Although he couldn't make out individual names, he was able to identify a handful of conference championships and some individual record-setting plaques. Hanging directly above the door was the one he'd been looking for.

Todd watched as Silk stood there staring at an overblown and somewhat grainy photo just below a faded banner announcing the

1977 boys basketball champions.

He took another step forward, trying to get a better look at the giant photo, which had been taken on this very court. The coach, a large man himself, was at center court holding a basketball. On either side of him were three boys, all dressed in their warm-ups, hands clasped behind their backs. The word CURWOOD in block letters was emblazoned on their chests. Silk looked at each boy and tried to envision what it must have been like to be on that team. They were all smiling from ear-to-ear. No names were listed but he recognized Roy Spurgeon, the last one on the right. Silk took a deep breath, closing his eyes to better imagine the historic moment.

"It must have been cool," said Todd, who had come up to stand next to him.

"Yeah, more than cool. I can only imagine."

"My mom said it was very cool."

"Your mom was a student here in 1977?"

Todd took a few dribbles. "Yes sir, Mr. Trevor. Her and my dad both."

"Was he on the team?" Silk asked, nodding to the photo above the door.

"No. He was a football player. He never played basketball."

"I see. Well, your little town has quite the legacy. This team," he said pointing up at the banner, "is historic. They're semi-famous, you know."

"I know."

"You don't sound very proud."

"Oh I'm proud, Mr. Trevor. That's my granddad up there."

"What?"

Todd nodded. "He was the coach. Grandpa Marlin."

"Holy sh…cow! You should definitely be proud then. May I ask if your grandfather is still alive?"

Todd lowered his head and turned back to Silk. "He is, Mr. Trevor, but I'd rather not talk about it."

The kid looked dejected. Head down, shoulders slumped. "Um…sorry if I asked a question I shouldn't have, but you said he's still alive; that's a good thing, isn't it?"

"Yeah, that's a good thing." The sound of bouncing basketballs echoed from the other gym. "Hey, Mr. Trevor, I gotta go. Sounds like practice is going to start in a few."

Silk put a hand on the boy's shoulder and they began walking back toward the main gym. "Yeah," Silk said, "you don't want to be late. Coaches don't like that. Believe me, I've been there." Silk extended his hand for a final goodbye, and Todd grabbed it with more intensity than Silk was expecting.

"Thanks for everything. I can't wait to show Coach my free throws now."

"You do that," Silk said, and gave him a thumbs-up. "Remember those two tips I gave you. And if you can keep that form on your jump shots, I think you'll find a few more of those going through the hoop as well."

"Gotcha. Thanks again. I really mean it." Todd said as he darted through the open door.

Silk turned, a ton of thoughts swirling in his head. He was halfway down the main hallway when he sensed someone coming up behind him and instinctively spun around. It was Todd, sweaty and speaking quickly. "Mr. Trevor, I need to ask you a favor."

"Sure, what can I do for you?"

The boy looked around to make sure they were alone. "I don't know how long you're here for, but if you could go see my granddad before you leave, that would be great. I didn't want to say anything, but he's got Alzheimer's and, well…he doesn't recognize me anymore. All he does is sit in his chair and stare. He doesn't know my mom either. I just think maybe a great basketball player like you could maybe help him or give him a chance to remember something. Maybe even me or mom."

The young man's plea was hard to deny. Silk knew there was only one correct response. "Well, I don't know about that, but I've got a little time this afternoon. Is he at your mom's house?"

"No. He's in a nursing home in Townsend. It's just down the highway about five miles south. You can't miss it. It's a pink building and there's a big sign out front. I sure would appreciate it if you could."

"You have my word. I'll go right from here."

Todd's smile was enormous. "Thanks," he shouted, sprinting

back down the hall toward the gym. Before he entered, he stopped and shouted to Silk, "Ask for Marlin Butters when you get there and tell them I told you to stop by for a visit."

Silk raised his right hand and gave Todd a thumbs-up. He checked the time on his cell phone and texted Viceroy not to wait for him for dinner. Back outside, the wind had increased and he shivered as he hurried to the pick-up. "Townsend. This is crazy," he muttered to himself as he put the truck in drive and headed back to the highway.

CHAPTER 28

The assassin strode into Syer's Sporting Goods in Auburn Hills, Michigan. The place was enormous, but huge signs hanging from the rafters made finding the item he was seeking very easy.

He saw the sign that said BASEBALL/SOFTBALL against the far wall to his right and headed over. Knowing that Louise Wink would be alone for the afternoon was comforting, but also served to increase his level of anticipation. A clerk asked if she could help him, but he waved her off and kept walking. The first bats he saw were aluminum; he paused to consider this alternative but quickly decided to stick with wood. *More authentic, more in line with the proper retribution.* When he got to the section he was looking for, he had to smile at the coincidence of his Jackie Robinson alias.

The bats were clearly labeled, and he found the 32-ounce size he was seeking without any problem. He checked the bottom of the handle and there was the number two. *Beautiful.* He kissed the bat and headed for the check-out counter. A couple of minutes later he was back in the Jeep.

It was a cloudy day, and he blasted the heat to ward off the late autumn chill as he headed for the warehouse district in nearby Pontiac, the adjacent community. A former auto manufacturing town filled with abandoned buildings and empty, overgrown parking lots, it provided the perfect transfer point. He pulled into the far corner of a big empty lot and parked behind a large dumpster that was positioned nearby an abandoned manufacturing plant where he knew he'd be hidden from the road. He grabbed the bat, locked the Jeep behind him, and walked to the Comcast Cable van he had commandeered earlier that morning. He tossed the bat on the passenger seat and went around to the equipment storage area in the back. Climbing inside, he opened the bag and pulled out the dead cable man's official uniform and dressed. *Perfect fit.* Happy with his disguise, he got behind the wheel and headed for the exit. As he passed a different small dumpster with POWER TO NO MAN spray-painted on the side, he tipped his cap in acknowledgment of the dead Comcast employee inside.

Twenty minutes later he was back in Auburn Hills on the road leading to the Wink residence. He pulled the van over to a green box at the entrance to the street and, with the efficiency of a cable engineer, opened it up and snipped the cable line with the cutting shears he'd found in the van. He waited a full fifteen minutes before cruising up the slight incline to the first street on the right. Five houses down stood the Winks' simple ranch-style home. Of all the killings, this one would be the easiest to pull off. The Winks' daughter was married and no longer living at home, and based on his lengthy surveillance, he knew that Bruce was gone sixteen hours of every day, either at the factory where he worked or at the bar down the street, leaving his wife at home alone.

He parked the van in the driveway and noticed a woman peeking out the front window. He opened his door and ducked behind it, pulling his cap down even farther before grabbing the dead man's tool belt and fastening it around his waist. Next, he picked up the clipboard and finally the bat, which he shoved under the tool belt at the small of his back. He closed his eyes, allowing himself the pleasure that came from the expectation of what he was about to do. *Batter up.* With the slow deliberation of someone who did this every day, he walked up to the front door of Bruce and Louise Wink's house and rang the bell.

CHAPTER 29

Big, heavy snowflakes were floating down across Highway 32 as a squall line came through the area. Small drifts were already forming along the shoulders and spilling onto the blacktop. Silk had the heat in the pick-up cranked as high as it would go and was leaning forward in his seat to get a better view of the road.

The lights of a snowmobile approached on the other side of the highway, and Silk slowed down as it passed. A small sign emerged ahead as he got closer announcing: "Welcome to Townsend. Population 1,803." About a quarter of a mile further on he finally saw the pink building. Even in all the snow he couldn't have missed it. With a sigh of relief he pulled in.

The odor hit him as soon as he walked through the door; a mix of stale food, old clothes, antiseptic, cigarettes, and urine that he remembered from visiting his grandmother in the nursing home where she had spent her final years. An elderly woman in nursing scrubs looked up at him from the front desk, and he could tell by her expression that a tall, black man was the last person she had expected to see. She took off her glasses and sat up a bit straighter as he approached.

"Good afternoon," Silk said with a warm smile, hoping to disarm her.

"Good afternoon, sir. Is there something I can help you with?

Do you need directions?" she asked.

"Um, no, ma'am. I think I'm at the right place. I was asked to come by to see Marlin Butters. I met his grandson earlier today and he asked if I would swing by for a chat with the coach."

There was an awkward silence during which the nurse seemed to be sizing him up, trying to figure out if he was telling the truth.

"His grandson?"

Silk cleared his throat. "Yes. Todd asked me to come. Todd Schneider."

"Your name?"

"Trevor Moreland, ma'am."

The woman nodded and directed him to take a seat in one of the chairs against the far wall. Silk strolled over and lowered his large frame into a chair that was meant for a much smaller person. A lamp sitting on a glass-topped side table provided the only illumination. The woman picked up her telephone and spoke in hushed tones. He couldn't make out what she was saying, so he just tried to look inconspicuous. Two nurses, one of whom was pushing a very old woman in a wheelchair, glanced at him as they passed through the lobby and continued down a hallway. The overheated air mixing with the smell of age and illness made him uncomfortable, so he stood to take off his coat, hoping that would help. He was startled by a shout coming from another hallway. By this time he was wondering if he shouldn't just leave and head back to the hotel. As if reading his mind, the woman at the desk called out to him.

"Mr. Moreland?"

"Yes?"

"One of our resident assistants will be by in a few minutes to take you to Mr. Butters."

"Thank you." Another shout came from down the hall but didn't seem to bother the woman at the desk in the slightest. Silk hoped it wasn't Marlin Butters.

After an endless ten minutes, a man with thin wisps of blond hair, who was also wearing scrubs and appeared to be in his mid-thirties, emerged from one of the hallways and walked toward Silk. They shook hands and he introduced himself as Dennis

143

Pinckney. "I understand you're here to see Coach Butters?"

"Yes. His grandson Todd asked me to swing by."

Pinckney looked at him and Silk could tell he was trying to frame his next question. "Are you...related?"

"No, no, I'm not related. I'm up here on some business from Milwaukee, but I'm an old high school basketball player, and Todd thought it might be good for his grandfather if I spent a little time with him. I've never met him before and, to be honest, it would be an honor. His coaching accomplishment is famous."

"Sure thing, Mr. Moreland. I'm his resident assistant and I'd be happy to escort you to Mr. Butters. Your timing is somewhat fortuitous. He just woke up from his afternoon nap and will be going to the dining hall in about an hour, so we can hopefully sneak in a brief meeting. Come with me," he said, inviting Silk to follow him. Pinckney walked slowly, with his hands clasped behind his back, and Silk decided that he was thinking of what to tell his patient's visitor.

"I'm going to give you a brief heads-up. I don't know what Todd told you, but Coach Butters is not well. He has Alzheimer's and is in a catatonic state most of the time. He very rarely speaks, and when he does it's usually unintelligible. He doesn't always recognize people he knows, even his own family. He's very frail and sometimes has trouble breathing, so he's on oxygen. He drools frequently. I have to feed him, wash him, and clothe him. In the rare moments when he has some degree of clarity, he's as cranky as they come. When we enter the room, let him absorb your presence before you try to talk. He knows me, but I'm not sure how he'll react to someone he doesn't know. He may be in one of his closed moments so, well... just be aware that he may not communicate at all. And any words he might speak are sure to be few and likely not to make sense." Pinckney stopped then, and turned to Silk. "I appreciate Todd's wanting you to come by, but just don't expect anything...anything at all."

"Understood."

About ten feet farther down the hall they stopped before a door with a number on it and the name MARLIN BUTTERS etched onto a faux-wood nameplate. Pinckney knocked gently and opened the door. A rush of warm air hit the two of them. The small room was dimly lit by a single floor lamp, and it took Silk's eyes a moment to adjust. A hospital bed sat against the left wall with an old, brown leather recliner next to it. Two standard-issue hospital waiting room chairs were stacked near the recliner. Silk saw another small door to his right and assumed it was the bathroom. A decent-sized window was positioned directly opposite the doorway and Silk noted that the snow was still falling and hitting the window with each gust of wind. And there, at the window, his back to the two of them, Coach Marlin Butters sat wrapped in a shawl and hunched over in a wheelchair with an oxygen pump spitting out emissions every five seconds. He was bald, except for a small matted patch at the very back of his head. His shoulders were stooped and his neck seemed too thin to support the weight of his head. A few photos and other memorabilia hung above the bed and more were displayed on the windowsill and atop the chest of drawers.

Pinckney pulled the top guest chair off the stack and motioned for Silk to sit. Then he squatted down next to the coach, placed a hand on his shoulder, and quietly said the man's name. When he got no response, he said it again. This time Butters turned ever so slightly and Pinckney pulled a tissue from his pocket and wiped the corner of the old man's mouth. Meanwhile, Silk sat in the uncomfortable plastic chair, not knowing quite what to do and dreading the thought of being in the old man's situation himself fifty years hence.

Pinckney gave it a moment and then spoke again. "Coach, there's someone I'd like you to meet. He's a friend of Todd's and he came by to talk to you. He's a basketball player and I think he'd like to ask you a few questions about his jump shot," he said, giving Silk a wink. Butters didn't stir, but Pinckney stood up and motioned Silk to pull his chair closer to the wheelchair. When he was seated next to the coach, Pinckney gave him an approving nod, indicating that he should say something

Silk extended his hand to within a few inches of Butters and began to speak. "Hello, Coach Butters. I'm Trevor Moreland and I've come all the way from Milwaukee just to see you." When Butters didn't move, Silk pulled his hand back and looked at Pinckney, who

145

shrugged and nodded his encouragement.

"Coach," Silk tried again, "I'm a friend of your grandson, Todd. He and I were playing a little basketball earlier today and I think I helped him with his free throw shooting." Butters sat in rigid stillness. "Anyway, I've played a lot of basketball and I just wanted to meet the famous Coach Butters. Todd said it would be okay if I stopped by and said hello." Still the man sat frozen in his wheelchair. Silk glanced again at Pinckney, who nodded to continue.

"I think your grandson is going to be a really good player this season. By the way, I saw the trophy at the school and I just wanted to tell you it's an honor to meet you, sir, and you should be very proud of winning that championship. It had to have been a thrill, yes?" Butters didn't stir and began drooling again. Pinckney wiped the man's chin. The awkwardness of the situation was getting to Silk, who wondered again why he had agreed to this visit.

Pinckney sensed that Silk was giving up and urged him to try one more time.

"So, Coach Butters, I'm really glad I'm here," he said, hoping just the continuous sound of his voice would be enough to elicit some small reaction. "The Curwood Bears are a legend thanks to you." He was about to give up again when he had an idea that he hoped would cut through the awkwardness and give him an easy exit. "Coach, do you mind if I take a look at your pictures and stuff? It would be great just to see some of your trophies and all." Butters' left hand moved slightly, and Pinckney jumped in to help solidify the connection.

"Coach, Mr. Moreland is going to take a look at your photos, okay?" The man's left index finger lifted ever so slightly; Pinckney took that as approval. "Go ahead, Mr. Moreland."

Silk moved to the head of the bed and began his visual journey through this slightly famous man's life. Above the bed were a dozen photos of his family, some in black-and-white, and some in color. He saw an old photo of the coach holding a little boy in his arms while standing next to a woman who Silk assumed was his wife. At her side and holding her hands were two slightly older girls, presumably his daughters. He tried to guess which one was the mother of Todd. He moved to his right a couple of steps and continued his photo scan. Many of the pictures were of Coach Butters standing on the sidelines of a basketball court at various stages of his career. The most amusing one was a grainy photo of a crew cut, young Marlin Butters in a t-shirt, grinning broadly and spinning a basketball on the tip of his finger.

Silk moved over to the chest of drawers. A miniature replica of the trophy honoring Curwood's 1977 championship formed the centerpiece of a display that included medals, a proclamation from the then governor of Wisconsin announcing 'Marlin Butters Day' on March 30th of 1978, and a copy of the *Sports Illustrated* issue that included the Curwood Bears story.

"Wow," Silk half whispered as he picked up the magazine. "This," he proclaimed, turning to Pinckney and Butters, "is really, *really* cool. It's like going through a museum," he said as he completed his tour. "This is really something, Coach Butters. You should be very proud." The coach stirred just enough for Silk to know he had understood. "I mean it. Your career and your life should be cherished," he said again, examining the few photos on the windowsill in front of the wheelchair. The last one on the far right was just far enough away that Silk had to pick it up and hold it near the lamp to see it clearly.

Watching from his spot near the wheelchair, Dennis Pinckney saw Silk's hands start to tremble ever so slightly. As he held out the photo in front of him, he looked as if he had just seen a ghost.

"Oh my God," Silk said under his breath, but loud enough for Pinckney to hear. He lowered the photo with excruciating slowness, and shifted his gaze to Marlin Butters, who simply stared straight ahead at the storm raging outside his window. Silk looked back down at the photo. There, in faded color, was one of Butters' basketball teams in the same pose Silk had seen on the gymnasium wall, but with two startling differences. The players were not wearing their warm-up jackets and the numbers on their jerseys called out to Silk, like warnings from the grave. There were numbers six through one, all in a row and all in order with Coach Butters in the middle. But all the way on the far left there was another player wearing number seven. The magnitude of what he was holding ripped through Silk's mind.

"What is it?" Pinckney asked as he stood.

"This photo," Silk said, stabbing the picture in front of Pinckney. "I'm pretty sure I know the answer, but what is this photo of?"

Pinckney stammered an unintelligible reply.

"Listen, Dennis, this photo is crucial to the reason I'm here. I'm a detective from Milwaukee," he said as he flashed his badge, "and I'm up here with two other detectives investigating a murder case. I really did come over here to see Coach Butters because Todd asked me to, but I truly believe this photo may be the key to the investigation."

"I'm sorry, Mr. Moreland, but your tone is becoming aggressive, and I'm not sure if, um, well…if, you see, um…."

"Dennis, I don't mean to upset you or Coach Butters, but this photo may be a very major piece of a very complex puzzle," Silk said in a quieter voice, hoping his change in tone would get him the answer he needed. "Do you know with one hundred percent certainty the year of this team photo?"

"Well, yes. It's a photo of the 1977 team. Why would that matter?"

"Unbelievable," Silk said to himself. He then kneeled in front of Marlin Butters and held the photo right up to the old man's face, prompting Pinckney to protest.

"Sir, please. Coach Butters is not well enough for this. If you continue this way I'm going to have to call security," he said as he took a step towards the door.

"Dennis," Silk said in a calm but firm voice, "I'm not going to do anything to Coach Butters. I promise. I just need to know who these guys are."

Pinckney stopped and turned.

"I promise, okay?"

"Okay, but I know all their names. Everyone in the area knows all their names."

"What?"

"Their names aren't a mystery. They're Curwood's most famous sons."

Silk stood up, wondering if he should call Viceroy before asking the critical question. But before he could finish his thought,

Pinckney piped up again.

"Here," he motioned to the two chairs. "Let's sit down and I'll answer all your questions."

They pulled the chairs together, and Silk held the photo between them. "Okay. This team, who are they? In order."

Pinckney took the photo from Silk and pointed at Bennett. "Well, this first fellow here, this number seven, is the one guy that's, well...not really considered one of the team, at least not by the locals. His name was Bennett Wang. I heard he was on the team back then, but I guess he never played; he was just sort of, well...on the team." Silk gave him a quizzical look and Pinckney continued. "I'm sorry that I can't give you much info on him. Coach Butters obviously could if he were able; all I know is the kid was on the team but something was weird."

"Why isn't he in the photo that's in the gym at the high school? The big one on the wall?"

Pinckney shifted slightly in his chair, trying to be tactful and wrestling in his mind with what he should or shouldn't say to this tall, black detective from Milwaukee. "I honestly don't know; I only moved to Curwood about ten years ago, but I gather that his Asian descent and the fact that he married a local girl were problems back then. Probably would be a little bit today, too, but back then it was rough waters. Her name was Greta Zumwald and apparently she was quite the catch. But something happened. The folks around here won't talk about it, but something bad happened a long time ago involving that boy."

"Okay, so is he still in the area? Can I go see him?"

Pinckney cleared his throat. "Um, no, that isn't possible. He died a long time ago."

"What happened?"

"All I know is that something occurred back in the eighties that was so bad no one will talk about it."

Silk sat back in his chair as he tried to determine how far he could push Pinckney without shutting him down entirely. He decided that one more question would be okay. "Final question on this Bennett Wang person, I promise. Okay?" Pinckney nodded and Silk continued, "How did he die?"

"Fire. He and his family—wife and son—all died in a house fire. The house is still up there in Curwood, but it's a burned out shell and hasn't been touched since the day it happened. I do know the house is owned by a charitable trust and for some reason they don't want it demolished, so it just sits there rotting year after year. And that, Mr. Moreland, is as much as I know. Believe me, I've tried to find out more, but I've learned that asking those kinds of questions is like walking down a very dark and dangerous alley, if you know what I mean, and it just wasn't worth it to me. Besides, no one will go near the house. It's as if the fire's still burning."

"Okay then, I guess I'll just have to get the police report and see what it says."

Pinckney leaned back and cleared his throat again. "Look, you can do what you want, but it's going to be a dead end. I told you that I came to the area about ten years ago, but I didn't tell you that I was a sheriff's deputy at the time, working out of the county dispatch office. A year into my job I got a tickle in my spine to sniff out the details of this unsolved mystery. I was sort of doing it on my own time just because it sounded so mysterious and it grabbed my imagination. One of the first things I did was to check the files on the case." Pinckney stopped and got up to close the door before continuing. "They don't exist. Whatever police report was filed, if there even was one, was either hidden or destroyed. My money would be on destroyed. I had a good friend in the records department at the time who confirmed to me that there wasn't anything in the files, but it got him asking some questions as well. Listen to me now, Mr. Moreland. Listen carefully. My friend was killed in a freak snowmobile accident a short time after he started asking questions. His body was found in a remote lake one February day after his snowmobile cracked through the ice and he supposedly drowned." Silk crossed his arms and leaned forward. "Problem is, he had a strict rule never to snowmobile on ice. About that time I was told by the sheriff to cease my inquiry immediately, and within two months I was fired on a trumped-up charge of insubordination."

"You're joking."

"Wish I were. The sheriff who fired me, Sherriff Huber, retired a while back and I heard he died last year at his condo somewhere down in Alabama. Anyway, I got the charge dropped, but I didn't get my job back. The only reason I'm here in front of you right now is that I simply fell in love with the north woods and I love the lifestyle. So I decided to stay and found this job which, to be honest, I rather enjoy. I've been working here at the home for the past five years."

Silk looked back at the photo and studied the face of the young Asian boy standing in the line of players. He was the only one not smiling. "Okay, Dennis. Let's put the Wang kid aside for a moment. I need you to give me the names of the rest of these players. I'm afraid I already know them, but let me have them in order."

Pinckney pointed a long, narrow finger at the photo and began the roll call with the player to the right of Bennett Wang. "Number six here is Howard Hale; five is Archie Schmitt; four is Kenny Kittleton; three...." Pinckney stopped when he noticed that Silk was getting agitated again. "Are you okay?"

"Yes." *Number six, start counting.* "Please just continue."

"Okay, well, where was I? Oh yes, three is Larry Udell, and two is Bruce Wink. You may know number one. He's probably the most famous of all of them. He's—"

"Roy Spurgeon."

"Why yes, yes it is. The governor's husband."

"Son-of-a-bitch!" Silk shot up and grabbed the photo from Pinckney's hands.

"Hey."

"Listen, Dennis, I don't have time for a lengthy explanation. I have to have this photo."

"But—"

"No time to explain, but you need to know that Coach Butters may be in grave danger. A few of these guys in the photo have recently died under strange circumstances. Is there some kind of security that can be sent over here to guard him?"

"Townsend doesn't have a police force, but I can probably find a few guys who would volunteer."

"Perfect. Get him twenty-four-hour protection." Silk grabbed his coat and yanked it on, knocking over a small potted plant on the chest of drawers, and took a giant stride over to the wheelchair.

"Coach Butters?" The man's demeanor didn't change, but Silk thought he saw a flicker of understanding in his eyes. "Coach, I'm going to take this photo, but I promise I'll bring it back to you, okay? It was a real, real pleasure to have met you. I'll tell Todd we had a great chat."

"This is crazy." Pinckney said. "You can't just take my patient's property."

Silk grabbed Pinckney by the shoulders to get his attention. "Listen, I'm not going to hurt you or the coach. You have no idea what this photo means, and I need it. I am who I say I am." He reached into his coat pocket, pulled out a business card, and slapped it into Pinckney's palm. "Are we on the same page?"

Pinckney swallowed. "Um, yes. Same page."

"Good. Now listen, I've got to go make some calls. Have your guys get over here right away."

Pinckney nodded and Silk went to open the door when a fragile, shaky voice sliced through the room.

"Penny."

Silk froze. He held his breath and turned his head ever so slowly toward the window. He saw Dennis Pinckney just standing there staring at the old coach with his mouth agape. Silk could hear his heart thumping in his chest and he looked from one to the other and finally managed to utter a single word: "What?"

Marlin Butters weakly moved his left hand and cocked his head ever so slightly. "Penny," he repeated.

CHAPTER 30

Wu Yin walks on the beach with his benefactor. He is a refugee from an orphanage with no understanding of where he came from. All he knows is that Tao Wang adopted him at a young age and he has lived his entire life in luxury. For Tao's part, it has been almost twenty years since he left Curwood and took up residence in the home that his now deceased son and family were building in the Cayman Islands. The dual heartbreak of losing his wife and son in a place that never wanted them to begin with made it an easy decision. In 1983, he packed it all in and sold off both properties, landing in the Cayman's to finish what his son had started. In the process, he adopted a young Chinese orphan in memory of Bennett and to continue a life that was taken from his only grandson.

Tao Wang moves with extreme difficulty on this day. The cancer has all but claimed his body. He has just enough strength to make it to the dock where his yacht is anchored. His wish to spend his final days in the master suite is being fulfilled. The gentle rocking of the boat will dull the pain and send him to join his wife, and maybe see Bennett once more. The hospice staff Wu has hired is already on the yacht.

They reach the dock and Wu carries Tao the final few yards. A wheelchair awaits them at the ramp to the boat. Wu slowly lowers Tao into the seat. Tao winces and then sighs heavily. A nurse pushes him up the ramp and along the length of the boat to the master suite, which lies just below the captain's deck. Wu follows, weeping silently. The only father he has ever known is dying.

Two nurses assist in transferring Tao as carefully as possible from the wheelchair to the bed. Once he is settled, the soft rocking of the boat puts him to sleep. Wu sits in a comfortable chair at the head of Tao's bed and nods his thanks to the nurses, who then leave the two of them alone. Wu stares at the old man's face and sees that, for the moment, it is free of pain. Inevitably, his mind is flooded with memories. The first one that comes is the day he first saw the vast ocean and the beach that goes on forever at Tao's estate. He thinks he was probably two or three years old. Where he was before that time he does not know. All he knows is that he was an orphan. The estate will soon be his, along with the fortune Tao has willed him.

All Wu understands is that his parents died when he was just a baby and Tao adopted him a short time after that. He knows Tao was a benefactor of the only orphanage on the Cayman Islands and has always assumed that their shared Chinese heritage is what moved him to do what he did. Beyond that he can only guess. Tao has also refused to leave the islands. In fact, Wu remembers his leaving only once in the entire time, and that was to consult an oncologist in Philadelphia in the United States. As a result, Wu has grown up surfing, sailing, and being educated by private tutors, but it has been an isolated life and he has no close friends.

Other than Tao, the person he's been close to in the world is Maryann Nadine, who has been there from the moment he was adopted and has helped raise him. Now getting on in years herself, she enters the room carrying a tray of juice and fruit, which she places on the bedside table next to Wu. She pats his hand and is about to leave when Wu pulls her close and begins to cry uncontrollably. Mrs. Nadine strokes his head until he is calm, then kisses him on the forehead, and leaves the bedroom. Not a word has been spoken between them.

Wu watches her go and turns back to Tao. Watching his chest

rise and fall, Wu soon falls asleep as well. When he awakens two hours later, Tao is also awake. Wu quickly goes to sit on the edge of the bed. Tao looks up and manages a painful smile. He lifts one shriveled arm and beckons for Wu to come closer. Wu leans down until his right ear is almost touching Tao's lips. The hoarse whisper floods his brain and he pulls back, looking at Tao as if to confirm that he has heard him correctly. Tao nods a few times and waves his right arm, motioning for Wu to do what he said. Wu goes to the bookcase on the far wall. There on the top shelf, as Tao has just described it, is a volume titled "The History of Curwood." Wu blows off the dust, and wipes his hand across the front. He looks back at Tao, who motions him to bring the book over to the bed.

Tao takes the book and holds it against his chest. As tears form and slowly roll down his cheeks, he opens the book. Wu looks down, expecting to see pages filled with photos and text. Instead, he sees a circular space cut out of the pages to hold a disk. Tao removes it and sets the book aside. Once more he motions Wu to come close. As more tears make their way down his wrinkled cheeks, Tao speaks softly, slipping into his native Mandarin, requiring Wu to strain in order to understand every word. After a few minutes Tao is hit with a bout of pain and has to stop until it has passed. When he begins again, it is once more in English.

"Promise," Tao implores.

"Yes, of course. Whatever you ask," Wu says.

Tao stares up at Wu and looks intently into his eyes. Finally satisfied that Wu will be true to his word, he lets his head relax on the pillow. "Remember, my dear child," he reiterates, "not until you are twenty-five."

"Twenty-five. You have my promise."

Tao closes his eyes and turns his head away from Wu as he cradles the disk against his chest.

Wu never speaks to him again.

CHAPTER 31

"Nothing. Not another word. Not so much as a sigh. He went catatonic, or at least he acted the part." The three were huddled in a small office belonging to the director of the nursing home. It was 6:00 a.m. and a nurse had just dropped off a large pot of coffee and a plate of bagels. Silk continued, "You can try to talk to him if you want, but I don't think the medical staff is going to let you near him. Besides, he's mostly a drool machine and only during that one moment did he get even close to human communication."

Viceroy and Regina had arrived about 10:00 p.m. the previous evening. None of them had had any sleep, and the smell of the place had so permeated Silk's brain that he felt as if he'd never get rid of it. He was on his way out the door to get some much needed fresh air when he bumped into the director, who had just gotten out of a staff meeting. Regina was sitting in a desk chair crammed into a corner doing as much research as she could on her laptop, but based on the sketchy information Silk had gotten from Pinckney, she didn't have very much to go on. Her head ached and she hoped the fresh coffee would at least take the edge off the throbbing in her temples. Viceroy was behind the desk staring at the photo Silk had taken from Coach Butters.

The director, a short and extremely thin man in his early sixties, had been roused out of bed at 1:00 a.m. After meeting with the three detectives he agreed to let them use his office as their temporary headquarters. A volunteer friend of Pinckney's had also arrived and, per Silk's instructions, stationed himself inside Marlin Butters' room. One nurse and an assistant had also taken positions along the corridor leading to the old coach's room, while the rest of the staff tried in vain to keep the other residents from finding out what was going on and the director did his best to maintain some kind of order in the midst of all the chaos.

"Excuse me, Detective Viceroy," he said as he entered the office. "I know you're doing your job and I apologize if my staff seems a little jittery. They're not trained for this sort of thing and they're just trying to do *their* jobs."

Viceroy got up and came around to sit on the corner of the desk as he squeezed cream cheese from a foil packet onto a bagel. "No problem. I appreciate the help…and the breakfast. In about an hour we're going to start making some phone calls, and I hope to be out of your hair by mid-morning. Before we leave, I'd like to have a chat with Mr. Butters, if that's possible."

"I'll see what I can do. But I must tell you that if, in my opinion, he's not up to it, I won't be able to let you bother him. Not without a warrant and his family present. I'm not saying I won't; I'm just saying that if, in my opinion, he shows signs of stress from the meeting with your man, I'm going to have to deny your request."

"Completely understood," Viceroy said. The director exited. Viceroy turned to Regina, who had a mug of coffee cupped in both hands and her head resting against the wall. "Well, I'm not sure he'll give us another shot, but I had to try. If it turns out we need a warrant, I'll set that up."

Regina's computer beeped suddenly, causing her to jump and spill coffee on her jeans. "Hell," she said as she grabbed a tissue from the desk and began swabbing at the stain. She opened the file that had just popped up. It was from the county newspaper's archives and there, in a grainy scan, was the only story apparently ever written about the house fire that had caused the deaths of the Wangs. Of the many archives she'd searched, this was the only one she'd come up with, and then she'd had to wait impatiently for it to download. "I keep telling you I need a new laptop, boss," she said as she watched the story come to life on her computer screen. There was a photo of the home taken the morning after the blaze. The story itself was written three days after the fire and simply stated the facts. The only quote came from the grandmother of the wife, who stated that the Zumwald family would like some privacy. Regina noted that Greta's funeral arrangements were already in place while there was zero mention of a funeral for the father, Bennett, and/or the son, John Wang. "Roger," she said, motioning with her head, "come look at this."

Viceroy bent to read the story over her shoulder and then stood up straight, trying to get his brain around the lack of information connected to the Wangs. "Weird. Well at least the gist of Pinckney's story seems to agree with this one. Silk mentioned that he said the marriage was a problem for the townsfolk. My hunch is that's the reason for the freeze-out on the Wangs. Did we find out if any Zumwalds or Wangs still live in the area?"

"No Wangs. In fact, nothing about any Wangs since the fire. Even the police say they have nothing about the incident in their files, which corroborates what Pinckney told Silk. As for the Zumwalds, the parents died eight years ago—just a few days apart—from natural causes, but Greta's brother is still living in the area. Eric Zumwald. Silk and I should be able to talk with him today if we can find him. Apparently he isn't at home much, but that isn't unusual according to Vogl. He has a few hunting cabins in the area and is probably at one of them. I'm told he's also a pretty good wildlife painter so he's known to leave town for weeks on end to who knows where and comes back with his paintings. Sells them here and around the whole county. Anyway, the police are looking for him now. He doesn't own a cell phone so it's a crapshoot on when they might be able to connect with him."

"Sounds like a plan. Thanks for all your good work."

"One more thing," Regina said as she glanced at the article again. "The fire was in 1982, for what it's worth."

They just stared at each other. He wanted to make a leap but his training told him to file it as a fact that might be only a coincidence.

Silk reentered with his hands up around his mouth as he blew some warmth onto them. "Almost sunrise. Still damn cold out there, but at least it's stopped snowing. What we got? Any word yet about the Wangs...Zumwalds...or any other local family that might know what the hell happened back then?"

Viceroy said, "Regina found an old newspaper article that seems to back up what that guy Pinckney told you. As soon as he comes in, I want you to go another round with him."

"On it," Silk said, somewhat savoring the opportunity. "I think he wants to be helpful. He got spooked when we were in Butters' room, but maybe he'll remember something more from his own little investigation that will help us out; also, Vogl will be here around nine-thirty to assist."

Viceroy took a bite of his bagel before picking up the team photo again. He still couldn't believe that the key to tying up all the loose ends of their investigation might be this decades-old photo that had been sitting on a windowsill in a smelly nursing home in nowheresville, discovered only because of Silk's chance encounter with a teenager in a high school gym. It gave him the chills just to think about it.

Regina's computer chirped once again, and he could hear her tapping away on the keyboard as he continued to stare at the faces of young Roy Spurgeon and his teammates.

"Oh my God. You're not going to believe this," Regina said. She shook her head as if she couldn't trust what she was seeing on the screen. "As you know, Archie Schmitt is number five in the photo. When I went to see Emily Udell's parents yesterday afternoon, and they weren't home, I was lucky enough to have a friendly chat with their neighbor. He's a lifelong resident of Curwood. Sort of fancied himself the local historian and a real nice guy, very eager to help. I called him last night after you asked me to track down Schmitt and he told me that he and his wife, Wanda, had moved to Buchanan, North Dakota, fifteen years ago. She inherited a family-owned fishery and they decided to move out there and run the place."

"Okay," Viceroy said, knowing there was more to come and fearing the worst. "So if the Schmitts are alive and well and living in North Dakota, maybe my theory is wrong. Regina?"

Regina stared up at him and began to shake her head. "It seems that Wanda Schmitt was murdered about five weeks ago. I just got the file from the Buchanan PD."

"Oh hell," Viceroy shouted. "How?"

"She was found in a row boat, strangled with a fishing line. The boat was found floating up against the shoreline, apparently at a spot on the lake that doesn't get much traffic. Some guy out fishing saw the boat and discovered her. The Buchanan police attached the crime scene photos. They're downloading now, so give it a minute. They say there must have been a struggle because some blood was found in the boat."

"Get that type ASAP," Viceroy said.

"It's coming, boss. The Buchanan police are at a dead end and only too happy to share anything that might help solve the crime. Anyway, there's an oddity here that…oh, no."

"What?" the two shouted in unison.

"Her fishing line was still in the water when the police got to the crime scene. When they pulled it out of the lake they found something very puzzling. Wait a second; the photos are coming through…. Oh my God. Look at this." She flipped her laptop around to show them.

The photo captured the end of the fishing line with a Ziploc bag attached to the hook. Inside the bag was a penny.

"I know what the answer's going to be, but—"

"It's eighty-two. That's the second photo attached."

"Damn, Preacher. Just…damn," Silk said, starting to pace as best he could in the confined space.

"Regina, call your guy in Buchanan again. See if there's anything else he can add. There's got to be a number five connection even if they don't understand it, and I'd like to know what it is. Is there a photo of the victim he can send?"

"Let's see," she said as she dialed. The other two listened to her portion of the conversation and when she rose from her chair in an incredulous moment they both gestured her a silent 'What?' All Regina could do was put her finger up, indicating that she'd tell them in a minute. "Well, thanks again," she said to the cop in North Dakota. "I'm sure I'll be in touch once we figure some things out over here. I'll look for those other photos, and thanks for the information. Okay. Bye."

Regina put the phone down and looked at the two men.

"He said that Wanda Schmitt was strangled with fishing line wrapped around her neck." Regina paused and let out a heavy sigh. "Five times. And, there's more. He said that Archie Schmitt's truck was discovered at an old gravel pit a few miles out of town that's been turned into a man-made lake. The vehicle was parked near the pit and he had tied some weights to his ankles and jumped into the water. He'd been missing for three weeks. Some teenagers out partying found the vehicle just last Thursday. The police sent down divers who found him at the bottom of the lake."

Silk poured himself a cup of coffee before leaving the room, smacking his fist on the doorframe as he went. Regina started to call after him, but Viceroy stopped her.

"Let him go. Sometimes he's better if you just let him be. Anyway, I think all three of us know where this is leading. If we keep counting, Governor Spurgeon is seemingly on the list. We have to get out of here and back to Madison. I've got a zillion calls to make, but right now the man on my most wanted list is Roy Spurgeon. I have to think this through, Regina. What if he's the guy we're looking for? What if there's some sick psycho reason he's involved in these murders? What if that fire in 1982 is tied to him? We're in a very dicey situation here, but I'm sure you know that."

Regina said, "I'm almost afraid to say this, but don't you think we should be trying to track down number two?" Regina consulted her notes. "Looks like that would be Louise Wink, wife of Bruce."

"Call her. Call her now, and get the local PD involved in whatever city she's in."

"According to the neighbor, the Winks are in Auburn Hills, Michigan, in the Detroit suburbs."

"You got a number for them?"

Regina rifled through a few pages of notes and pulled out the sheet she was looking for. "Not yet, but I'm on it."

"Okay, call the Auburn Hills police and get someone over there right away." Viceroy picked up his jacket and left the room.

His head was swimming as he stepped outside. The morning chill stabbed at his senses. He quickly zipped up his jacket and walked around to the side of the building to be alone. There, under the wintry October sky, he closed his eyes for a moment. The sun was just starting to peek above the tree line. After several minutes of complete immersion in the moment, he began to calm down. He looked up to the sun, its light stabbing through the ebbing dusk. A momentary peace welled up in him for the first time in he didn't know how long. *Your subtlety is overstated. But thanks for the lesson. So now please cover me. Protect my staff until we finish this. And as long as I'm asking for things, I'll need a little light on my marriage when you can spare it. It's pitch black whenever I look in that direction.* He let go a robust exhale and watched the mist hover then dissipate into the morning air and made his way back inside to find Silk.

A visit with the Zumwald brother was now critical, and with him and Regina on their way back to Milwaukee soon, it looked like Silk was going to be the man for the job.

CHAPTER 32

Viceroy was doing ninety miles an hour as he and Regina approached the Milwaukee city limits. Adrenaline from their recent discoveries was still flowing through his body, but the three-hour drive had given him some time to settle down. When he'd called Kay Spurgeon at 8:00 a.m. she was at the governor's residence in Madison and informed him that her husband had resurfaced. She relayed her husband was at their condo in Milwaukee and would probably be in his office around noon, which precipitated the duo's hasty departure from Curwood.

There was a lengthy list of details to take care of—the first being a call to Jerry King telling him priority one was to order additional security for the governor.

Viceroy exited the Fourth Street ramp into the downtown area. A few turns and he screeched to a halt in front of the MRSCU offices. "Sorry for the rough last couple of miles, but I have to try to get to Roy Spurgeon before he has a chance to become unavailable in his office."

Regina gathered her belongings and stepped out. "No problem, boss. I'll be on the office phone, so call my cell if you need me."

"Thanks. I'll call you after I talk to Spurgeon. Meanwhile, Jerry might check in, so please keep him updated. And make sure DeWitt is clued in just in case we need his team. See you later."

Regina exited and Viceroy headed for Roy Spurgeon's law offices in the Pabst Building on the lakefront. Five minutes later, he pulled into the parking lot and entered the lobby at just after 11:30 a.m. He was welcomed by a burly, black security guard with a thin mustache who made him sign the visitor's log, then steered him to the elevator bank.

At the twenty-sixth floor he stepped out into the elevator lobby. The only way to go was to his left through a glass door into the posh wood-paneled offices of Spurgeon, Carleton & Mann. Large framed portraits of the three principals were positioned directly behind the reception desk. *Eerie.* A young woman with dangling hoop earrings looked up and gave him a polite but plastic welcoming smile.

"Good morning. I'm Roger Viceroy, with the Midwest Region Special Crimes Unit," he said as he gave her his card. "I'm here to see Roy Spurgeon."

She took the card, gave it a glance, and placed it next to her phone. "I'm sorry, Mr. Viceroy, but Mr. Spurgeon isn't here at the moment."

"The governor said earlier this morning that he would be in around noon, so, if you don't mind, I'll just wait until he gets here."

"I'm sorry, sir, but Mr. Spurgeon called earlier this morning as well and said he had a client emergency and was on his way to London."

"Excuse me?"

"He's on his way to London on business. He said he wasn't sure when he would be back in town."

Viceroy stared at the woman for an awkward moment, then spun on his heel and ran for the elevators as he speed-dialed Jerry King on his cell phone. Before it clicked through he saw a call coming in from Silk as he pushed through the glass door. He took it knowing he would call Jerry back as soon as he could.

"Yo, Preacher," Silk started. "Where are you?"

"I'm at Spurgeon's offices. What can you tell me?"

"Lots, and you're not going to believe it."

"Lay it on me," he said, as he began to pace in the elevator lobby.

"I went to Eric Zumwald's house about two miles out of town. More like a cabin than a house. Checked around the property but no car, no nothing, so clearly he wasn't home. Thinking I'm in a small town so a local has to have some info on the guy, what better place to find out than the town diner, right?"

"That's what I would've done."

"So I pull into this joint back in town. A few wary eyeballs follow me to the counter, but I strike up a conversation with the owner, a gray-haired bowling ball named Olivia. The perfect person. Born and raised in Curwood. Knows everything and isn't too shy about letting you know it. I explained who I was and tried my damn best to get the skinny on Eric Zumwald, but she wasn't biting. I ordered up a sandwich just to thaw her out a bit as she's barking out short orders in between talking to me. Best I could find out was he's a red-haired guy with a massive chip on his shoulder. She was getting irritated with me poking around too much so I called in the cavalry and got Vogl to drive over. As soon as he joined me, she warmed up."

"Good. So, what've you got?"

"It's a long story and not very pretty."

"Okay, so…?"

"Well, she took us to a corner booth and let loose. It seems that the Wang family was seen as a scourge on the town. Reviled, hated, despised, ostracized. Race, ethnicity, religion…that sort of ugliness. The mother and father had only the one son, Bennett. The kid had maybe one friend in the entire north woods until Zumwald's sister, Greta, took a liking to him. They ended up becoming lovers and eventually got married. The town went berserk and most people marginalized the new couple. She said that over time things began to thaw a bit, but the bias was still pretty thick. Fast forward a few years and Bennett and Greta Zumwald conceived a child. They named him John. Shortly after his birth there was an incident at the house. All three of them died from the fire that somehow erupted, but we knew that. Arson was suspected, but Olivia said the whole town went into lockdown immediately following the tragedy. The police evidently did a cursory investigation but by the second day it was ruled an accident. Greta's body was put in a casket and buried. She doesn't know what happened to the other two. She claims the story was that neither of the Zumwald parents even got to see their daughter's body. Ready for another zinger? The doctor in town who did all three autopsies says they died from smoke inhalation and that the bodies were all burned beyond recognition. That doctor was Edgar Spurgeon, father of Roy."

"You're kidding me, right?"

"No joke. The autopsy results seem reasonable enough, but why were there no photos of the bodies? And why no police file? She then went on to say that the Wangs were essentially erased from existence. Old man Wang, a widower, left the area shortly after the fire, but neither she nor Vogl knew where he went. And before you ask me, Dr. Spurgeon died in 1999; his wife in '98."

"Okay, Silk, I'm all ears. What else you got?"

"Well, there's a small twist. Not even Vogl knew about this. Olivia said that just prior to Greta's involvement with Bennett Wang, she was dating someone else. The man whose office you're in right now."

"What?"

"Yeah. Roy Spurgeon."

"Now you've really got to be kidding me."

"Ain't got to the best parts yet, so hold on. There are two more things, and they're both a gut punch. She tells us that Eric Zumwald always called his sister by her given name, but the rest of the town had a nickname for her." Viceroy held his breath. "Penny. Because of her copper-colored hair, the town knew her as Penny. Son-of-a-bitch, Preacher. Penny!"

"Son-of-a-bitch is right." *Molecules.* "I'm not sure you can top that, but what's the second thing?"

"Well, I explained to her that as part of the investigation both me and the sheriff would really like to talk to Eric Zumwald. I relayed that I already went to his house but he wasn't home, and asked if she might have any idea where else he might be able to be found. Without hesitation she says, 'one of his cabins, most likely the one near Crandon. He spends almost all his time there' then gives us the directions. It's about fifteen miles straight east, so we shoot over there and find the same thing upon arrival. No one home and no vehicle around. The front of this place is mostly logs with small windows head high, each covered with a curtain. Nothing to see. Vogl goes to the detached garage to check that out while I walk behind the cabin just to see what can be seen. Come across a bay window with no curtain, so naturally I peer inside. You ready?"

"What? What are you going to tell me?" Viceroy asked with a flashing thought of another dead body like Kenny Kittleton.

Silk replied in a slow observational pace as if he still couldn't believe what he saw. "On almost every square inch of this one room cabin he has glass jars. Across the entire mantle of the fireplace, on the headboard of the bed, the dining table, the top of the refrigerator, and on and on. Each one ain't empty. Each one is filled to the brim."

"With what?"

"Pennies."

CHAPTER 33

"I'm ready."

It was the sixth meeting between Ox and Debbie, this one at a small coffee and deli called The Holy Roast Café that Ox liked to go to around the corner from the church. It opened two years prior by a church member and he found its décor and aroma provided a conducive atmosphere for productive talks. It was mid-morning and Debbie had carved out a few hours from her new job. She arrived first and purposely took the seat facing the back wall; he entered a few minutes behind her. They were sitting in a small corner booth, one of four in the entire place.

Ox said, "Yes, I believe you are. The question is going to be... is Roger?"

She had both hands cupped around her coffee to warm them. Her Florida blood still too thin to keep the cold at bay.

"I'm scared, Pastor. I don't know the answer to your question and probably won't until the moment arrives."

"Let's talk through that, okay?"

She nodded and took a sip.

"I said I believe you're ready and I mean it. Your spiritual journey since you returned has been nothing short of amazing. Almost two months ago I met a woman who was full of conviction about changing her life and regaining her marriage, but also completely aware, maybe in a subconscious sensory way, that a vital but missing piece was God's grace. Grace is a straightforward thing; simply an acceptance that God gives us what we don't deserve. Unearned blessings. I say this with no condemnation that you left the marriage. Rather, that your exit ultimately opened the avenue that allowed you to now have a deeper relationship with God. He used your fall to raise you higher. In this way, your spiritual depth and emboldened faith will provide you the pillars to abide your husband's decision, if it means the end to the marriage. That's what I meant by 'I believe you're ready.'"

"Well, thank you, I guess. I was just trying to sew back together the ripped apart pieces."

"You have. Save for one."

"Do you think he's ready?"

Ox crossed his arms and leaned back, looking at her for a few beats before he replied. Debbie was fully aware of his friendship with her husband and the unbelievable manner in which they each had found their way to him and the church. She and Ox both conceded that random coincidence had nothing to do with that fact. From the moment she found out the situation she had full faith and trust in Pastor Greg Oxenhaus. He was a living, breathing messenger in her eyes. She also knew he hadn't told Roger of her return. Yet.

Ox said, "Honestly, I don't know. As I indicated last time, he seems a bit detached from God right now. Probably not dissimilar to where you were not that long ago. His spiritual connection is weaker than when you last saw him, if I had to put a finger on it. The investigation is taking its toll on his faith as well. Unfortunately, in that condition, God's voice can seem distant or distorted. I'm really not sure at all how he's going to react."

"I understand, but I have to try. I miss him."

"Of course you do. And try you will. I'll help."

"What do you suggest?"

"Well, I think it best that he finishes the investigation for however long that takes before you reveal your return. He deserves the chance to complete the task without the jolt that I'm sure your reappearance will cause."

"I'm a jolt?"

Ox smiled. "I didn't mean that in any negative way."

"I know. I was just trying to be funny."

"Eventually you can jolt him. But giving him his space to do what he needs to do is the right thing. And that's my official pastoral response to your question. In other words, Roger's not ready."

"So...?"

"So we wait. I'll continue to walk alongside him, and once the investigation is over, I'll arrange for a meeting."

"How and where?"

"Not sure on that, but let's see what God has in store. I'm confident the 'how and where' will become evident."

The two chatted for another fifteen minutes. Another parishioner entered, saw Ox in the corner, and walked over to chit-chat. After a quick introduction Debbie excused herself to return to work. The slightly chilly breeze hit her as she exited the door. It felt like a thousand knives. She fumbled with her keys before finding the right one and hurriedly jumped in and drove off. Once she was out of sight the floodgates opened and she had to pull into a nearby subdivision and let it out. It was a good cry, but not the sort that leaves the soul in tatters; instead, she felt cleansed and uplifted.

I'm ready. And I pray he will be.

She put the car in drive and headed back to work.

CHAPTER 34

Bruce Wink downed the last of his beer. It had been a week since he buried Louise and he'd taken a few days off to wallow in self-pity and alcohol. Tomorrow he had to return to the assembly line, and the boys had taken him out to Victor's Tavern for a night of man fun. He was cleared by the police just yesterday and the combined shit-mill of that investigation, plus the package he'd recently received in the mail, gave him more than enough reason to spend six hours on a bar stool. He lifted his right side and let out some gas as a heavy hand landed on his shoulder. "Yo, BW. I gotta get home, man. We're the last ones standing." Wink turned and clasped hands with his union brother. "You'll be okay. They'll find the asshole that did it."

"Thanks, Pete," Wink said as he stood and gave him a bear hug. "See you in the morning."

"It is morning, butthead."

"Shit, it is," he replied as he looked at his watch. "I gotta go too."

"You okay to drive?"

"Hell, yeah."

They both headed for the rear exit, giving Victor a faux punch as they walked by. Victor nodded and went back to his gin and tonic. In the parking lot, Wink stumbled on a raised crack in the cement and just missed slamming his left knee into a fire hydrant. Cursing, he got up, gave the hydrant the finger, and pulled his car key out of his coat pocket as he continued on a few more yards to his rusted pick-up. There weren't many other cars around at that hour, so he didn't hit anything on his way out despite a few swerves.

The ten minute drive to his house was a blur. He kept seeing Louise in her casket, gray hair curled, wearing her only nice dress, and looking better in death than he remembered her in life. They had grown apart over the past decade, but losing her wasn't something he wanted. She had kept their house running smoothly and paid the bills. Now that he would have to take care of everything himself, he admittedly didn't have a clue where to begin.

The next image that popped into his brain was that of her lying in their front hall covered in blood. Her face was untouched but the rest of her body was horribly beaten. The weapon, a wooden baseball bat, leaned against the wall next to the front door. He started to sob, but then fought back the tears as he made the turn into his driveway. He stopped a few feet short of the garage door and had to get out and open it because the electric door opener had been broken for months and he had been too lazy to fix it. He slipped as he stepped out of the pick-up and landed square on his rear.

"Damnit."

He got up, swatted off the snow, lifted the door, then went back to the truck and drove it inside, banging the front bumper against a wheelbarrow he had left sitting there far too long. The door from the attached garage led to a narrow hallway where he hung up his coat on a rack already full of outerwear. His boots came off, but not without difficulty, and he swore at them once he was able to plop them on the floor. The hallway led to the kitchen, where he flicked on the light and headed straight for the refrigerator. He grabbed a Bud and walked into the living room, groaning as he more or less fell into his favorite chair and took a long swig before reaching up to turn on the floor lamp. Across the room, another light went on. There was a man sitting in Louise's rocking chair.

"Holy shit!" Bruce yelled as he tried to stand up, but two other guys he hadn't seen shoved him back into the recliner, one of them pointing a gun at his head. "Hey, hey, I got nothing! I got nothing! No money, no anything!" He went from drunk to panicked in the blink of an eye, flailing his arms in an effort to protect his head.

"Settle down, Brucie," said the man in the chair.

Wink immediately shut up. The voice sounded familiar. He lowered his arms and looked across the room. Roy Spurgeon stared back at him.

"Hello Bruce."

"R…Ro…Roy?"

Spurgeon uncrossed his legs and leaned forward a bit. "Yeah. Been a long time."

"Roy. What the hell are you doing here? Holy shit. You scared the bejesus out of me. What the…? Damn, Roy!"

"Settle down, Brucie," Spurgeon said. "I'll explain everything in a minute." He nodded to his two goons, who backed away and sat down on the couch. "Sorry to pop in on you like this, but I had to. You look good for an old man."

"Hell, you look good too. What's it been, twenty years?"

"Thirty-one, to be exact."

Wink scratched his head trying to do the math. "Well, hell, it's a long time no matter how you count 'em. Hey, hey, can I get you guys something to drink? Want a beer?"

"No, Brucie, we don't. We're here for a reason."

"You in town for something? How did you know where I live?"

"I'm in town for something, yes. Sorry about Louise."

Wink's jaw dropped. "You know about her? Ah, hell, Roy, it was awful. The asshole beat her to death right there in my foyer," he shouted and gestured to his left.

"I know."

"You know? Well, what the…? How do you know that? You keep tabs on all us guys?"

"No, Brucie, I don't. But I know about Louise. In fact, that's why I came to town."

Wink scratched his head again, rubbed his eyes, and said softly, "Well, sorry, but her funeral already happened. I can take you to the cemetery if you want."

"That won't be necessary. It's you I want to talk to."

There was a long silence as Roy Spurgeon stared down Bruce Wink. After half a minute Wink understood. Roy Spurgeon wasn't here to console his old friend. He wanted something else. Wink sighed and leaned back into the chair, trying to diminish himself. "What do you want?"

"We scoured the place while you were out. I was hoping to find it so I wouldn't even have to talk to you. It would be better if I wasn't here. But we came up empty."

"What the hell are you talking about, Roy? What is it you're looking for? I'm a poor S-O-B, so I don't have any money stashed here."

"I'm not looking for money, Brucie. I believe you possess something else that's far more valuable to me right now."

"What? I don't understand."

Spurgeon rose and walked across the room to stand over Wink. The man's height made him look gigantic in the small living room, and Wink unconsciously tried to bury himself even deeper in the chair as Spurgeon reached into his coat and drew out a gun.

Wink instinctively raised both arms to cover his face and started bawling. "What? *What?* I'll help you any way I can, just don't shoot. What is it you want, Roy?"

"Where's the picture?"

Wink lowered his arms. "Wh…what?"

"The photograph, Bruce. Where is it?"

Wink looked away, racking his brain to come up with the right answer. Three guns were now pointed at him and he knew he had to give them what they wanted, but his beer-soaked brain couldn't figure out exactly what that was.

"I'll give you thirty more seconds."

He looked up at Spurgeon, tears streaming down his cheeks, knowing this could be his final moment. Then it hit him.

"Oh shit. You're looking for the photo of that old Wang place in Curwood, aren't you?"

Spurgeon smiled and knelt down so that they were face-to-face. "Yes, Brucie, that's what I'm here for."

Now that he knew the right answer, Wink began laughing. "Damn, Roy, why didn't you just come out and say so? Did you send that to me? I couldn't for the life of me figure out why I got it. It just arrived this morning. Shit, was it supposed to go to you? That thing scared the living crap out of me."

Spurgeon raised his gun and lifted Wink's chin with it. "Where is it?"

Wink gulped and pointed directly down with a shaking hand. "It's in the basement?"

Wink shook his head no and then pointed down one more time. "I'm not in the mood for charades, Brucie. Where exactly is it?"

"May I get up?" Spurgeon nodded and stood up himself. Wink hoisted himself out of the chair and clumsily got down on his hands and knees. He reached under the chair and pulled out the photo. "I didn't know what to do with it so I just shoved it under here. Did you send this to me?"

Spurgeon grabbed it and handed it to one of his goons. "No, Brucie, I didn't. But use your brain and figure it out."

Wink shifted himself to a sitting position in front of the chair and tried to come up with an answer. "I…I don't know. I'm afraid. Is it a bad thing?"

Spurgeon squatted next to Wink so they could again face each other. "Yeah, Brucie, it's bad. You got your head in the sand? You been keeping up on the news?"

"Well, I know Howard's new wife was killed, and so was Clare, but what does that have to do with me or that stupid photo?"

"Think, Brucie, think. Howard's wife was killed, then Archie's, Kenny's, and Larry's. And now yours." He paused to let that sink in before adding, "That makes Kay next."

Wink sat there for a minute trying to absorb what Spurgeon had just told him, and then it hit him. "Oh my God. Wanda and Emily are dead, too? What the hell, Roy?"

"Shh, Brucie. Let me explain. Someone knows what happened that night. Old man Wang is long gone, but someone knows and, whoever it is, they're killing off our wives just like we killed Greta, even though that was an accident. Whoever it is sends that photo after they do their murders. Whoever it is wants us to know they know. And if they know, then others could know. And I'll be damned if any of you idiots are going to spill the beans. We took a blood oath, Brucie, never to tell."

Wink blinked rapidly as he absorbed all this. "Roy, I never told anyone. Never."

Spurgeon sat back down in Louise's chair before firing off his response. "Well, someone did, Brucie. And that photo is the message. If that photo, in the circumstances in which it was received, ever made it to the authorities, we would all be facing a shit heap of questions, and I can't risk one of you breaking under that kind of pressure. So I had to come, Brucie. I had to come see you. To be honest, I was hoping the authorities would have caught up with this guy by now, because I know I could make sure the bastard was silenced once he was in custody. It's got to be someone from Curwood. I even gave the cops a lead, hoping they'd get him. But, unfortunately for you, the creep is still out there, and I'm not going to let the past catch up with me."

"Shit. I ain't breaking. You got the photo so we're good."

"With all due respect, we aren't good. My risk is just too great."

"What do you mean?"

"You see, Howard, Archie, Kenny, and Larry all had a similar problem. Howard was the first. He was freaked out and he showed me the photo the day he got it in the mail. I understood immediately what was happening and I've stayed one step ahead of it ever since. All of them, Bruce; they all got a photo. Funny thing is, they all were so distraught over the loss of their wives that they couldn't go on living."

"What do you mean? They all committed suicide?"

"You're not much of a news watcher are you? Unfortunately, yes. Howard shot himself. Kenny hung himself. Larry died of asphyxiation in his garage."

"Well, what about Archie? I don't even know where he lives."

"I didn't either, Brucie. I'd lost contact with him a very long time ago, sort of like you. Only difference is, he was in some outpost in the Dakotas, so it took me longer than I had hoped to track him down."

"Good thing you found him. But…he did something too?"

"Yeah, he did. He jumped into a deep lake with weights on his legs."

"That's horrible."

"Yeah, it was horrible. It was hard to get him to stop kicking long enough for us to tie the weights on. The poor guy just kept kicking and squirming."

The room went silent. Bruce Wink couldn't move.

"You see…you, too, are distraught over poor Louise's death."

Wink struggled to speak. "Roy—"

"Ah, Brucie. It's a fact. You loved her so much that you couldn't handle it."

"Roy…what about your wife? Does she know?"

"Enough. I've been here too long as it is. Hell no, she doesn't know, and I'm not about to tell her. Kay's on the hit list; the last one to be avenged. Too bad. She's a good governor and a decent wife. But I've got a plane to catch. I'm going to Mexico, where I'll be living out my days on a beach. Everyone in my world thinks I'm on a plane to London at this very minute when all the while I'm right here in little old Auburn Hills, Michigan. As soon as we're done I'm off to the airport where my good friend Miguel has a plane waiting for me. Did you know that Miguel is the largest heroin provider in Wisconsin? His uncle runs the operation out of Guadalajara. It's truly amazing how many people you get to know just by becoming a lawyer. You, on the other hand, are in need of becoming dead." Spurgeon smiled as he pulled his gun out one more time. The two goons stood and pulled theirs as well. Wink began to sob once again. "But, like the others, we have to make this look accidental. Your cooperation would be much appreciated, Bruce."

Wink started shaking.

Spurgeon stood and began a forward-and-back pace, lecturing as if he were teaching a class. "Each one has been an interesting challenge for me. You see, I couldn't simply have each of you shoot yourself like I did with Howard. That would not only be too easy, it would start to look like a pattern, and that wouldn't be good. So tonight I'm going to take advantage of the weather conditions. Here's how this is going to go down. You're going to take off all your clothes and march straight out your back door into the woods behind your house and stay there until dawn."

Between heaving sobs, Wink protested, "But, Roy, it's freezing out there."

"Why, yes. Yes, it is. Last we checked it's about ten degrees above zero. That should put you frozen to death in about an hour or two.

And since you're half in the tank from that bar you were at, my plan is quite perfect."

Wink summoned all his courage and stood up. "And if I say no?"

Spurgeon stopped pacing and turned to face him. "Well, I've got another guy a mile away sitting in a car ready to enter your daughter's house and kill her, her husband, and your granddaughter. All he needs is a phone call from me. Which option would you prefer?"

Wink stared at Spurgeon. Tears poured down his cheeks as he slowly unbuttoned his shirt. Within five minutes he was standing naked outside his back door. The bite of winter didn't even register as he looked back over his right shoulder to Roy Spurgeon, who was standing at the window holding up his cell phone. Wink wiped away a tear, lowered his head, and began to walk. His extremities began the death march as he stumbled into the forest and fell. A snowdrift cushioned his fall, and he lay face down for a moment. He knew his time was short, and in the icy blanket gripping his body a small ember of an idea flared up. His arms and legs were already numb, but he managed to get to his feet. He took ten steps through the trees to a clearing and hooked his elbow around the limb of a small poplar to steady himself. His right leg gave way as it shut down, but he willed it back to life and staggered into the open space.

Through the window, Roy Spurgeon watched him lurch around for another minute, and then saw him fall to the ground one final time. After five minutes the body hadn't moved. Spurgeon pulled out a chair from the kitchen table and sat down at the door wall looking out to Bruce Wink. He crossed his legs and sat in silence for ninety minutes. Satisfied that his old high school friend had taken his last breath, he and his goons exited the house and returned to the car they had left at a gas station three blocks away.

A few minutes later, the moon broke through the cloud cover and lit up the clearing. In the snow trail behind the body of Bruce Wink three letters were carved in the snow. His feet lay at the base of the letter Y. To the left were an R and an O.

CHAPTER 35

Silk ran up the stairs of the Wisconsin State Capitol Building. The temperature was slowly climbing back to normal, but the air was still cold enough to pierce his lungs, causing him to gulp for air by the time he reached the top landing. It was Monday, October twenty-third, and the entire lower plaza was festooned with decorations ranging from cornstalks and pumpkins to giant music notes and inflatable badgers. He could see a few of the smaller music stages that had already been set up on the side streets leading to the plaza, and a giant pile of construction materials lay at the base of the steps, waiting to be assembled. In the plaza itself a work crew was just putting the finishing touches on the ice rink, and an enormous banner reading BADGER FEST had already been hung from the balcony above the front entrance to the building. Everywhere people were busy preparing for the weekend's festivities. Plainclothes security teams and uniformed policemen roamed the entire area. Silk leaned on the heavy revolving door with both hands to get it moving. Viceroy, Regina, and Jerry were waiting for him to arrive so that they could start their meeting with the governor.

Once inside, a security guard led him to the office where his colleagues were already gathered. Viceroy was scrolling through the messages on his cell phone and Regina was talking into hers.

Jerry King stood up and gave Silk a friendly handshake and a hug.

"Sorry, boys," Regina said, after quickly ending her call. "My sister needed to know if I was going to man the candy station for Halloween, and I had to tell her I might be otherwise engaged. She wasn't pleased."

Viceroy said, "Alright, alright, now that Silk has decided to report for duty," with a bit of a smirk towards the big man, "let's get our heads together before we see the governor. Regina has some more info to share."

She flipped open her computer to reference her notes as she spoke. "I had confirmation late yesterday that Louise Wink was killed about a week and a half ago. She was bludgeoned to death in her home and the perpetrator left the weapon in the foyer near the body. A wooden baseball bat. The penny was taped to the bat."

Silk blew forcefully out of his mouth and was about to say something when Viceroy interjected, "Yes, Silk, unfortunately. The bat was a 32 weight. The number two was etched into the bottom of the handle as all bat companies do to indicate the weight of their bats, so we have the number two. We're trying to get some forensic evidence through the PD over there. Right now they think they have a shoe print off the snow, and a neighbor thinks he saw a cable company van in the driveway around the time they believe it happened. There is no evidence inside of the perpetrator."

"And the husband?" Jerry asked.

Viceroy glanced over to Regina. "His daughter found him over the weekend in a wooded area behind his house. He froze to death. He was naked and had a rather high blood alcohol content."

"Damn," Silk said.

"He walked there, Silk," Regina said. "His footprints lead from the back door to the place he was found. But before he died, he left a note."

"Well, do we have a copy? Did their PD send you a scan or anything? That could be huge." Silk was impatient.

Viceroy nodded, pulled a photograph out of a manila folder, took a look, and flipped it around for Jerry and Silk to see.

"Oh, my holy God," Jerry said. Silk shoved his chair away from the table and stood, arms hanging straight and loose from his shoulders as he stared.

Viceroy spoke next in a measured tone. "As you know, we've made every effort to find out what flight Spurgeon took to London. I've pulled in the FBI and the FAA along with any and all contacts I have to find him. We've checked every flight to London from anywhere in the USA over the last ten days. Roy Spurgeon's name isn't on any of the manifests. We've also pinged his cell phone but it's been silent for a few days. The last known ping was from downtown Milwaukee. My hunch? He never intended to go to London at all; however, my FAA buddy in Chicago has been very helpful. The night of Bruce Wink's death this past Thursday a private Lear jet registered to a wealthy Mexican departed an executive airport in the Detroit area. All we know is that there were three passengers. I'm assuming one of them was Spurgeon. In cooperation with the Mexican government we've been able to track the plane to Guadalajara."

Regina already knew where Viceroy was headed. Jerry and Silk just waited for him to continue, and after an awkward silence Silk spoke up, "And...?"

"And I need both of you to pack your bags. Hopefully you haven't put your summer clothes in storage yet. Guadalajara is in the eighties right now." Viceroy was about to add to his comment when his cell phone buzzed. He took it and hung up. "That was Governor Spurgeon. You two guys are getting off easy, quite honestly. Regina and I are going to have to break the news to her. You're expected at the airport in two hours. When you get there, go right to the FAA office. They'll have a private jet waiting for you." He flipped them each a file, adding, "You can read these on the plane. There's information on the Modero family. They're the owners of the plane I believe Spurgeon was on. They're rich, but it's dirty money; drugs mostly. You're there to find Spurgeon, but proceed with caution. The Moderos aren't to be taken lightly." The two men nodded their understanding and headed out to their cars. As they hit the atrium lobby they heard Viceroy calling out from down the hall. "Stay in touch, boys. Godspeed."

Jerry got to the revolving door and pushed. Silk followed right behind, asking him if he knew any Spanish.

CHAPTER 36

Viceroy and Regina could only wait as Governor Spurgeon sat behind her desk in silence. It had been a good five minutes since they delivered the update on their investigation along with the awful news about her husband and the photo they'd received from the Auburn Hills police. She had turned her chair sideways and was staring out the window. She was dressed casually in jeans, stylish winter boots, and a sweater that accented the blue of her eyes. The silence was uncomfortable, but Viceroy had come to understand that this was her way of processing information. Finally, she cleared her throat, stood up, and walked to the window. Regina looked questioningly at Viceroy, who gestured for her to be patient. After a few more minutes, the governor turned back to the desk.

"I'm beyond shocked. You know I trust you two implicitly. Jerry has been great at keeping me up to date, but this news, as I'm sure you can imagine, is very difficult for me to absorb."

In as compassionate a tone as he could muster, Viceroy said, "Governor, I'm sorry you had to hear it, particularly when you have so much else on your plate. My heart goes out to you on a personal level."

"Thank you. I'll descend into despair tonight when I'm home, but right now let's talk about where we go from here."

"Anything you want, anything at all."

She sat back down, put her elbows on the desk and clasped her hands in front of her. The governor was about to deliver her official thoughts, and both Viceroy and Regina understood that they were simply to listen and accept whatever she had decided.

"Again," she began, "I want to thank you both and the rest of your staff for the efforts you have made over the past two months to solve the bombing at Pine Creek that started this whole mess. Now it seems that my own life is in danger. My husband, who appears to have murdered at least one person and quite probably more, has fled the country, and my signature public event is scheduled to take place in five days. I've had better moments. However, let's take one thing at a time and deal with each piece as the facts warrant."

"Okay," Viceroy said.

"Of course," Regina echoed.

"First, on a personal level, I'm devastated. Roy and I have had our struggles, and now that I know what I know, I can see why he's pulled away from me even more since Howard and Mary's passing. He was different when he returned from seeing Howard the day after the bombing. Now I know that he must have discovered something that made him snap. Hopefully we'll find out what it was. But, that said, I want you to find him and bring him in. You say you think you know where he is, but because of our professional relationship you prefer not to tell me. I respect that. All I ask is that you conduct your search in a discrete manner. Should he call me, you will be the first to know, and I will try to find out where he is. However, I have no intention of canceling the festival and I will not allow any of this to be made public until after the weekend, so if you do find him before then, he can sit in a jail cell and wait. I'm sure you have a place to keep him that no one knows about."

Viceroy nodded.

"Good. You have been very forthright with me, and I appreciate that. I hope you realize that I'm not a part of Roy's twisted scheming and I certainly am not protecting him. Are we of the same mindset here?"

Viceroy nodded again.

"Good. So we will proceed with Badger Fest as planned, and I do not want to hear any protests from you."

"But Governor—"

She slapped her palm on her desk to drive home her point. "Roger, this is not negotiable."

"You are on a hit list, for goodness sake. And as the head of MRSCU, I have to protect you."

"This festival has been planned since the moment I took office, and nothing is going to stop it. Nothing."

"We don't know who we're looking for or even if—"

"I do not care. Wisconsin is going to celebrate this weekend, and I will not budge on that."

Regina had been quietly observing the noisy battle between her boss and the governor, trying to keep her head down to avoid any verbal shrapnel. But hearing what the governor had just said, she knew she had to speak up.

"Roger...?"

As the battle of wills continued, she tried again.

"Roger. Governor...?"

It was no use. If she wanted to be heard, she'd have to outshout them.

"Governor Spurgeon and Roger Viceroy," she said in a clear, strong voice.

Both went silent and turned to see Regina Cortez in full battle mode. "The attempt on your life will be this weekend, Governor."

"Regina..." Viceroy interjected, trying to cover for his trusted employee.

"Please listen to me. Governor, Roger is simply trying to ensure your complete safety. The killer will attempt to carry out his or her assassination this weekend because that's what murderers who want attention do. He or she will attempt to kill you at the festival, and since you will appear right here on the Capitol steps to kick off the celebration, in my humble opinion, that is where the attack will occur. Someone's been counting down from six to one, and while I'm not sure how that ties into this weekend, I can only hope that we don't find out the answer after the fact." When she had finished, Regina lowered her head as if in apology for sassing her elders, and added in a quieter voice, "There won't be much to celebrate if the killer succeeds."

Viceroy could only stare at her in silent admiration.

"Well, well, Regina," the governor said after a moment, "it's good to hear you speaking up. And, for what it's worth, what you say makes sense to me."

"So clearly," Viceroy jumped in, seizing the moment, "you have to cancel." Then he turned to Regina. "Thank you," he said.

"Clearly, Roger, I will not cancel. In fact, just the opposite. I want you to use me as bait. I can wear a bulletproof vest and no one will know, since I'll be wearing a coat anyway, and you'll have your greatest opportunity to find the murderer. If whoever this is uses a firearm, I'll be protected; if there's another method, then your army will have to suffice in ensuring that method is not successful."

Viceroy said, "You can't risk your life like that."

"Oh, yes I can. And, yes, I will."

"But we don't even know how, when, or where the attempt will be made."

"Then you'll just have to prepare for every possibility."

Viceroy wasn't ready to give up, but after a few minutes he knew he was fighting a losing battle. In just five days Governor Kay Spurgeon would be standing on those steps speaking to a crowd of thousands.

"Very well then, it's settled," she said. "Now if you'll excuse me, I have a night of ungodly emotions concerning my husband to attend to. Thank you both for everything, and I mean that with all sincerity. I have every confidence in your talents and your instincts. You will find this person. Pull in whatever police resources you need to get the job done, and if the festival is the stage, then so be it."

The two exited.

When he knew they were out of earshot, he first told her how proud he was of what she had said and then added that he hoped her own bulletproof vest still fit, because she would be standing next to the governor on the Capitol steps on Saturday.

CHAPTER 37

Wu Yin awakens to a much-anticipated day. The teen has become a young man. It has been seven long years since Tao Wang's passing. Seven years to contemplate what is on the disk. Seven years to hold his promise intact. Seven years to think up a thousand scenarios of the secrets the disk holds, now to be revealed. In his life of mostly solitude, he needed to fill the gap between receiving the disk and watching it. *Seven years.* Time for learning—to paint, to golf, to sail, to play the piano, to invest, to find a lover, to lose a lover, to master firearms, to read, to travel, to think, and to do anything else that comes to mind on any given day. Except for this day. This day is predetermined.

It is mid-morning on the day of his twenty-fifth birthday. The wait is over. Now, in the comfort of his den with the sound of the ocean in the background, he takes a deep breath and settles into the sofa with the remote in his hand.

He presses the play button and Tao's image appears. He is seated on a stool wearing a plain, gray t-shirt and jeans. Wu recognizes the room is the one he is sitting in now. Based on his physical appearance, Wu guesses that he must have made the video just after he was diagnosed with cancer. Tao's head is bowed and after a moment he raises it and looks directly into the camera. He begins to speak in a quiet, steady voice.

He starts by telling Wu that the video he's going to be watching has been pieced together from photographs, home movie footage, and tapes collected over a lifetime.

He says that he knows, since Wu is watching, that he, Tao, has died. He urges Wu not to mourn his passing as he watches.

He says that he is going to explain Wu's family history and tell him the truth about the fate of his parents. Hearing those words, Wu sits bolt upright on the couch.

Tao tells Wu that everything he knows is a lie. He apologizes but asks for Wu's forbearance and forgiveness. He affirms he is rich, but not from an inheritance as he had led Wu to believe all of his life. The lie they have lived was a necessary gambit.

He takes Wu back to his start in China and about his own wife, Jiaying, explaining they met at engineering school in Shanghai. Once graduated they were allowed to leave for continued studies at the University of Chicago in the United States. A year later their first and only child was born. A few more images appear of Tao and Jiaying in those years, followed by pictures of a baby boy. Tao then looks straight at the camera and tells Wu that the baby in the pictures is his father, Bennett, Tao's son.

Wu's finger hits the pause button. He is frozen, trying to process the knowledge that the man he had always considered his benefactor was actually his grandfather and that he had never been in an orphanage. The image of his boy-father is paused on the TV screen, and tears stream down Wu's face as he stares at it, knowing for the first time that he indeed had a family. He slowly slides to the floor with his back against the sofa. After another minute, he moves a trembling hand to the remote and pushes the play button.

Tao tells him that his true name is John. John Wang. He asks John once again to forgive him for making up the story about the orphanage, but what had befallen his father and mother was so terrible that he needed to keep the truth secret until such time as they could have this conversation. He was hoping it would be in person, but once the cancer was discovered he decided this would be the best way.

187

He continues pulling together the pieces for John, outlining that he had an opportunity with a paper company that ultimately led the family to move to Curwood, Wisconsin, in 1964.

John then views many images of a beautiful house on a tree-lined street. Images of his father, his grandmother, and his grandfather fill the screen. The film traces the family's activities all the way through Bennett's high school years.

Tao explains that their life in Curwood had been extremely challenging but his father had always held his head up and walked the high ground. There was deep prejudice against Asians and his father was robbed of a happy childhood. What kept them there was the lucrative job, which ultimately blessed the family with the fortune.

Tao then wipes away a tear and opines that life is always clear when one looks back on it. It is rare, however, to look forward and know where all roads lead.

The bright side was the relationship John's father had started in high school with a beautiful young lady named Greta Zumwald. He explains the marriage, the aftermath his parents had to battle, and their decision to stay in hopes of changing hearts and minds.

John sees images of his mother and father—the wedding, their lives, and finally a photo of him being held in a hospital bed as a newborn. Tao tells John to be proud to have inherited his red hair from his mother, known to everyone as Penny.

In a shakier voice, Tao says that the images he is about to show next are of his parent's house in Curwood taken just a number of years ago. He asks if John remembers the week he left the island and explains that it wasn't really to see a doctor in Philadelphia as he had said. He'd needed to visit Curwood one more time to capture this footage. The same tree-lined street that had been in the photos of his parent's house appears on the screen. The footage is being shot from a moving car. The car stops and the camera pans to the burnt-out shell of a house. All the windows are shattered, part of the roof has caved in, and the vegetation has gone wild, covering the stone walls and the porch and growing though the missing windows. A "Keep Out" sign is posted in the overgrown front yard. John stares at the image and a tingle runs down his spine.

The screen goes dark and Tao reappears to explain that the house is still there on Juniper Street in Curwood, given as their gift to Bennett and Greta when they got married. It's where John was born, and it is still owned by Ji Zhu Trust. John has always been intrigued as to why the trust had been named after the Chinese word for "remember"; now he knows why. Tao has kept the house in its condition as a permanent reminder to everyone.

Tao relates that his parents were so aware of the hostility towards them in the community, his father took the precaution of installing a sophisticated recording system for security. It was on when his parents met their fate, and the footage John is about to see was taken that night.

He reminds his grandson to stay strong and watch so that he understands what happened and who was responsible. He simply wants John to know the truth. Tao explains that a phone call awakened him that night. The caller didn't identify himself but Tao was told to get over to the house immediately. He still doesn't know who made the call, but he's always suspected that it was a man named Marlin Butters, his father's high school basketball coach. When he arrived, the house was in flames. He found a way in through the basement and took John out, but he couldn't save his son or daughter-in-law. The video, he says, will explain everything.

John sees it all. The six young men. The brutal force. The jerseys. The numbers. The names. The assault on his father. His limp body. His mother tied to the bed. The knife. The rapes. The crushing blows. The burns to her body. The gunshot. The curtain aflame. The picture then fades and goes black as smoke eventually blankets the screen.

John pauses the video and sets down the remote. Nausea wells up like a volcano in his gut and he runs outside to vomit over the patio rail into the bay below. Finally, he sinks to the floor and curls into a fetal position. He stays there, unaware of time and even place, for several hours. Eventually he stirs. With a gargantuan effort he gets to his feet and goes back inside. He summons the strength to return to the disk.

He hits the play button once again. Tao is once more sitting on the stool explaining that he didn't discover the tapes until a week after the event when he remembered the recorder in the basement. He took it to the police, but they were not interested. The autopsy done by the town doctor said his parents had died of smoke inhalation resulting from an electrical fire. John was also listed as deceased, the assumption being that his body had been consumed in the fire. The police remained adamant that they had no desire to learn the truth. Given their insolence, Tao never told them about the phone call he had received or that he had rescued his grandchild. One month later, he moved with baby John to the estate his son had been building in the Cayman Islands. He makes clear to John that leaving was the best way to ensure his future and that the lies over the past twenty-five years were for his protection.

The recording ends with Tao expressing his love for John, reminding him to live with honor in the islands and use his wealth to do good for others, thus securing a new legacy for the Wang family. Tao then holds up leather-bound copies of both the Holy Bible and the Tao Te Ching. He finishes with a final instruction from grandfather to grandson. "These books will always help you. Christianity and Taoism are your heritage from your parents union. Continue to learn, absorb them both, and then live them well." The screen fades to black.

When John turns off the disk, he cries for a long time. He lets out a scream of emotion. Inside him a foreign feeling stirs. His grandfather's final words wither quickly away.

CHAPTER 38

The assassin held the paint brush ever so delicately as he put the finishing touches on the picture. *It's a masterpiece!* He had arrived in Milwaukee on Sunday, October twenty-second, and he was hotel-hopping every night so as not to become noticeable in any one place. His choices were random and he always paid in cash. On Monday night he was hunkered down at the Marc Plaza just a few blocks from MRSCU headquarters. The news anchor was in the middle of a year-to-date story and was recapping the original bombing at the golf club as well as the Kittleton and Udell murders. Of course, the media had not been given any information that would have connected the three crimes. He knew the great Roger Viceroy was too smart for that.

He held the photo up for a final inspection and approved what he saw. *For you, Spurgeon, I'm going to make it very clear.* Then he repeated the artistic addition on the last photo. *And yes, white knight, you get one too, because taking the risk is thrilling.* Ten minutes and a few extra paint strokes later, he was done. He capped the paint jar, opened his window, and let it fall down into the alley near a dumpster. The brush he put in the trash can by the vending machine in the hallway. By the time he returned to his room, the paint had dried so he boxed up both photos, attached the delivery addresses, and went to the bar across the street.

On Tuesday he ate a large breakfast and spent the entire day at a multiplex in a mall watching the fall blockbusters before finding another hotel.

Wednesday morning he climbed into his Jeep, stopped at a post office, and headed west towards Madison. The first exit he came upon was for a road named Kaykill. He laughed out loud and stepped on the gas pedal.

CHAPTER 39

On Friday morning Viceroy arrived at the office a good two hours earlier than normal. He had some paperwork to complete for Strongsmith before driving over to Madison and the final preparations for Badger Fest. It was warmer out than it had been for days, and he was hoping the weather would hold through the weekend. Security was going to be tough enough without having to freeze all day. Along the way he called Jerry and Silk as he had done every morning since their arrival in Mexico. They'd made some progress but still didn't know Spurgeon's exact location. The international connection took a while to ring through and he heard Jerry's voice just as he hit the on-ramp to the freeway.

"Roger?"

"Hey, Jerry, how's it going?"

"I'm wearing shorts and a t-shirt. The sun's already getting hot, and the hotel pool has some awesome sights. You?"

Viceroy said, "That sucks. You're missing a temperature reading of thirty-seven degrees on a nice, crisp morning. I'm wearing khakis, a scarf, Timberland boots, and a button-down shirt under a nice argyle sweater. I also have my black leather gloves at the ready for when I exit my vehicle."

He heard Jerry laugh on the other end and then say "Hey, Silk's here. We're wolfing down a breakfast and then heading over to our friend's office at the Mexican federal authorities building."

Viceroy heard a "Yo, Preacher" in the background before Jerry continued.

"We got a call last night and we think we may finally have a solid lead. I don't know the details yet, but we may be on the move. Our boy is definitely in the country. We just have to find out where. We'll keep you posted."

"Thanks, Jerry. I'll wait for your call. And remind Silk not to drink the water."

"Will do, boss. Call you later."

Viceroy heard the connection go dead and he maneuvered over to the faster left lane while dialing Sheriff Vogl, who answered on the first ring. The two had a standing daily phone call to update Viceroy on the search for Eric Zumwald. There was a chance Zumwald was camping in the wilderness up in Canada—a frequent activity of his they came to learn. Vogl had contacted the Canadian authorities, but to date no information came back. More concerning to Viceroy, however, was that Zumwald was nowhere they were looking but instead was stalking Governor Spurgeon. Vogl reconfirmed they had the three cabins and the house on constant stake-out. No news either from any Wisconsin police departments on spotting Zumwald's vehicle. To date, the man was off the grid. He disconnected with Vogl and was through his office door a few minutes before nine o'clock. He had spotted Regina's car in the parking lot but she wasn't in her office, so he grabbed the morning paper off her chair for a quick scan. He fired up his computer, hoping there would be no interruptions and he would be on the road to Madison by one. A half hour into his report, Regina poked her head in and said a brief, "Good morning."

An hour later, his assistant tapped softly on the doorframe and Viceroy looked up over his glasses.

"There's a package for you," she said as she placed it on his desk. "It just arrived a few minutes ago."

"Thanks. Who's it from?"

She turned the package to get a better read on the label. "No name, but the return address is Juniper Lane, Curwood, Wisconsin."

A startled Viceroy said, "Um, look, I'm not quite sure what

you've got there, but I wasn't expecting anything from Curwood."

She shook the package gingerly trying to discern its contents— loose or something solid. He took it from her, not sure if he should call the bomb squad or simply open it up.

"Thanks," he said. "And would you please ask Regina to come in here?"

Within thirty seconds Regina was at his door. She could see that he didn't look happy as he stared at the package on his desk.

"The label says it's from Curwood, but the postmark is right here in Milwaukee."

Regina moved into the office and took a seat. "So what are you waiting for?"

"Trying to decide if I want the bomb squad to check it out or simply see what we have here."

"Well," Regina said, "I vote for opening it. The post office is supposed to scan and sniff out any and all mail coming our way, so let's trust they did their job."

Viceroy picked up the package, grabbed the rip strip on the top, and tugged just enough to get it started. He peeled it back an inch, and when he was satisfied that his fingers were going to remain attached to his hand, he finished ripping it off. Looking inside, he saw what looked like a wooden picture frame. He pulled it out and stared at the burned-out Wang house.

"Oh crap," Regina said.

He flipped the frame around to see if there was anything on the back, but there wasn't. Regina grabbed the box and looked inside. Seeing nothing, she shook it just in case, but again, nothing. Viceroy carefully removed the frame to examine the back of the photo. Still nothing. He put the frame back on, placed the photo on his desk, and stood over it.

"This person is not only crazy but taunting us as well. Why the hell would he send this to me?"

"I don't know. Maybe it's supposed to be some kind of message. Maybe the killer is hoping you'll figure something out that he wants you to know about. It's like leaving the pennies and the numbers countdown. He's communicating."

Viceroy rubbed his chin as he sat down to stare at the photo.

195

"Maybe. Let's think."

After a few minutes he went to the file cabinet to pull out the notes and photos he and the team had produced during their stay in Curwood. He pulled out their own photo of the house and flipped it to Regina. "Look," he said, with a not-very-successful attempt to inject some humor into the situation, "we've already got one." She placed the two photos side-by-side.

Regina said, "Oh, God."

His head snapped up. "What?"

"Look."

Viceroy walked around the desk and stared straight down at the two photos. Regina pointed to a small dark spot on the framed photo that was not on the file photo. He had to get so close that his nose was almost touching it to see the tiny added detail. There, in one of the burned out windows on the second floor, stood the finely painted silhouette of a human being; just below it, on the arch over the front door, were barely visible brush strokes that to the naked eye looked like they might be letters. Grabbing his magnifying glass, he was able to clearly see "Romans 12:19" on the arch above the door. Oddly, the artist had painted a thin, black line through it.

"It's scripture," he said to Regina.

"What?"

"Yeah. Romans twelve, verse nineteen, but there's a line through it."

"I'm confused."

"Me too. Can you look that up on your phone?"

"Give me a sec," Regina said, while her fingers flew. "Um, it reads, 'Do not avenge yourselves, my friends, but give place to wrath, for it is written 'Vengeance is Mine, I will repay' says the Lord.'"

"Okay, this just took on another level," Viceroy said as the clue kicked in. He shouted out the door to his assistant, "Get Strongsmith on the line and tell him I won't be getting his report to him today," then continued his verbal analysis with Regina. "The person who sent this wants us to know that the Wang family has some connection to the investigation. We may have an individual of Asian descent to track down along with Zumwald. Call the Madison

PD. The security around the governor's event tomorrow just got more specific. And my brain's telling me the verse being crossed out was purposeful. We've got a revenge serial killer on our hands."

As Regina went to her desk to start making phone calls and sending emails to everyone on the event security staff, a few blocks away a similar package was being delivered to the offices of Spurgeon, Carleton & Mann.

CHAPTER 40

The rest of Friday was spent with everyone on the MRSCU team looking for anyone of Asian descent who could possibly be involved with the case. Their database indicated there were eighty-seven individuals in Wisconsin named Wang, but all of them checked out clean. A search of hotels in the capital for any guest with an Asian-sounding name came up with close to two hundred, and it took the entire day to vet them. By nightfall they were reasonably comfortable that none of them posed a danger to the event or to the governor. Additionally, the photo of Eric Zumwald had been delivered to every hotel in the greater Madison area with the hope that, if he's the one, he would mess up and rent a room at one of them.

That same morning, the assassin awoke in his Jeep in the middle of a disused, dilapidated barn on the outskirts of Madison. He'd spotted it from the freeway on his way into town and decided it would be a perfect place for him to hide out. The roof was caved in at one end and half the slats were missing along one of the sides, but it provided a place to park his vehicle and stay out of sight. He had let the engine run all night with the heater on so that he wouldn't freeze. Now the tank was almost on empty, and after stepping outside to relieve himself, he got back in the car and went looking for a gas station. From there he would proceed to the State Street parking garage on the campus of the University of Wisconsin, where a man carrying a backpack would look like just another university student or professor. The only difference was, his backpack was loaded with ammo, a tripod, a high-powered gun, and a telescopic lens. Also in his Jeep were a heavy blanket and a battery-operated heater for his Friday night stay in the blighted building he had selected for his perch. *Tomorrow I finish.* He pulled a Pop Tart out of the glove compartment and ate his breakfast.

CHAPTER 41

Governor Spurgeon arrived at the Capitol under heavy police escort at 8:00 a.m. on Saturday morning. The temperature was hovering around fifty degrees and the forecast was for sunny skies. Despite all the potential dangers and her own personal heartaches, she was excited for this day to finally arrive and would not allow anything to diminish the occasion she'd worked so hard to create. Festivals and outreach efforts had been planned in communities throughout the state. People of all ages and from all walks of life would be uniting to celebrate the simple joy of being Wisconsinites. Her vision was vast and her expectations were high. For the past two years she had worked tirelessly to persuade big cities and small towns to engage. As a result of her efforts, she knew this inaugural year would be a fantastic success. Even more important, future events would build off this one until, ultimately, the festival's annual celebration of unity would become a daily way of life, or so she hoped.

The police escort dropped her off at a side entrance, and as soon as the driver opened her door, the media pounced. She was beaming when she stepped out of the car dressed in a full-length, chocolate-brown coat, an orange scarf with green accents, and sleek, brown leather boots. She was in full governor mode as she walked to the bank of microphones her communications director had set up as a press conference area. The questions went on for fifteen minutes before an aide intervened, telling the media that the governor had to get inside for the live television interviews that were scheduled to start at 8:30 a.m. One reporter launched a final question about her husband's conspicuous absence, but the governor was ready with her response. She let it be known that he had taken ill and was resting at home under doctor's orders. Hopefully he would be back at it next week, she added. And with that, she headed inside.

On the massive stage in front of the Capitol a local band was warming up and doing sound checks. The plaza was ablaze with color. On the north side, local restaurants had set up food trucks for "A Taste of Wisconsin," and the south end had a plethora of interactive games and creative arts displays. The giant middle of the plaza was left open for people to walk around and listen to the music that would play all day. The steps leading up from the plaza to the Capitol's main entrance were covered in bright red carpet, and the massive Badger Fest banner hanging from the balcony flapped lightly in a soft breeze. People were already pouring into the area even though the festivities wouldn't officially begin until 10:00 a.m. with an address from Governor Spurgeon given on the landing below the banner. There, a podium was in place with chairs and bleachers that would soon be filled with politicians and VIPs.

From a window on the second floor of an abandoned building a few blocks away, the assassin kept watch, making sure to remain hidden from the security personnel he knew would be patrolling the area. He had avoided their sweep of the building earlier that morning by hiding out in the ceiling panels. Once cleared, he quietly repositioned himself. He had chosen this particular window with precision. It provided the best angle for a clear shot to the podium. The floors above him would have narrowed the sightline and increased the percentage of missing his target. As he watched the final preparations, it gave him great joy to know that his glorious mission would soon be completed. His legs were cramping from crouching down below the windowsill, so he crawled to a corner where he knew he couldn't be seen and stood up, stomping his feet to get the blood flowing, and then crawled once again to the other side of the room with two cans of spray paint.

After a few minutes, he stepped back and admired his handiwork. On the wall in black paint were the names of all six women, in order from top to bottom, with their corresponding numbers. Kay Spurgeon's name was the last one, and the largest. Just below, he taped a penny; positioned beneath it, in red spray paint, he'd written GRETA ZUMWALD WANG 1982. Placement of the gun and scope was next. Seeing the sheer number of eyewitnesses pouring in to witness his final glorious act of revenge gave him a thrill. He also knew there was an army of security personnel looking for him in this gigantic haystack. He opened the gun case.

A few blocks away, in a heated tent off the northwest corner of the plaza, Roger Viceroy and Regina Cortez were going over the final security details with a hundred armed uniformed officers. Regina shifted the bulletproof vest under her coat. It was uncomfortable but she knew she had to have it. Viceroy had one on as well. When he finished what he had to say, he asked the four captains to stay a moment for a final briefing, after which he and Regina headed straight to the Capitol for a meeting with the governor. As they exited the tent, Viceroy saw the huge crowd that had already gathered and felt a tingle; the kind that screams danger.

The governor welcomed them into her office just as a half dozen staff people were leaving. "You look good, you two."

Viceroy said, "You look good as well and I truly pray this day becomes all you've been hoping it would be. I know how important it is to you."

"Thank you. I appreciate that."

"And, by the way, I think you'll look even better with this on," he said, holding out a bulletproof vest.

She knew she had to wear it, but she didn't want to spoil the upbeat mood of the moment. "Do you have one in orange to match my scarf?"

Viceroy cracked a slight grin then shook his head and held it out to her.

They sat down for the update and he chose not to tell her about the doctored photograph, but instead took the moment to summarize the gravity of the situation.

"If this is going to happen, just a reminder that it's our opinion the killer will strike when you're standing on the steps giving your kick-off speech. It's the time you will be at your most vulnerable and most exposed. We have done all we can to secure the Capitol grounds and we have a small army of uniformed and undercover officers blanketing the building and the plaza, as well as the surrounding streets. Regina is going to stand as close to you as she can so that she can watch the crowd from your sightline. I promise she'll not be in your way, nor impede your own bodyguards, but I want her there and, frankly, you do, too."

"Thank you. I know you're against this, and I appreciate all you've done. Let's just put today in God's hands, okay?"

"I already have."

"Good, then that makes two of us."

"Three," Regina joined in.

"Then we're set. Where will you be during the speech?" the governor asked.

Viceroy said, "I've thought about that, and I think somewhere to the back would be best. Watching from behind serves a few purposes. I've had a small platform constructed near the skating rink so I can see above the crowd. In fact, I need to get going now to secure my position. I also want you to know that we have the entire area hooked up to security cameras. I've got a team in a trailer on a side street watching a bank of screens. Wisconsin's best uniformed sharpshooters are on all the rooftops surrounding the plaza as well."

"Well, that's comforting."

"It helps. Anyway, I wish you well and pray to God I'll see you in about an hour."

He shook her hand and walked out, leaving it to Regina to make sure the governor put on her vest. As he walked down the hallway, he inserted his earpiece, set his radio to the proper channel, and gave it a try. "Regina, making sure you can hear me. Everyone else on this channel stay silent."

"I'm here. The governor is properly vested and her communications people just arrived to escort her downstairs. We'll be leaving in fifteen minutes."

Her voice crackled a bit, but he knew that the communication would be crystal clear once they were outside. "Great news. I'm just now heading out. Tell the governor that her event is going to be a huge success. The crowd is gigantic."

"On it, boss. I'll let you know when we head out."

"Ten-four." Viceroy took a deep breath of brisk morning air and made his way down to the sidewalk that ran the length of the plaza. Coming from the main stage, he could hear the sounds of mic checks and a few dissonant chords. It was 9:45 a.m. and his heart started to beat a little faster as the hour of the speech approached. He thought he recognized a few of the plainclothes police in the crowd, but he couldn't be sure. In any case, he knew they numbered in the hundreds. At the end of the sidewalk, past the food truck line, he turned right and headed for the ice rink. There stood his small, four-foot-high platform. He nodded his thanks to the security officer who was guarding it.

From the platform, Viceroy could see above the heads of the people in front of him. It was positioned dead center at the west end, between the plaza and the ice rink, and about one hundred yards from the podium. Once he was in position, he radioed Regina, who informed him that the governor would be delayed by about ten minutes because the make-up person had arrived later than planned. This was actually welcome news as it gave him more time to scan the crowd. He relaxed a bit after a visual sweep. He also noted that all the seats and bleachers around the podium were already packed.

At 10:05 a.m., Regina radioed that they were on their way downstairs. In a perfectly timed moment, four fighter jets would be making their flyover, and he could hear the hum already coming from the east. Within a minute the jets were closing in and the noise level was building, along with a very palpable excitement emanating from the plaza. Viceroy could see people start pointing at the sky, and soon enough the jets were buzzing over the Capitol and the plaza. The noise was ear-shattering as the planes flew over and disappeared past the buildings. On the stage, the band was playing the governor's introductory music and the masses turned back around to face the Capitol. Everyone except for Roger Viceroy.

As he watched the jets disappear from sight, the last one on the left veered south and caught his eye as it made its bank. His gaze followed as it disappeared over a dingy old building about two blocks away. Every nerve in his body was on high alert, but it still took him a couple of seconds to process what he was seeing. Then it hit him. *Oh God.* Painted on the small brick façade above an arched doorway, chipped and barely legible, were the words WISCONSIN ONE BANK.

Viceroy sprang from the platform and screamed into his radio. "Everyone listen. Do not, repeat do *not*, let the governor out of the building."

Regina radioed. "Too late."

As her voice came through his earpiece he heard the crowd erupt in response to Governor Spurgeon's appearance. Music and cheers rang through the plaza. Viceroy was running full tilt, pushing past the startled spectators coming towards him as he made his way around the ice rink in a mad dash for the building.

"Get her out of there if you can," he shouted without breaking stride. Regina shouted back, trying to get clarification, but between the static and the cheering, Viceroy couldn't hear her and vice versa. What he did hear as he rounded the skating rink was the governor's voice welcoming everyone to Badger Fest. The crowds erupted again.

"She's already talking. What's going on? What do you have? Where are you?" Regina yelled into the radio as she stepped about six feet away from the governor, trying to hear.

Viceroy shouted into his mouthpiece again. "All security on the west end. I need all hands at the old Wisconsin One Bank building about two blocks south from the plaza. That's it, that's the spot. Any snipers with an eyesight to the building? Scan the windows, now!"

A round of confirmation came through and he heard that eight men were racing their way on foot.

"Any window on the corner with a view of the plaza. One of them is where he is," he screamed as he pumped his legs as fast as he could in a beeline for the building.

He reached the front entrance and pulled frantically on the door before realizing it was locked. He yanked his gun out and fired two shots into the lock. Across the plaza, the music and crowd noise were loud enough to drown out the sound. The door burst open and Viceroy pushed through. "All security coming to the building, I'm entering now and heading to the second floor. Everyone else head upstairs and check the upper floors. Remember, he's got to be at a window on the northeast corner. They're the only ones with a view of the plaza."

A round of "ten-fours" pierced through his earpiece. Regina's voice came through next as he ascended the first flight of stairs.

"I'm putting myself closer to the governor. I see the building you're talking about and... Oh Lord. Roger, it's the second-floor window facing the intersection. I can see something in the window."

"No clear shot," came ringing en masse through the radio from the snipers.

Viceroy heard it all as he pushed through the second floor fire door into the hallway with his gun drawn. He turned to his right and ran full speed to the open doorway directly ahead of him.

Inside, the assassin squinted into the scope and positioned his right index finger on the trigger. Governor Kay Spurgeon was in the crosshairs at the podium.

Viceroy bowled into the room and hurled himself at the figure in the window, knocking him off balance at the moment the trigger was pulled.

Simultaneously, Regina Cortez threw herself at the governor, grabbing her as they tumbled to the ground in a heap. There was a collective gasp from the people below followed by immediate pandemonium in the plaza as people ran in every direction while an army of security sprang into action from all angles. As the VIPs and politicians fled their seats, police and SWAT teams appeared out of thin air to secure the landing.

The governor lay on her back and felt blood on her cheek and in her hair. Her coat was also splattered. Within seconds, twelve security officers had her surrounded. She sat up and wiped her cheek. Her hand came away dripping with blood but she felt no pain. It was then she understood. As the security team frantically tried to keep her calm and assess her injuries, she screamed at them to move and made her way on hands and knees to Regina, who lay on the ground with her head in a pool of blood. The bullet had pierced her neck just beneath her jaw.

"Help, help! We need help, emergency!" she screamed at the top of her lungs, putting her hand on Regina's neck in a futile attempt to stop the bleeding. "Oh God, help!"

In less than a minute an EMT unit was there, and the security team was pulling the governor away and hustling her into the Capitol building.

Inside the bank building a few blocks away, Viceroy was breathing heavily as he stood over the body of the assassin, gun hanging limply from his right hand.

When Viceroy slammed into him, the momentum had flung them both into the tripod and crashed them into the wall next to the window, separating as they bounced off. The assassin was the first to scramble to his feet, and he lunged at Viceroy, who deflected the impact with his left forearm, pitching him over his head. Viceroy managed to grab his loose gun and rolled onto his stomach to face him. The assassin rose and was about to spring at him again. From his position on the ground, Viceroy fired at the man's hip to maim him, but the assassin ducked at the same instant, causing the bullet to land an inch above the heart.

Now he straddled the man, who looked up at him with his life dissipating. The only thing Viceroy could think of was to ask a question.

"Why?"

The assassin blinked and tried to say something, but he couldn't get a word out. The man went limp…then still.

Viceroy switched off his radio and lowered himself to the ground with his back against the wall. Two security men rushed into the room with their guns drawn, saw the body, and then turned to him.

"I'm alright," he said. "Just a little cut up. But I thought I heard a shot as I hit him. Please tell me the governor is alive."

The shorter one responded. "She's alive."

"That's great news."

"But I'm afraid he did get a shot off. Your girl was hit. I don't know the details but it doesn't sound good. They'll be rushing her over to University Hospital."

207

Viceroy stared at the two men for a moment, then leaned his head against the wall and allowed the emotions he'd been holding in check to engulf him. He closed his eyes for a moment, and when he opened them he noticed the spray painted names and the penny taped to the opposite wall. *Lord, God...* He looked from the wall to the dead man on the floor and back again, leaving the two officers to deal with the aftermath as he raced to the street and then made his way in the pandemonium to the hospital, praying all the way.

CHAPTER 42

The room was dark and quiet. Pain seared through her neck. She was lying down and covered with a blanket; therefore, she thought, she must be in a bed. As she became more conscious, she felt a mask covering her nose and mouth. Opening her eyes, she realized she was staring at a white ceiling, and in her peripheral vision she could see that there was a white curtain all around her. *Am I in heaven?* She swallowed and a stabbing pain shot through her jaw and neck, piercing down into her chest and arcing across her cheeks and forehead. She closed her eyes and opened them again, hoping the view would be different. *I'm thirsty.* Her right pinkie finger twitched, and with that a shadowy figure appeared above her and moved closer.

"Hi," the figure said.

She recognized the voice and squinted to try to see him.

He placed one hand on her forehead and softly laid his other hand over hers. "It's me, Regina. It's Roger. You're going to be okay now. You made it."

Regina tried to squeeze his hand and, sensing this, he squeezed back.

"You're in University Hospital and you're a very fortunate woman."

With her free hand she weakly fumbled with the oxygen mask.

Knowing that she wanted to communicate, Viceroy gently removed it. In a raspy, painful voice she slowly and simply said, "Explain."

"I don't know how much you remember, but five days ago you were standing outside the Capitol with the governor when the assassin got a shot off. It hit you in the neck. They got you into surgery in the nick of time. The doctors say you'll be here for another week or so, but they expect you to make a full recovery. She owes you her life, and she's asked us to let her know when you wake up so that she can come and thank you in person. You're a hero. The media's been here twenty-four-seven. I also owe you a lifetime of friendship and loyalty." He squeezed her hand again.

Another stab of pain shot through her jaw and she grimaced, then asked for more information.

"First, I want you to know that we got him. His name was John Wang." Regina's eyes opened wider at the news. "He was Bennett and Greta's son. Apparently, he didn't die back in 1982, and he was taking revenge on the people who were responsible for the deaths of his parents."

She blinked rapidly and tried to form another word. Not wanting her to struggle, and knowing that she was trying to ask the obvious questions, Viceroy continued.

"Early yesterday morning I was in the office when a small overnight package was delivered. I was knee-deep in a summary report for Strongsmith and didn't even look at it right away. When I did eventually get to it, I saw that the return address was from a Maryann Nadine in the Cayman Islands. Curiosity got the best of me and I opened it up. The only thing inside was a disk. No note, no explanation. So I popped it into my computer and you aren't going to believe what was on it."

Regina motioned with her hand to continue.

"Tao Wang, Bennett's father, made a video for his grandson explaining everything: the deaths of Bennett and Greta Wang and how it all went down back in 1982. They were victims of a horrible assault, which was captured on a surveillance video Bennett had installed. They were alive when the fire broke out, but Bennett was only semi-conscious and Greta had been tied to the bed and had been sexually assaulted and tortured. Neither of them could move and they died of smoke inhalation."

Regina closed her eyes as he continued, "The assault was perpetrated by the six young men on that famous basketball team. The ringleader, who is clearly visible on the disc, was Roy Spurgeon. John Wang murdered their wives according to the numbers on their jerseys, starting with Mary Hale, number six. Number one would have been Kay Spurgeon. I know that all their husbands supposedly committed suicide, but the note Bruce Wink left in the snow seems to indicate that something a lot more diabolical happened to them."

Regina closed her eyes and clung to Viceroy's hand as she let the information sink in. He tightened his grip and leaned a little closer.

"One more thing. John Wang's methods for killing those women were based on the ways their husbands had assaulted his mother. The bomb that killed Mary Hale that started this mess correlates with Howard Hale's actions that night in Curwood. The video shows him tossing a firecracker at the sleeping Wangs. Once you see the video, you'll understand. John Wang was excruciatingly methodical. And we finally had contact with Eric Zumwald three days ago. He resurfaced after a wilderness hunting expedition in Canada. He was, well…shocked after finding out the entire story, and his alibi checks out so I'm confident he and Wang weren't connected."

"Pennies?"

"Ah, the pennies. He simply had been collecting them all his life since the death of his sister. He said it was his way of having a tangible memory. The last piece of news I have for you is that we were able to locate and contact Maryann Nadine. She was the Wangs' nanny and housekeeper. Fortunately, she's agreed to fly up here to talk. She wants to help and will be on a flight tomorrow afternoon."

Regina squeezed his hand one more time and summoned the strength to whisper a final question. "The building…how did you know?"

"Well, call it luck, call it happenstance or, if you're like me, you can call it God's providence. I know you couldn't see it clearly from the landing but, from my vantage point, I could. As I was following the path of the jets doing their flyover, I happened to notice an old building a block away. It used to be a bank that closed its doors a long time ago. The name painted along an arch was barely legible, but it read Wisconsin One Bank. Number one. Start counting, right?"

An ever-so-slight smile appeared at the corners of her mouth.

"Madison PD had swept the building that morning but somehow he eluded us. Publicly I'm saying we just happened to be sweeping that particular building at that exact moment."

Regina patted her chest with her free hand to relay her emotions. Viceroy understood and patted his own chest in reply. "Now you need to rest, and so do I. That chair over there isn't very comfortable for sleeping. By the way, I asked Pastor Oxenhaus to come here the night it happened to pray over you. He'll be thrilled to know you've pulled through and will probably pop in sometime tomorrow. I'm going home now that I know you're alright," he concluded, putting on his coat.

A nurse entered the room and her face lit up when she saw Regina awake. She helped her drink a bit of water and gave her some medication, straightened her pillows and put the oxygen mask back in place, then exited.

Before Viceroy left, he provided one more piece of news. "I'm sure you'll be glad to know that we're catching up to Roy Spurgeon. Silk and Jerry are pretty sure they have him in their sights, so, hopefully, there will be more good news soon." Regina blinked once more and then closed her eyes. Viceroy leaned down and whispered in her ear, "Thank God you're alive. Sleep now, okay?" He squeezed her hand one last time and left the room.

On his way down to the car he checked his cell phone and saw a text from Ox. He texted back about Regina and to confirm that he would come by on Thursday evening to finally meet with the woman his friend had been counseling. Ox texted back a picture of the sheet music for the "Hallelujah Chorus." Viceroy could only shake his head in amusement.

CHAPTER 43

Roy Spurgeon stretched his legs out on the lounge chair outside his casita. He had just finished a breakfast of papaya root mash and a coffee, followed by a short swim in his private pool. The sun was shining, as it had done every day since he arrived in Troncones a few weeks ago. And now, in addition to the consistently gorgeous weather, there was the added value of a beautiful woman still asleep in his bed. He had met her the night before and was immediately struck by the dramatic white streak in her otherwise dark and wavy hair. And to put the cherry on the cake of his pleasure, her bedroom skills turned out to be as exceptional as her appearance. Remembering the night, Spurgeon sighed deeply, knowing that this would be his life from now on.

He reflected on his high school friends and the unfortunate ending each of them had come to. Howard's was the most painful for him; their lifelong friendship obliterated when he made him pull the trigger. Incredibly sad, but eminently necessary. True, he had initially hoped to save his old life with Kay by putting an end to the murders back home. That had been his intention when he gave the cops a heads-up about Clare Kittleton. If they'd caught the killer in time, Kay would no longer have been in danger and they could have gone on with their lives as Wisconsin's first family. Too bad things hadn't worked out quite as he had planned, but he had to admit that his new life was promising to be even better.

A young servant came by to clear his plate and ask if he would like a drink. "Absolutely. A vodka and lemonade would be great."

As the boy went off to fetch it, Spurgeon lay back and took off his dark glasses to let the sun warm his face. A gentle ocean breeze stroked his skin as he allowed his past life—Curwood, Greta, Milwaukee, Kay, the murders, the law firm, all of it—wash out to sea.

Eyes still closed, he heard the boy return and set his drink on the table next to his lounge chair. "Thank you," he said, without bothering to look up.

"You're welcome," came the reply.

Spurgeon's eyes flashed open to see a 6'5" black man standing over him.

CHAPTER 44

On that same evening, Viceroy walked into the Bread of Life Church and was greeted at the front door by Ox. No words were spoken as they clasped hands.

Smiling as never before, Ox said, "Man, it's great to see you. Thanks for letting me know Regina's back with us. Amen and Amen, huh?"

"You have no idea. Thanks again for coming over to Madison that night. I needed you but, more importantly, she did."

"An answered prayer is always a welcome bit of news. I'm going to go see her again tomorrow morning. You're looking good. I can already see the weight's been lifted off your shoulders. Why don't you come into my office so I can fill you in on the woman I told you about before you meet with her?"

Viceroy had spent countless hours in that office during counseling sessions with Ox, which he hoped he could resume in the coming weeks. He settled into the chair closest to the window and thought it odd when Ox grabbed the chair next to his instead of sitting at his desk.

Ox said, "So, I'm going to begin tonight by asking you a simple question. Do you trust me?"

Viceroy replied, "What? Of course."

"Good, because there's something I have to confess to you. I haven't been completely transparent, but I...well...I believe I had a very good reason."

"What are you talking about? I thought you asked me here to speak with a woman who's new to the church."

"I did, and I do. But she's someone who's going to need some special handling, particularly if you agree to speak with her." Viceroy gave him a quizzical look. "Listen, this is hard for me because I feel like I've been keeping something from you; I guess, in reality, I have. But, again, not without cause. Your investigation over the past couple of months was priority one, and as it wore on it became clear to me that nothing, and I mean absolutely *nothing*, should be allowed to interfere with that. So, forgive me, but I was just trying to guard your backside as you ran full speed ahead, and I think you would've done the same thing if our roles were reversed."

"What are you getting at?"

"I think this will help," Ox said as he went to his desk and pulled a small box out of a drawer. He lifted the top, letting the contents fall into his massive palm and closing his fist before Viceroy could see what he was holding.

"She showed up here around the time your investigation was getting underway and I've been counseling her ever since. She, um...well...she wants to put her life back in order and found her way through our front doors, just as you did."

"Alright, well then, maybe I can help."

"Maybe," Ox said with a sheepish grin. "Roger...God has a way of appearing when we least expect Him. In the midst of our lowest moments we don't always realize that He's right next to us and, often times, carrying us through without our even being aware of Him. You came here a year ago seeking answers and grasping to recover your spiritual footing. You and I have made some progress, but you also have your sights set on divorce. You're standing at the divide. Yet, buried in the rubble of your heart, you also desire to salvage your marriage." Ox reached over and gently grabbed his hand. Then he held his other hand over Viceroy's and let something fall into his palm. "She hopes for the same."

Viceroy let his gaze drop to the wedding band that lay cradled in his palm. He stared at the ring; its gold reflection acting like a

216

magnet. He couldn't pull away, he couldn't even move.

Ox reached over after a minute and gently closed his friend's fingers around the ring. Viceroy raised his head, eyes filled with tears wanting to escape, to look into the face of his mentor.

Ox spoke softly as he delicately guided him to the next step. "It's understood that you may not want to see her. She's already accepted that as a possibility. She's also come to accept the possibility that you may simply want the divorce finalized, and she's prepared to sign the papers today if that's what you choose. She's down in the Prayer Room now, but you don't have to see her if you don't want to."

Viceroy's breathing became a bit labored as he attempted to formulate his words.

Ox continued, "I've been praying about how to handle this, and for the last month or so no clear answer came. On the one hand, Debbie came to me quite innocently for counseling with no idea that you had joined our congregation, and certainly no idea that the two of us had become friends. I finally explained the situation during our third or fourth session. Her reaction was, well…one of hope, and she took it as a sign that she had done the right thing; that God had guided her to this church. On the other hand, you were chasing down a killer, all the while seeking an end to your personal grief and an official release from your marriage. I found myself in an awkward spot, until God finally spoke. I find that His voice, most times, is one of quiet wisdom. He simply said, 'Attend to Debbie and I'll handle Roger.' So that's the path I followed."

Viceroy swiped at a tear that had run away down his left cheek. He grabbed a tissue from the end table and stood at the window looking out over the parking lot.

"When she realized the enormity of her decision to flee, she felt that she couldn't reverse course. She ended up back in Florida and, as you suspected, was with Donna the whole time. Her employer was gracious enough to let her have her previous sales territory back down there. Then, sometime into the separation, her heart began to change or, as I'd like to believe, the Holy Spirit made Himself known. She moved back here in September determined to salvage everything, if you're willing."

"But why did she leave in the first place?" Viceroy said.

217

"She was afraid."

"Afraid? Of what? If she was afraid of something, why didn't she tell me?"

"She was afraid that one day she would come home to an empty house. She confessed that every day you left for work she couldn't shake the feeling that it might be your last. Once that thought took hold, I think she thought the best way to handle it would be to run before the feeling completely consumed her."

Viceroy reached for the armrest of the chair and lowered himself in slow motion, all the while staring blankly to the floor.

"And how do I know she's resolved her fears? What would prevent her from taking off again and ripping my heart out one more time? Would *you* take that chance?" he asked, raising his eyes to Ox for an answer.

"Well…"

"I mean it, Ox. If there were ever a time to make an objective decision, one not based on emotion, this is it."

"What I was going to say was that, as your friend and pastor, I believe the spirit of reconciliation and grace now shine on her. I don't think she would have returned without it. I don't think she would be here if her fears weren't conquered."

With that, Pastor Greg rose slowly and went to his desk to retrieve his bible. "I'm going to be in the church praying for a while. Whatever you decide, all I ask is that you also go to prayer beforehand. I love you as my brother, Roger. I'll stand alongside you in whatever decision you make, but know that I'll be there for her as well."

Ox made his way to the door.

"Before I leave, allow me a biblical truth." Viceroy nodded as Ox softened his voice. "It's one I often speak about during premarital counseling but I think the theme is applicable with you and Debbie now as well. It's simply this: A rope of one strand is vulnerable to all manner of harm. It can be cut, frayed, chopped or sliced without much effort. A rope of two strands is stronger, but still vulnerable. A two-stranded rope can be easily untwined once that process is started. But a rope of three strands has the strength to endure anything. That's how God designed marriage. Husband and wife entwined with the strand of God." Ox let his final sentence hang and then left quietly. Viceroy heard his footsteps recede down the hallway.

He opened his hand to look again at the ring. With the echoes of all his heartaches pounding inside him, he couldn't believe that Debbie was now a mere fifty feet away. It had been a year and a half of feeling utterly powerless, and their reunion now depended on his decision. *A strand of three. Being married to you overwhelmed me.*

Viceroy stood, holding the ring in front of him like an offering. He walked to the office doorway and stepped out into the hallway. A small crucifix hung on the wall directly opposite. The hands of the Jesus figure nailed to the crossbar were cast such that the index fingers hung limply, seemingly pointing east and west. He stared at it. Fifteen paces to his right was the prayer room; the lobby and exit doors were a short distance to his left.

He bowed his head and lowered his arms as his fingers closed around the ring.

God...

ACKNOWLEDGEMENTS

After a very long voyage, my debut novel has found fresh waters in which to sail. As with any journey, without those who provided support it simply wouldn't have happened. I would today be shipwrecked or sunk in the vast ocean of literature.

So to all of my crew of family, friends, and a new publisher, a bursting heart of thanks...

I have to start by thanking my beautiful wife, Lori. Your unwavering support while I've been tethered to a keyboard makes you an important part of this book getting published and any future success that may come.

And to my daughters, Lauren Lietaert and Joelle Baldwin, knowing you're cheering me on provides an immense tailwind in which to push forward. Thank you and your husbands, Zack and Collin, for the blessings that you are.

I want to extend an enormous thanks to my agents, Liza Fleissig and Ginger Harris from Liza Royce Agency. You saw potential when most others did not and took a chance early on. Despite the headwinds, you steered me true with patience and optimism all the way to a published novel and this relaunch.

Also to John and Shannon Raab of Suspense Publishing, for your friendly, authentically straightforward approach in wanting the second book in this series (coming soon) which led to this relaunch moment and your invitation to join your house. I look forward to working with you on what lies ahead with renewed hope and vigor.

Thanks to all of my support group of extended family and friends and the encouragement and well wishes you send my way. To Dave and Cathy Jolly for the simple gift of their cottage on a hill. Four days in solitude while writing the final chapters was perfect. Also to Janet Hill Talbert, an enormous reservoir of guidance and support, not only for her literary acumen, but more importantly for her faith in God that she imparted to me—it kept me afloat when I least expected it but definitively needed it. And not at all the least, my beta readers—Constance Ovesen, Amy Peterson, Mark Crockford, Cathy Jolly, Lauren Lietaert, Joelle Baldwin, Lori Harms, and all the LRA readers—who helped shape the final product.

And not least, the talent I may possess, such as it is, that God has bestowed on me. My deep gratitude and unending acknowledgment of the source.

ABOUT THE AUTHOR

Steven C. Harms is a professional sports, broadcast and digital media business executive with a career spanning over thirty years across the NBA, NFL, and MLB. He's dealt with Fortune 500 companies, major consumer brands, professional athletes, and multi-platform integrated sports partnerships and media advertising campaigns.

He's an accomplished playwright having written and produced a wildly successful theatrical production which led him to tackling his debut novel, Give Place to Wrath, the first in the *Roger Viceroy* detective series. The second book, *The Counsel of the Cunning*, is due out in fall of 2021.

A native of Wisconsin, he graduated from the University of Wisconsin–La Crosse. He now resides in Oxford, Michigan, a small, rural suburb of Detroit.

AUTHOR'S NOTE

Dear Reader,

I hope you enjoyed reading *Give Place to Wrath* as much as I enjoyed writing it. Support from readers like yourself is crucial for any author to succeed, particularly in this e-book era.

If you enjoyed this book, please consider writing a review at amazon.com and if you are inclined, follow me on Facebook at https://www.facebook.com/authorstevencharms. You can also go to my website at www.stevencharms.com.

The reviews are important and your support is greatly appreciated.

Thank you,
Steven C. Harms

THE COUNSEL OF THE CUNNING

A *ROGER VICEROY* NOVEL: BOOK 2

CHAPTER 1

A howler monkey screeched, its shrill pitch adding to the endless cacophony.

Dr. Catarina Amador watched the animal move through the trees until it vanished in the dense canopy below, then drew a last puff on her cigarette, crushing the butt with the heel of her worn-out tennis shoe. Her eyes shifted to the ancient ruins sprawling in every direction; eroded, gray slabs of rock covered with vines, others crumbled beyond recognition.

Her prison.

Atop the temple mount, the slight breeze and mid-morning sunlight provided a respite from the enclave of stone ruins and paths that weaved through the jungle of whatever country she was in. To the east, the sun reflected off the lone glimpse of the river, catching her eye. The faint sparkles shimmering off the surface forever calling her home. Six years and counting. But each passing moment chipped away at her will, replacing those pieces with an ever-increasing hopelessness. She had become mostly devoid of thought save for the world-class talents she employed for her captor.

The youngest daughter of a large family from the slums of Mexico City, her intellect and scientific acumen made her a prodigy. World-renowned in academic circles by the age of fourteen. At fifteen she began her studies at Johns Hopkins University in Baltimore; flying through, she graduated just five years later with a PhD in biomedical engineering. Her human molecular manipulation thesis elevated her into the scientific world's stratosphere. Upon graduation, blank check offers from a hundred different companies and research labs spanning the globe filled her mailbox. All she had to do was pick one. Her parents had come to Baltimore for the graduation and to help with the decision. Over dinner, the list was pared down to four opportunities in the western hemisphere. When the evening came to a close, they parted company—her parents back to the hotel and Catarina to a local establishment to celebrate graduation with her peers. She was never seen again.

Sighing, she took a few steps forward to look out over the plaza area, resting her arms at chest height on the massive stone wall encircling the space. Standing just over five feet, her stature matched her frame. A lithe body and long, black hair kept in a ponytail most days accentuated her stunning facial features. A foot taller and she would have graced magazine covers instead of medical journals.

She peered down at a bird-faced stone sentry near one of the plaza's entryways and the eyeless human statue set a few yards to its left. A variety of bizarre figures were sprinkled throughout the ruins. She felt the strangest ones were the two tall snakes, standing erect at twice her height with human feet, holding large blackish orbs of polished rock in their massive jaws. Positioned on either side of "Main Street," as she had nicknamed it, they guarded a small but steady waterfall spilling in front of a steep rock wall. The falls travelled over the rock above creating a wall of water ten feet high, cutting off the path with no way forward. A five-foot-wide chasm stood between the path's end and the water wall. She once had peered into it. No splash sound, the rushing water just disappeared into an eternal abyss. Beyond the water wall was the forbidden canyon and the treasure of the ancient ruins.

She closed her eyes tight and bowed her head, reflecting on the moment she first penetrated the water wall, not knowing what was on the other side.

Two men had tossed her over the chasm where she landed on hard ground and found herself in a dank cave, lit only by a torch on each wall. Soaking, she followed the orders she was given and took ten steps forward to a turn in the cave, which led to the opening on the other side. About sixty feet ahead was the jagged mouth of the exit, perfectly outlined by the sunshine stabbing through on the other side. Picking her way carefully towards it, the temperature warmed until she was standing at the cave's exit. She took the final step, ducking slightly into the beyond, and took in the wonderment of her surroundings.

It was a smallish canyon with sheer, steep sides and thick vines growing in bunches among the rocks. Clinging in arbitrary clumps was a fruit she had never seen before, displayed in a spectrum of light green to black and every variation in-between. Above the canyon the jungle had formed a natural ceiling of branches; not overly dense, but enough to provide a protective layer yet still allow the sun to push through to the polished, black-stained stone floor in various spots.

And there, in the middle of it all, stood a man of some years with his hands clasped behind his back. Wearing a panama hat, unassuming slacks and a floral print button-down, the hat's shadow cut across his face making his mouth the only discernible feature.

He gestured to her to come and sit at a small wooden table to his left. She had walked with slow, unsure steps towards him. What would he do? Was this the end? As she neared, his persona became clear. A man of Hispanic descent, well-manicured, with an air of self-assurance that clung to him like an invisible but tangible layer.

Once she sat, the man took his own seat and lit a cigar, drew a

226

few puffs, and spoke.

"Good afternoon, Dr. Amador," he had said. "Welcome to my kingdom," he added, with a sweeping hand gesture.

"Where am I?" she remembered asking, as if in a dream.

"Where you were *born* to be."

"Who…who are you?" she asked.

Her mind's eye recalled the memory of his response at this particular moment. A smile. Cryptic.

"My name you will never know. But take heart. You are here to lead a significant advancement in a little science project I have a vested interest in. You, Dr. Amador, will be its shining star." Then came his explanation for her kidnapping and what he wanted.

He began with a cloaked apology for his men taking her off the streets of Baltimore and blindfolding her for two days.

Her memory replayed the horrible experience. Someone coming from behind as she passed an alley. A hood suddenly coming down over her face. A vice-grip hand that quickly covered her mouth. The man whispering something in her ear—a throaty, aged timbre—before hustling her into a vehicle. Once inside, he let go but ordered her to be silent as she felt the unmistakable hardness of the barrel of a gun being pressed against her temple. She recalled the vehicle speeding up, taking a number of tight turns before zooming along a straight path, then slowing to a stop and taking a final turn. The last slice of recollection was a breeze touching her arms as she was pulled out of the vehicle, being carried up a flight of stairs and into an enclosed space, as the sound of an airplane's engine roared to life. For a brief moment the hood was removed, but an instant later, a man she assumed was her captor, sprayed something in her face. That was it. Her recollection of a hazy, in-and-out consciousness was the only vestige of the bridge between boarding that plane and coming off it some amount of time later. Once again hooded and placed back in a vehicle for a short ride, she was then in a helicopter—the sound of its rotors were unmistakable. She remembered the flight being incredibly long. Upon landing, the same throaty voice said something she couldn't understand and then her hood was removed.

The bright stab of lush greenery walling in a sunlight-splashed landing pad pierced her vision. She recalled squinting, trying to discern the environment. The warmth of the climate immediately registered. Baltimore and her parents were the first thought that came to mind and then the understanding that they and the city were now thousands of miles away.

Two different men, not so gently, had taken her arms and steered her to a pathway that directly led into what she then was able to realize was a tropical forest, and finally to the waterfall and the eventual meeting with the man in the panama hat.

With another puff of the cigar, he then presented her with the whole tale of what lay ahead.

She was to develop a new drug, and he had stated that her opportunity to use her intellect and talent when it came to molecular manipulation was going to be unfettered. "Anything and everything is at your disposal," he had said with firmness and a hint of delight.

Next was a tour of the compound and her new living quarters—a luxurious penthouse adjacent to the ancient temple featuring a grand view. It was stocked with a closet full of clothes, toiletries, a hot tub on the small balcony, a desk, books for reading, and a computer to be used for her research. Following that came an introduction to the world-class lab with five qualified scientists, also prisoners. Her operation to run. Her scientists to lead. A deadline of three years.

Included in the "tour" was a modern, plain brick building housing more prisoners, each given a simple cell. Haggard-looking people. Further on came the trails, the statues, the ruins. Another cement block building looking completely out of place, with a large "F" scratched into the door, and behind it the three men and one woman chained to the wall. Final stop, a spherical hut off the southwest corner of the plaza, secured by barbed wire and an armed guard.

"Sometime in the coming weeks I will escort you here again," the man had said in a different, almost reverential tone. "The treasure inside is truly priceless. Perhaps the single greatest discovery in the long, brutal history of this ancient empire."

His final comment echoed in her mind, reverberating, before she